The End of a Dynasty

By

Andrew Maloney

Note for Librarians: a cataloguing record for this book that includes Dewey Classification and US Library of Congress numbers is available from the National Library of Canada. The complete cataloguing record can be obtained from the National Library s online database at:
www.nlc-bnc.ca/amicus/index-e.html

ISBN 1-4120-2210-X

TRAFFORD

This book was published on-demand in cooperation with Trafford Publishing.
On-demand publishing is a unique process and service of making a book available for retail sale to the public taking advantage of on-demand manufacturing and Internet marketing. On-demand publishing includes promotions, retail sales, manufacturing, order fulfilment, accounting and collecting royalties on behalf of the author.

Suite 6E, 2333 Government St., Victoria, B.C. V8T 4P4, CANADA
Phone   250-383-6864   Toll-free   1-888-232-4444 (Canada & US)
Fax   250-383-6804   E-mail   sales@trafford.com
Web site www.trafford.com   TRAFFORD PUBLISHING IS A DIVISION OF TRAFFORD HOLDINGS LTD.
Trafford Catalogue #04-0038   www.trafford.com/robots/04-0038.html
10   9   8   7   6   5   4   3

For my brother Dave, whose inane conversations inspired much of this story

PI⚾NEERS Fan Card

Welcome to Game 4 of the 2003 World Series!!

After another successful regular season, the Buffalo Pioneers look for their third consecutive World Series Championship tonight at Pioneer Stadium

Below are the eight Pioneers who made the American League All-star team:

Pos	Player	Avg	Hr	Rbi	Sb
SS	Benjy Alvarez	.317	2	67	73
C	Terry Miller	.321	5	82	0
LF	Scott Harper	.336	33	126	30
1B	Eddie Griffin	.294	35	128	2
CF	Pete Sampson	.285	31	105	11

	Pitcher	W-L	Era	
SP	Frank Ringler	24-3	1.82	
SP	Chris Norton	17-8	2.94	

	Reliever	W-L	Era	Saves
RP	Conan O'Shea	2-0	0.53	46

Manager: Jack Vaughn, 4th season   All-time: 1088-693   .611
                                               Buffalo: 401-247   .619

CHAPTER 1

"Welcome back folks! The Pioneers need just one more out here to put the finishing touches on another dazzling season and their third consecutive championship! I don't think there could be a pitcher the Buffalo fans would rather see out there than Conan O'Shea."

"You said it Chuck, these fans are on their feet yelling and screaming and why wouldn't they? Conan 'The Barbarian' has been lights out as the closer this season. When this guy comes in you might as well put the wife and kids to bed because it's time to say good night!"

The robust reliever finished his warm-up pitches and eyed his prey in the on-deck circle. He was an imposing figure with long, red curly hair flowing out from behind his cap and a face composed of muscular symmetry. When he glared at the batters, there wasn't a more intimidating pitcher to look at with a game on the line.

"Troy Timmons steps to the plate for Atlanta. This is a confrontation of power versus power."

The bank tower across the street loomed over the field with the inscription "Go Pioneers" turned on in the lights of its offices.

"O'Shea sets.....the pitch......swing and a miss, strike one!"

"YEAH!!!" The crowd thundered.

A sea of white towels twirled in a dizzying fashion. Faster and faster they went, propelled by the emotional charge of the moment.

"O'Shea made Timmons look sick on that one! He put a heater right down the pipe and Timmons couldn't catch up."

The camera panned the stadium and scanned a multitude of faces; the frenzied fans with painted faces, the players overhanging the dugout, and finally the owner. The benign old man and his wife were sitting in their private box holding hands. There was a time-honoured graciousness about him, a gentle face and full head of white hair that fostered a venerable image.

"You can only be happy for an owner like Jonathan Jenkins. He represents everything good about this game."

"This crowd is on their feet! 3-0 Pioneers, 2 outs, one strike. O'Shea sets.....he winds and delivers.....strike two!"

"YEAH!!!" The crowd erupted again.

Suddenly, the entire stadium stood up in one collective motion. The noise became deafening.

"One strike away from glory! There is a lot of nervous energy in this stadium right now."

The manager sat in the dugout with a blank expression as he calmly sipped his coffee. He had a battle-scarred face that was coarse and gruff, giving him the unflinching gaze of a man who had been here many times before.

"Take a look at Jack Vaughn down in the dugout. If there is a more composed person in the world, I have yet to meet him."

"O'Shea is ready to go....he sets....the pitch....swing and a miss, strike three!"

"YEAH!!" The stadium exploded in celebration.

Fans overran security guards by the thousands and piled onto the field in a sea of pandemonium.

"Three-peat! The Buffalo Pioneers are the 2003 World Series Champions! What a team, what a town!"

Players jubilantly ran out to mob O'Shea on the mound. At the bottom of the pile, the hulking reliever crawled his way out to give manager Jack Vaughn a bear hug.

The manager's usually dour face cracked a rare grin. He even forced a smile for general manager Trent Blair, despite rumours they had not been getting along in recent months. The two men shook hands with unrestrained jubilation.

"Get over here you son of a bitch!" Vaughn beamed.

"You've held this team together," Trent smiled. "You're the best manager in baseball."

Jonathan and Rose Jenkins slowly made their way down to the field. The owner's arthritic hands cradled the World Series trophy as the Commissioner handed it to him in front of the television cameras. As the old man turned to Jack Vaughn, the two men could only smile at each other.

"We did it for you, Johnny," Vaughn said, as he warmly put his arm around the owner's shoulder.

It was one of the many moments over the past few seasons when everything seemed right with the world. The Buffalo Pioneers were the envy of baseball and they got there by being a classy organization at every level.

It started at the top with Jonathan Jenkins, the benevolent grandfather, who was willing to pay for a championship baseball team without meddling in every aspect of it. He was a grocery man and a baseball fan, but he never confused the two. Now over 80 years of age, he was best known for the large and profitable chain of supermarkets he had established in Western New York. Jenkins' roots in the community went deep and he was loved accordingly by the Buffalo faithful.

Upon buying the club nearly a decade earlier, the old man's best move was his first one, hiring the dynamic Trent Blair away from the Los Angeles Dodgers to be the Pioneers' general manager. Recognized as the best young baseball mind in the business, the mid-thirties, clean cut Blair turned out to be the perfect fit. Born and raised in San Francisco, Blair had nonetheless received most of his baseball education in the Los Angeles organization. With him came Al Ferreira, another scout whom he brought along from L.A. to be his assistant.

Together they represented the new style of general managers, not necessarily bred in the game but versed in it. Both were avid proponents of sabermetrics, a method for evaluating players that places a higher emphasis on numbers and statistics than scouting reports. Although the philosophy was shunned by the old guard baseball establishment, it did not take long for the results of their work to become tangible on the field.

The farm system began overflowing with talent scouted, drafted and signed from the United States, the Dominican, Puerto Rico, and beyond. After a few seasons of initial struggles, Blair and his scouting staff assembled one of the most impressive collections of young talent in baseball: outfielders Pete Sampson and Scott Harper, starter Chris Norton, and speedy shortstop Benjy Alvarez. In Alvarez's case, Blair had plucked the Gold Glove winning shortstop out of the Dominican using a controversial loophole clause. Benjy knew little English, but spoke the language of baseball fluently.

Eventually there were only a few missing ingredients to the mix, and with Jonathan Jenkins' blessing, the general manager decided to go shopping for the high priced talent that could take the ball-club to the next level.

Blair started in the dugout by hiring a veteran manager to steer the club into the playoffs. There was only one man who could fill that job: Jack Vaughn. The Hall-of-Fame skipper was a winner, plain and simple. As an all-star outfielder for the great Los Angeles Dodger teams of an earlier era, Vaughn had earned a reputation for himself as a hard-nosed, intense player who had made the most of his average size and skill. As a manager, he had more than distinguished himself with several teams and had the World Series rings to prove it.

On the field, Blair vaulted the Pioneers into contention by signing 36-year-old free-agent first baseman Eddie Griffin from the New York Yankees and acquiring veteran catcher Terry Miller from the Los Angeles Dodgers. Griffin's leadership skills and not to mention his 35-home run bat, combined with the savvy defensive abilities of Terry Miller behind the plate were just the kind of veteran intangibles that would transform the Pioneers into a World Series Contender.

With an exciting young team and a proven manager directing the show, the Buffalo Pioneers dominated the baseball world during those halcyon years. It was a time remembered fondly by everyone, especially the way things went sour so fast.

CHAPTER 2

"On behalf of the Baseball Writers of America, it is my privilege to present Jack Vaughn with the award for the 2003 AL Manager of the Year!"

The members of the media roared their approval as the manager made his way to the microphone. Jack Vaughn was the type of man who garnered respect everywhere he went, combining an old style of curmudgeonly charm with a dry wit that seemed to have an astute sense of timing. There was no denying he was a winner, but even with his faults, the drinking habit, the public divorce, and his sometimes snide disposition, the blue-collar city had taken an instant liking to him. Vaughn was old-school, yet there was something timeless about him.

"Thank you very much," Vaughn said.

The applause refused to die down.

Next to the podium, Commissioner Richard Smalls began glad-handing the manager and smiling profusely as cameras buzzed incessantly around them.

"Are you gonna let go of my hand?" Vaughn muttered under his breath.

"Just shut up and smile," the Commissioner said through his teeth.

The Commissioner finally released his hand.

"Thank you everyone. Thank you, really," Vaughn said, almost ashamed of the praise being heaped upon him.

The manager never sought the attention, but the applause refused to die down. The media was fawning over him.

"Thank you. I can't tell you what a great honour this is, but I want to remind everyone that this really represents the accomplishments of a group of people. Jonathan Jenkins....you're one of them."

Vaughn took his coarse right hand and blew a respectful kiss to the owner standing at the back of the room. He then looked at pitching coach and long time friend Grant Robinson.

"Then there is Grant Robinson who has done a great job with the pitching staff. I can't stress that enough....."

Sitting next to Vaughn at the podium, an eager looking Trent Blair appeared like an expectant father.

"Finally, I can't forget the players...."

Blair frowned.

"I've always been a believer that a manager can't magically turn a bad team into a championship squad, but he can sure screw things up!"

The whole room laughed.

"Thankfully that hasn't happened. This award means a lot to me and hopefully we can come back next year and make it four in a row."

As Jack stepped down from the podium, a sea of reporters blocked his path to the exit. They merely wanted to shake the man's hand.

Off in the corner of the room, *Buffalo News* columnist Chet Thomas stood by himself. The physically rotund writer may have been the only person in the room who seemed genuinely unhappy that day. Vaughn was never one to play the media game and his sarcastic responses certainly hadn't endeared him to Thomas over the years. The writer walked out of the room without saying a word to anyone.

A few days later, Frank Ringler was named the 2003 American League Cy Young Award winner. At 38, he still had the best heater in the game and managed to fool hitters at an age when most pitchers were finished.

"I never thought I'd win another one at this age," Ringler said, as he stroked his moustache. "But here I am. It's been a great season."

The accolades were a fitting way to cap off three years of excellence. The epiphany came in early November when the Mayor of Buffalo, Mr. Art Dingleman, put on a grand black-tie dinner to honour the Pioneers at the Buffalo Convention Centre on Pearl Street. It was a chance for the city's elite to hobnob with the players and executives of the flourishing baseball team.

No expenses were spared in the preparation of this sumptuous feast. The buffet tables were lined with the choice meats and the wine was among the finest the world had to offer. It was a dinner fit for champions.

At table five, the Pioneer veterans sat with Jack Vaughn. Every few minutes a corporate executive or politician would come by to shake the manager's hand or say a kind word. It seemed that everyone at the dinner wanted to see or be seen with Jack that night.

Next to the manager sat Eddie Griffin. The gregarious first baseman loved the spotlight and enjoyed being the centre of attention, either through his extensive public charity efforts or his generous responses to reporters' questions. He donated heavily to

African-American charities and wasn't afraid to let people know about it. Some people thought he was a hero, others thought he was a phoney. Either way, Eddie certainly had cultivated tastes. He liked his wine red and his women white.

Across the table sat rambunctious closer Conan O'Shea. Affectionately known by Buffalo fans as Conan 'The Barbarian,' the hulking reliever was a paragon of fitness. Never afraid to impose his opinion, either verbally or physically, the Irishman gained infamy in Buffalo sports lore after he blew up and charged a batter following a rare late-inning home-run. Suffice to say, his little blow-up, while frowned upon by the Commissioner's Office, earned him a special spot in the hearts of Buffalo fans for years to come.

Then there was Frank Ringler. The wily veteran was one of Jack Vaughn's favourite people and it wasn't hard to understand why. He was a four-time Cy Young Award winner, three-time World Series champion and one of the fiercest competitors ever to take the mound. Frank may have been a Hall-of-Fame pitcher, but he was no less a person. For years, he had deferred contracts and taken less money to finish his career in Buffalo.

As the night wore on, the three men listened with tacit amusement as Vaughn told one of his classic yarns.

"Okay boys....if you have fifty lesbians and fifty civil servants in a room, what does that give you?" The manager yelled without any regard for who might be listening nearby.

Nobody knew the answer.

"A hundred people who don't do dick!" Vaughn barked.

The table erupted in laughter as guests throughout the dining hall looked on in curiosity as to what the uproar was all about.

Only an hour into the ceremonies, Vaughn already had a few too many. The old manager drank hard and liked his liquor even harder. With the players hanging on his every word, it seemed that Eddie Griffin's thunderous laugh became louder as the evening progressed.

Across the dining hall at table thirteen, Trent Blair sat with Scott Harper's agent Eli Ginsberg to talk business.

In four short seasons, Scott Harper had developed into the best left fielder in the game. He was an athletic kid who had a dangerous combination of power and speed that seemed to get better each year. The only problem was that Harper was also a year away from free-agency and everyone knew it would cost the Pioneers dearly to lock him up.

After a few minutes of uncomfortable silence, Blair decided to break the ice.

"I hear that Marcus Dillard filed for free-agency today," Blair induced.

"Did he?" Ginsberg replied. "He's going to command quite a bit. It'll be interesting to see where he goes."

"Well....we could use a right fielder of his calibre," Blair slyly added.

"Anyone could use a Marcus Dillard," the agent replied dismissively.

Everything about Trent Blair was so meticulously polished, from his clean cut face and short blonde hair right down to the conniving salesman's voice. When he wanted to test the waters, he never just jumped right in. Blair always conducted himself with cruel efficiency. He wanted to start these talks off on his terms.

"I almost forgot to ask. What are your plans for Scott?"

"Scott?" Blair replied with a shocked look. "That's something I wasn't even thinking about. But....uh.....I'd have to say Scott's definitely high on our list of priorities."

It was an award winning performance on his part.

"I know Scott loves it in Buffalo," the agent added. "He told me that if you sign him now, he'll take a discount to stay here. In this day and age, sacrifice like that is rare, especially from a guy who can hit 35 homers and steal another 35."

Blair pondered to himself for a moment.

"What kind of discount are we talking about here?"

"$70 million over 5 years....on the open market I figure we can get at least $90 million."

Blair rolled his eyes.

"Are you sure we're getting the discount?"

"Buffalo is his first choice," Ginsberg insisted.

"I respect that, but at this price my hands are tied. I'll bring it to ownership and if Jenkins approves, I'll see what I can do. The ball is in the old man's court."

"When should I expect to hear from you on this? I know Scott is anxious to get something done."

Blair tried to conceal his annoyance.

"All I can tell you is this. Scott is our number one priority and we want to lock him up. That's a personal promise between me and you."

At the head table sat owner Jonathan Jenkins, Mayor Art Dingleman and New York Governor Tom Murdoch. The men bantered on for most of the evening about trivial topics, but it was impossible to put three movers and shakers together without the conversation shifting to business. The easy smiles, small talk and political charm from earlier in the evening had given way to grim faces.

"Tom, what do you think of that proposal I put before you last summer?" Jenkins asked. "Have you given it much thought?"

"I have," the Governor replied, while chewing the fat, "and it is something I have put before my people."

"What do they think of it?" the owner asked, as he bit a piece of steak.

"Well.....there seems to be a general consensus that it needs to be done."

"What kind of time frame are we looking at?"

Murdoch paused for a moment. It was a difficult subject to broach with the state elections just around the corner. Jonathan Jenkins understood the Governor's plight and attempted to put him at ease. He knew when to pry and when to conciliate.

"Tom, you know I don't make threats. I'm not going to claim we've lost tens of millions or that I'll move the team, because that's bullshit. I know it, you know it, and Art knows it. I love this city too much to leave. Something needs to be done though. We can't sustain this thing forever. We need a new stadium. I can't tell you how important this is to the future of baseball in Buffalo and western New York."

Pioneer Stadium only seated 32 000 and had limited luxury boxes, which was bad enough for the team financially, but the fifty-five year old stadium was literally falling apart. Only three months earlier, a huge concrete block smashed onto the upper deck a few hours before a home game.

Public safety officials eventually cleared the stadium for public use, but the fear still existed that something bad might happen once more. As melodramatic as it might have seemed to talk about the future of the Pioneers after they had just won three consecutive championships, the Governor seemed sympathetic.

"I understand your team's plight Johnny and I'm strongly in favour of the state helping out, but only if the municipality is behind this all the way."

"The municipality?" Dingleman guffawed. "The City of Buffalo is the last thing you guys should worry about! We've been behind this thing from the start. I'm with you through thick and thin."

Both men looked at the Mayor awkwardly. They had been inclined to believe him before his over-the-top performance. Dingleman's golden-toothed smile and slick hair gave him the appearance of a man who had never met a person he didn't immediately try to impress. Art Dingleman was a man of images and clearly they meant a lot to him.

A former Navy seal during his youth, Governor Murdoch could not have been more different. His word was his bond and for twelve years the one thing that had always gotten him elected was his straight-forward honesty. He was a man the people could trust. He also knew better than to trust others blindly.

"If you're not on board, Art, tell us now. We can't have you bailing on us when the temperature rises."

"Governor Murdoch, I resent any implication...."

"Are you on board or not?" The Governor interrupted more forcefully.

The mayor grimaced before making the commitment.

"I'm with you," Dingleman said.

"In that case," the Governor said, "it sounds like a done deal to me. After the state elections next fall, I'll push this thing through no problem. You have my word."

Later in the evening, the owner left the table to speak with Trent Blair.

"Trent," Jenkins put his hands on the young general manager's shoulders. "If you've got a minute, let's take a walk."

After excusing himself from the table with a forced smile, Blair joined the owner in the room outside the convention hall.

"Jonathan!" Blair said eagerly. "How are you doing?"

"I just wanted to....."

"What's up?" Blair persisted ingratiatingly.

"I was speaking with the Governor tonight, and he seemed very enthusiastic about the idea of building a new stadium."

"Did he promise anything?"

"He'll make it public after the state elections next fall."

Blair sighed.

"And if he doesn't get re-elected?"

"That won't happen," the owner dismissed the notion. "Nobody can touch Tom. He owns this state."

"Did he at least give you a firm promise? I wouldn't trust those Albany bastards farther than I can throw them."

"Not to worry," Jenkins replied in a hushed tone. "Tom and I have been friends for a long time. We have a firm understanding. Just keep it quiet. This thing is very politically sensitive."

The two looked around to make sure nobody was listening. Blair paused for a few moments to think.

"I guess its good news, especially with Eli Ginsberg breathing down my neck. He's been harassing me all night."

"What does he want?" The owner asked curiously.

"He's trying to get a new deal for Harper. He's hinted that if we do it now, Scott will be more apt to take a hometown discount."

"That's great news."

"Not really," Blair said. "He wants $70 million over five years."

The old man's eyes widened and his breathing became noticeably heavy.

"My God, that's a discount?"

Jenkins thought about it for a moment. The money was more than he could fathom, yet the old man's will to win was even greater.

"Let's do it," the owner said cheerfully.

"Really?" Blair replied less enthusiastically. "What about the money?"

"Money is less of a problem now," Jenkins said. "The stadium will take care of everything."

Trent paused. He had something else in mind.

"In that case, why don't we go after Marcus Dillard? He just filed for free-agency today."

The older gentleman gave a great sigh.

"Before fixing up Harper first? That doesn't seem right."

"We'll worry about Scotty at the end of the season," Blair assured him. "Marcus Dillard needs to be our priority. He'll jumpstart this club."

The old man wore confusion on his face.

"I didn't know we needed a jumpstart," he remarked.

"We can't be complacent, Johnny. I built this team by being aggressive, only aggression can sustain us. Everyone in the league would like nothing better than to take us down. I'll never let that happen."

The old man breathed heavily

"You know, Trent, this doesn't make any sense to me at all. But you're the baseball man. I give you the budget, you make the call."

"Fabulous. We get Dillard now and then when word comes down from Albany about the stadium, we'll talk long-term with Harper. Maybe his agent will pull his head out of his ass by then."

The old man wasn't sure how Trent would pull it off, but he was too tired to try and figure it out. He sighed wearily.

"Whatever you say, Trent."

Over the next week, the team started making the necessary preparations for the upcoming season. Statistics needed to be analyzed, scouting reports needed to be looked over and preparations had to be made in case any changes were going to be made to the roster.

In mid-November, the Pioneers held their annual organizational meetings. It was a chance for all the personnel from the team's baseball side (the scouts, directors, manager Jack Vaughn, G.M Trent Blair, assistant G.M Al Ferreira, and Jonathan Jenkins) to meet in one room and lay out the plan for the upcoming season. Coming off a third consecutive World Series Championship, there was definitely a jubilant feeling in the air.

Team accountant Paula Lombardi started the proceedings off by addressing the team's financial situation in 2003.

"Although gate and related stadium revenues were stagnant this year, increased television exposure allowed us to make a modest profit of $4 million this past season. Based on these figures, an increase in player payroll to $60 million is feasible for the coming season."

The accountant was an attractive, late twenties brunette who frequently wore short skirts and seemed like a walking sexual harassment case. Listening to her speak revealed the depth of her knowledge and the seriousness she went about her profession.

Paula Lombardi was the type of woman who knew what she wanted in life and understood how to get it.

"However," she continued, "it is my opinion that this organization needs to quickly find new revenue streams to keep up with rapidly increasing costs."

Following her short presentation, the first hours were spent discussing minor-league development and a new scouting initiative in the Far East.

"Scouting is important for any organization," Trent Blair cheerily told the room. "While we rely heavily on statistical evaluation around here, it is always good to have the physical evaluation to along with it. All of you are indispensable to our success."

An agreeable atmosphere permeated the room until conversation turned to the major league talent available on the free-agent market. Assistant general manager Al Ferreira started discussing a pitcher he believed the Yankees were pursuing, but the conversation quickly shifted to Florida slugger Marcus Dillard.

"I think this guy's our best bet," Blair said. "Dillard, Scott Harper, Eddie Griffin, and Pete Sampson would form a murderers' row in the middle of our lineup."

"I agree," scouting director Luis Toca proclaimed. "I saw this guy in Florida, and he delivers the goods."

"Regardless of what you saw," Al Ferreira interrupted arrogantly. "The guy hit 49 homeruns last year and had a .380 on-base percentage. What more do we need to know?"

"It helps to have seen him in person," Toca defended himself.

"Whatever," Ferreira interrupted again, as he stroked his thin fox-like moustache. "The bottom line is his asking price. What is it?"

"He wants about $40 million over 4 years," replied Blair, "and Florida's last offer to him was well below that. They're a last place club, they can't keep him."

Another scout piped up.

"I saw him in a game in late-September where he hit five home runs. It was one of the greatest displays of sheer power I've seen in all my years in this game."

Jack Vaughn was silent. He sat slumped in his chair, sipping coffee and keeping quiet. He knew the conversation was about to swing his way.

"Well guys," Blair said. "I think we should definitely go after him. What do you think of all this, Jack?"

The manager remained still and calmly sipped his coffee. The room waited in breathless anticipation.

14

"What do I think?" Vaughn responded curtly. "I don't like the guy. I think he's a prima donna."

The whole room was taken aback.

"Come on Jack," Blair argued. "He's been known to have a bit of an ego, but it isn't that much of a problem. Nothing you can't deal with."

Jack laughed under his breath.

"Don't blow smoke up my ass, Trent. I've heard enough stories about this guy to know he'll be a poison to this team."

"One guy can't destroy a clubhouse," Blair shook his head. "I don't buy it, not for a minute."

Vaughn began to look irritated.

"Look. You asked my opinion. I gave it," Jack said crustily. "I don't think we need him."

"The sabermetrics on Dillard are fantastic," assistant G.M. Al Ferreira said. "The guy gets on base and hits homeruns. That's all we should care about."

"Come on Al," Vaughn retorted. "You know I don't buy into that bullshit."

At that moment, team accountant Paula Lombardi boldly took it upon herself to convince Vaughn of Dillard's worth.

"I think you have to look at this from a few different perspectives," Lombardi said. "There's more to this than just baseball. Marcus has a certain charisma about him. He's flashy, and flash is what sells in this business. We've got a local television deal coming up for review after next season. With a guy like Dillard, we can make a real killing on the networks."

The manager looked at her in utter disbelief. His interest began and ended on the field.

"Who the fuck invited you to this meeting," Vaughn snapped. "You've got a pretty face and a nice ass, honey. But this is a baseball meeting. Hit the road."

On the verge of tears, Lombardi sat down bitterly.

"She's got a point, Jack," Blair added. "We need to look at this from a broader perspective."

"You mean to tell me you're actually defending this nonsense?" Vaughn said in astonishment. "I'm amazed Trent. I always thought you cared more about the on-field product."

Down at the end of the table, Jonathan Jenkins looked uneasy. At this stage in his life, the old man was more than content to accept World Series trophies and appear at ribbon cutting ceremonies. He wanted nothing to do with this.

"Surely you can stop this Johnny," Jack pleaded with him. "What's Scotty Harper going to think? He's given his heart and soul to this team. Let's extend his contract now instead of throwing money at this head case."

The strain on the owner's face was obvious. Jenkins liked to tell the story of how, in his younger days, he would wake up every morning to pick the finest produce for his grocery stores because he couldn't trust anyone else to do an honest job of it. He always said that when an owner ceded control of operations he was susceptible to being betrayed. Whether he had forgotten his old maxim or was simply too weary to care anymore, the old man nodded at Trent and remained silent.

"Let us worry about that," interrupted Blair. "We can deal with Harper at a later date. I'll admit Dillard may be a little screwed in the head, but he's a great slugger. Just looking at his stats makes me weak in the knees."

Vaughn shook his head.

"You're making a big mistake."

"Look Jack. I'm the general manager and you're the manager! You do your job and I'll do mine. It's a pretty simple fucking arrangement!"

The stunned room looked on. All the rumours about Blair and Vaughn not getting along were finally being validated.

The manager slowly stood up, put his coffee down and calmly stared Blair square in the eyes. The tension was palpable.

"Don't order me around, son. I won't stand for it. Obviously you don't care what I think, but let me tell you one thing. Marcus Dillard will be the ruination of this team. You can mark my words on that."

He gave a disgusted look at the accountant sitting across the table and walked out of the room.

CHAPTER 3

"It's very rare that we can acquire such a quality individual as a Marcus Dillard. He is not just a great player, but a great man....."

There was mild applause from the media. The diminutive general manager had the attention of the baseball world and was more than dressed for the occasion. He had recently ordered some of the newest and most fashionable European suits imported from Milan. With the way he flaunted them, he almost seemed to be modelling himself.

"....Humble in the way he conducts himself, the example Marcus Dillard set in his previous six seasons in South Florida is something we should teach all of our kids. There really isn't a guy who exemplifies the word 'team' more than he does, and there isn't a guy who could be a greater addition to both the moral and communal fabric of Buffalo than the man standing right here. It is therefore with great pleasure that I announce the Buffalo Pioneers have signed right-fielder Marcus Dillard to a 4 year/$44 million deal."

Dillard stood up and posed for the cameras as his agent, Rodrigue Salazar, and Trent Blair held a Pioneer jersey in front of his massive frame. Each man's flashy attire seemed motivated by an unspoken desire to upstage the other. A few minutes passed as the cameras kept buzzing away.

As Marcus strutted up to the microphone, he carried an air of contradiction. There was his braggadocio, his swagger and open cockiness; his shirt seemed to be tailored specifically for the maximum exposure of his bulging upper body and his conversational habits tended towards the third person. But beneath his dark skin seemed to hide something even darker; he had a brooding way about him, almost an inclination that he wanted to be left alone.

"Where do you think you fit in the lineup of a three-time defending champion?" A reporter from the *Buffalo News* asked.

"I think you've got it backwards," Dillard responded quickly. "The question isn't where Marcus Dillard fits into the lineup; the question is where the lineup fits around Marcus. Marcus sees himself batting clean-up, everything else is rudimentary......it's all perfectly elementary. With the weak American League pitching, Marcus will hit 80 home runs this season, no problem."

A few chuckles were heard throughout the media gallery. Seated to the left of the microphone, Jack Vaughn could only shake his head.

The next question came from a *USA Today* reporter.

"What about Jack Vaughn? Do you think you will get along with him?"

"Marcus doesn't see a problem with Mr. Vaughn. As long as Marcus gets what's his, there ain't gonna be no problem."

"You said you will only bat cleanup? That's been Eddie Griffin's slot for the past three years, and Scott Harper has been hitting third. Do you really think you can displace them?"

"Marcus will bat cleanup and that's that. Marcus is......"

Dillard's agent, Rodrigue Salazar, sensing an unwanted controversy, impatiently interrupted.

"That will be worked out by the manager in spring training. We're not here to discuss that, sir. Could you pick another topic?"

A reporter from the *New York Times* was up next.

"What do you think your new teammates think of you?"

The big man wasted no time responding.

"They look at Marcus and they realize that Marcus is the guy who will lead them back to the promise land....."

"They've already been to the promised land three times," a few reporters snickered under their breaths.

Dillard's agent anxiously interrupted once more. His face gave the impression that he could suffer no greater joy than the knowledge that his client's mouth had been permanently screwed shut.

"At this point gentleman, I think we need to be moving on. However, before this press conference concludes, I'd like to state how happy both Marcus and I are to be joining the Buffalo Pioneers. Playing in such a great baseball city is every player's dream. It was an easy decision to make."

Suddenly it was Jack Vaughn's turn to speak. The crusty manager was slumped in his chair and looked like he wanted to be elsewhere. He slowly took a sip of his coffee and walked to the microphone.

Chet Thomas of the *Buffalo News* was the first in line to ask the manager a question. As the reporter began to speak, a vicious smile spread across his chubby face. The distaste each man held for the other was obvious in their faces.

"Do I sense a possible spring training controversy if Dillard doesn't hit cleanup?"

"I don't know, Chet," Vaughn responded snidely. "Do I sense you have nothing to write about today?"

The press gallery erupted in laughter as the heavy writer made his way to the back of the gallery. A reporter from the *Buffalo Sports Network* was next in line for questioning.

"This doesn't really pertain to anything...."

"That's all right," Jack interjected. "Most of the questions you guys ask me don't pertain to anything."

A few more laughs.

"....but I was wondering why you always have a cup of coffee with you?"

The manager thought to himself for a moment and looked on sombrely. The smile had fallen off his face as he rubbed his bulbous red nose, the product of many nights of hard drinking. He was still struggling to put those days behind him.

"Well....it sure beats a bottle of booze, especially after what I've been through."

The members of the media nodded their heads understandingly.

The final question of the night went to a *Sports Illustrated* reporter.

"Could you assess your team's chances of a fourth straight championship with this addition?"

Vaughn thought for a moment then gave the writer a subtle smirk that portended a heavy dose of sarcasm.

"We all heard it from Marcus himself. Apparently we're headed to the promise land, everything else is elementary."

The room burst into laughter. Jack Vaughn was not always the easiest person for media types to deal with, but when he was in the mood he could always provide a lively quote. He stepped down from the podium and walked past Marcus Dillard with nary a word to the slugger.

The next day, Trent Blair received a phone call in his office from Eli Ginsberg.

"You son of a bitch! You lied to me!"

"Relax," answered Blair, somewhat startled. "We had a change of plans, but Scott is still high on our list."

"Don't tell me to relax! You fucked me, and I don't like that one bit. I told Scott what you told me two weeks ago and do you know what he thinks now?"

"I don't know, what does he think?" Blair rolled his eyes.

"He thinks you guys don't want him, he's hurt," the agent responded.

"I think you're overreacting. Once certain issues are finalized next fall, we can talk extension."

"Next fall? Next fall! Not next fall! NOW!" the agent demanded

"There are certain things that need to be dealt with first."

"That's what you told me two weeks ago and look what happened!"

Blair sighed haughtily.

"We had a change of plans. This time I mean it."

"Look Blair. I don't like you. I think you're a callous, manipulative prick, but I'm going to give you one more chance. If you screw me on this one, Scotty is as good as gone. I mean it. After the season he's on a red-eye out of town."

"I'll get back to you after the state elections. That's a promise."

"Don't patronize me, Blair. Your promises are worth nothing. Next fall or else."

Click.

In mid-December, the team owners gathered in Nashville for the annual winter meetings. There were several issues on the agenda, but the state of economics in the game took precedence. The conference did not go well. Several owners began shouting at each other over the discrepancy between small and large markets. As usual, nothing was solved.

The conference had become a gathering of greed, with player agents milling about the hotel to negotiate multi-million dollar deals with the highest bidder and orchestrate trades for their disgruntled clients. The gala dinner on Saturday night was the one place where the owners, executives, and league officials could take refuge.

As Jonathan and Rose Jenkins walked over to one of the tables to snatch up some of the finger food, they reluctantly bumped into someone they would rather not have seen.

"Oh Jesus, its Vince," Rose said under her breath. "I guess we have to say the obligatory hellos and pretend we're happy to see him."

The owner would have none of it.

"Or we can just turn away now and not say anything," Jonathan replied.

The couple quickly scurried over to another table.

There was no man Jonathan Jenkins found more odious than New York Yankees owner Vince D'Antoni. His seedy reputation as a Manhattan construction magnate spoke for itself. Both may have been self-made men, but the similarities ended there. The unpredictable D'Antoni was Jenkins' complete opposite. He was an arrogant meddler who liked the sound of his own voice and needed his fingerprints on everything. For Vince D'Antoni anything less than the best was unacceptable.

Turning to an executive from another team standing nearby, the Yankees owner was visibly upset at being ignored.

"Would you believe that," D'Antoni spouted off in his silky smooth New York accent. "Jenkins won't even say hello."

"And why would he say hello to a jerk like you?" The executive laughed.

"Nobody snubs Vince D'Antoni. Nobody."

"Take it easy, Vince. Jenkins is a good man."

"He's an old man...."

"Maybe so, but a lot of people respect him."

"If he's so smart," D'Antoni stammered on, "then why does he keep that little attack dog of his around?"

"Who?" The executive asked. "Trent Blair?"

"Do you know any other midgets running baseball teams? He's like a little Napoleon. I'd like to bury that puke in one of my buildings!"

The executive looked around to see if anyone was listening.

"From what I hear he has broken some of baseball's rules."

"What rules?" D'Antoni demanded.

"They tell me he's been a little too aggressive in his recruiting."

"Oh?" The Yankee owner perked up

"Remember when Blair signed Benjy Alvarez as a loophole free-agent a few years ago? Apparently there were some birth certificate shenanigans that took place."

The Yankee owner spit his drink out.

"Son of a bitch! I knew the guy was a jackass, but he's a cheat as well!"

"Okay, just keep it down."

"Keep it down? Are you kidding me? The Commissioner will hear about this immediately!"

"Vince, I'm asking you not to make a big fuss about this," the executive pleaded, while looking around the room once more. "It'll be resolved in due course."

"Trent Blair has verbally insulted my baseball people on multiple occasions, he stole Eddie Griffin three years ago, and the bottom line is that I don't like him."

"I think you're spewing sour grapes."

"You're damn right it's sour grapes! Now he's jacked up the salaries by signing Marcus Dillard!"

The executive let out a hearty laugh.

"Well if it isn't the cat calling the kettle black," he said. "Every year your team spends the most money in baseball."

"You know as well as I do that if Blair had the same information about us, he'd spill the beans."

"Probably."

"There ain't no probably about it!" D'Antoni shouted. "I hate losing, and there is nothing I hate more than losing to a piece of shit like Trent Blair."

"Well," the executive laughed, "with Marcus Dillard you can expect at least a few more years of that."

The Yankees owner shook his head.

"You can have your fun, but the Yankees won't be down for very long. There's nothing I hate more than losing. Not a goddamn thing."

CHAPTER 4

The sounds of spring

By: Chet Thomas (Buffalo News)

There is something refreshing about spring training. It is a revival of sorts, a rebirth for all those who have fallen in years gone by to redeem themselves. It is a time of optimism, a time to hope rookies pan out and wily veterans still have some gas left in the tank. It is a time of great balance, as all teams start with a clean slate and with even records. The Buffalo Pioneers spring training represents all of these things and more. Led by the impeccable direction of mastermind Trent Blair and coming off the heels of three consecutive World Series triumphs, it is easy to assume that the team's outlook is great, especially with the gifted Marcus Dillard bringing his immense talents to town. But we are taught at a very early age never to assume. Never assume that what should happen does happen, especially when the comatose Jack Vaughn is running the show. It was a miracle the Pioneers won so much with his questionable on-field decisions, but now his calls off the field may hurt the team as well. His complete and utter disrespect for Marcus Dillard during his introduction to the Buffalo media was disgraceful. To mock and insult a man with as much character as Dillard is not only an injustice to a man who has humbly come to Buffalo in search of a World Series ring, but it is an insult to baseball. Vaughn has had a great career, but its over and he might be the last person to realize it. Spring training is about the return to a paradise of green grass and sunshine. With Jack Vaughn's recent gaffes however, it appears that there may be trouble in paradise.

"Did you read today's paper?" Pitching coach Grant Robinson asked. "That blowhard Thomas is sounding off about you again."

The black pitching coach had a quiet, humble demeanour. His hair was greying and his old body was slowing down, but his mind remained sharp and he possessed a simple niceness and quiet serenity to him that put those in his company at ease.

"What else is new," responded Vaughn nonchalantly. "He's still mad I wouldn't do that exclusive with him two years ago."

"I wonder who appointed him the baseball authority in this city," Robinson wondered.

Vaughn scratched his head in frustration.

"Nothing surprises me anymore."

"You have to admit that shelling out $11 million to put Dillard in right field was a bold move. Mr. J came up huge this winter."

"Johnny's a great man, but he listens to the wrong people. Getting Dillard was a big mistake."

"He should help us."

"The guy is a virus," Vaughn responded indignantly. "Blair and Ferreira think you can evaluate a player based on his statistics alone. But I've heard actual reports about this kid and he's bad news. I don't need a laptop to tell me that."

Vaughn took a sip of his coffee. The more he thought about it the angrier he became.

"Besides, do you think they signed him to help us? No! They signed him because some wench up in accounting thinks he can help us strike a better deal with the fucking television networks! Do you believe that? It's the biggest bunch of nonsense I've ever heard!"

The pitching coach laughed.

"You're still mad about that accountant," Robinson smiled.

"That broad would be wise to just keep her mouth shut."

"She was trying to help."

"I can do without, let me tell you. Do you think Vince D'Antoni listens to his accountant before making a trade? People say he's a bastard, but I bet he'd give his first born child for a World Series ring."

"He'd probably give all his children away," Robinson said wryly.

"Meanwhile, we're busy alienating Scotty Harper. We've got a home grown superstar a year from free-agency and nothing is being done about it."

The pitching coach was taken aback

"I don't understand it either."

"The more I think about it," Vaughn ranted, "The more I'm amazed that Trent didn't fuck this thing up earlier. The guy never even played in the majors."

The pitching coach attempted to soothe his friend's uneasiness.

"I'll tell you one thing, Jack. I look up and down our line-up and I see some powerful hitters. Trent must have done something right."

Jack sipped his coffee.

"Power hitters don't win championships. You win by making plays, executing the hit and run, the sacrifice fly, the clutch single and playing good defence. Anyone who played the game would know that."

"You might as well give Marcus a chance," the pitching coach said. "He might even surprise you."

Few people could disagree with Vaughn and get away with it, but Grant Robinson was one of them. There was a brief silence as Jack looked outside at the sun rising over another gorgeous Florida morning. A few pitchers were already warming up on the diamond.

"Maybe you're right, maybe I'm overreacting," Vaughn replied, running his hands through his thinning hair. "But I don't know......I just can't shake the feeling that this club is headed in the wrong direction."

The pitchers and catchers reported to spring training on February 19th, with the rest of the players due into camp a week later. Some showed up ahead of time.

Conan O'Shea, the ultimate fitness buff, was in early to work out. Despite already sporting one of the most well toned bodies in the game, the reliever had come to camp with an extra fifteen pounds of pure muscle while reducing his body fat to below 3%. It could hardly have been natural, and more than a few people took notice.

Musclemax Magazine sent a photographer to the Pioneers spring training camp to take a few pictures of the well-built reliever for the cover of their March edition. Some of the pictures bordered on the ridiculous, particularly the pullout that featured Conan throwing from a mound in nothing but his boxers. It did not take long for the magazine to find its way into Jack Vaughn's hands. Everyone knew what the crusty manager's reaction would be.

"Hey Fabio," Jack bellowed across the field. "Don't strain yourself. You've got a modelling career to worry about!"

The reliever walked over and put his bulky arms around the manager. The two had become like father and son.

"Any hitter that sees these pictures will fear the Barbarian."

"Is that so?" Vaughn retorted.

"Every bar needs its bouncer and every baseball team needs it closer. Somebody has to shut the door when its time to go home."

"Where the hell did we find you?" The manager laughed gruffly.

Catcher Terry Miller and starter Chris Norton were also in camp ahead of time. The battery-mates had developed a deep camaraderie with Miller's veteran influence behind the plate harnessing Norton's prodigious raw talent. Both were eager to get on with the season.

When the time had come for the regular players to report to spring training on February 26th, there was only one player missing. Days went by as February gave way to March, without word or even a phone call. It was the talk of camp that someone would have the audacity to show up not just a few days late, but over a week. The news spread quickly, both in the papers and on television. It was becoming an embarrassment for the team and the manager.

"Where the fuck is he?" Vaughn demanded.

Each day, the assistant general manager was dispatched to the clubhouse to explain for the unexcused absence.

"We're working on it, Jack," Al Ferreira responded. "You gotta be patient on this."

"You guys have your heads so far up your asses it's sickening," the manager barked back. "I'm sickened."

Eventually, the front-office tracked down the player in question at a resort in the Bahamas and arranged for him to report to camp on March 9th.

At first sight of his car, a sea of reporters parted in the parking lot outside of Jacksonville Field, the spring training home for the Pioneers. Slowly and painstakingly the yellow Ferrari pulled into the lot through the huge media scrum. When the car finally stopped it parallel parked across three parking spaces.

Out came a beautiful, scantily clad black woman in high heels and tight skirt followed by another. Then, with gold chains around his neck and chest, the man of the hour stepped out onto the pavement. One week and four days after his scheduled reporting date, an unprecedented length of time without an excuse, Marcus Dillard reported to camp.

The team was already so far into its training that their first Grapefruit League game was that very afternoon. Besieged by questions from the media hordes that surrounded him, Marcus put his arms in the air to signal to everyone present that his highness was ready to speak. He was not going to speak until everyone was silent.

After two long minutes, the parking lot was at last in complete silence. He put his arms down and immediately threw them around both women.

"I am here today to tell you all that Marcus Dillard is fit of body and mind. I have spent the last three months training at home in Miami and am ready to begin playing today."

Dillard grabbed the escorts' arms and walked into the clubhouse as the media threw question after question at him. Most of the team was already out on the field, but many of the players remaining in the dressing room had nothing but cold stares for the newcomer. Oblivious to them, Marcus mounted himself up onto one of the many stools proliferated throughout the room.

"The Saviour has arrived!" He proclaimed proudly.

A few moments of silence followed.

"Could have fooled me," a sarcastic voice came from the manager's office. "It sounds more like the village idiot."

The comment lit a fuse in the cocky slugger, who dismounted the stool and stormed over to where the voice had originated.

"Who dares to talk about Marcus Dillard like this?" He demanded.

As he entered the doorway of the office, he was greeted face to face by none other than manager Jack Vaughn. There was no welcome in his eyes.

"Glad you could make it Marcus," he said snidely. "Why don't you tone down the bullshit though. Its still early and I'm already getting a bit of a headache."

He tossed a uniform at the bulging slugger and slammed the door in his face. The sound reverberated around the room.

Marcus sauntered over to his stall in disbelief.

"That's how it's going to be, huh?"

His locker was completely empty with the exception of a baby pacifier that somebody had evidently hung from a hook in jest. He ripped it down angrily.

One of the trainers came over with some uniforms.

"Mr. Dillard, it really is an honour. I've been watching you for...."

"Put them down here," interrupted Marcus coldly, "and get me some water. Damn! What's a brother have to do to get some service around here?"

"Right away Mr. Dillard," responded the trainer, quickly rushing off to the water cooler.

Moments later, the trainer came back with the water.

"Here you go Mr. Dillard."

Marcus snatched the cup from his hand and walked outside.

On the field, hitting coach Norm Watkins was running the players through some intense endurance drills. A former marine-corps officer, Watkins was not the type of man who inspired respect, but he certainly tried to demand it. He relished the role of authoritarian.

"Come on boys, Pick it up!" Watkins barked at them. "I don't care how you guys feel, move it!"

The only thing stopping many of the players from revolting against the hitting coach was the threat of Jack Vaughn coming out onto the field. There was fear and there was respect. Norm Watkins instilled neither of them.

"Imagine Watkins ran this team?" Eddie Griffin remarked to catcher Terry Miller between breaths.

"The guy still thinks he's in 'Nam," Miller responded.

The hitting coach noticed the two veterans slowing down.

"Move it, move it, move it!" He barked at them like a guard dog.

A few minutes later, Marcus Dillard sauntered onto the field. As Watkins caught sight of the tardy newcomer, he sped down the field to greet him. His rough looking face suddenly gave way to an eager smile. He could be sycophantic with the best of them.

"Marcus! It's a pleasure!"

Dillard didn't say anything, preferring to wear his customary frown.

"How are you doing?" The hitting coach kept saying in an ingratiating tone. "Do you feel up to running today?"

Dillard had little interest in pursuing conversation.

"No I'm good, coach. I'll stay right here."

"Suit yourself. It's great to have you here!"

As Watkins made his way back to the drills, he found the team staring at Marcus motionlessly. His face morphed back into that of a general.

"Ok boys let's get going, we don't have all day here!"

The whole field remained dead silent.

"Let's go! Nobody gets a free ride around here!"

"Oh yeah?" Conan O'Shea piped up. "How come he's getting one? We're not doing anything until his royal highness decides to join us."

"What!?" Watkins screamed. "O'Shea give me ten right now!"

"Blow me, Watkins."

The hulking reliever brushed by the hitting coach and walked aggressively towards Dillard. He pointed his index finger directly in the slugger's face.

"I don't know who you think you are, but you'd better get your ass out here!"

Dillard stepped closer to O'Shea and brushed his face against him. The two exchanged bad breath.

"Excuse me boy, are you talking to me?"

"You know damn well I'm talking to you and if you don't start running, I'm going to haul your ass over there myself."

"I'll run with you," Dillard replied, "but first I'd like to do this."

He sucker punched O'Shea, slightly dazing 'The Barbarian' before the reliever regrouped to tackle Dillard to the ground. The two exchanged blows until first baseman Eddie Griffin and others came in to break it up.

"What the hell is wrong with you two?" Griffin yelled.

"I don't know Eddie," O'Shea responded, "why don't you ask the pretty boy over here!"

"Kiss my black ass!" Dillard yelled back. "I ain't the one posing in no magazines!"

One of the attendants burst into the clubhouse to alert Vaughn of the fight. The manager slowly made his way onto the field.

"Oh great," shouted O'Shea. "Now Jack's coming."

The manager calmly made his way through the crowd of players and inspected the scarred faces of both players for a minute without saying a word. Suddenly everything seemed under control.

"O'Shea, I'm fining you $1000," Jack said. "As for you Marcus, come with me to my office."

"What did I do?" Marcus shot back in disbelief.

"Just come with me."

"You expect me to take this shit? Your boy had roid rage."

"Marcus....come with me," Jack insisted.

"What kind of...."

The manager now reached up to grab the ears of the six-foot-four outfielder. It was a comical scene: a senior man of such modest size with the nerve to physically scold a player of Dillard's huge stature.

"If you're going to act like a schoolgirl, I'm going to treat you like one. Now get the fuck in here!"

Vaughn released Marcus' ears to snickers as the two men walked back into the clubhouse. The situation, which had spiralled out of control under Watkins, was quickly and concisely handled by the veteran skipper.

Vaughn sat down behind his desk and was followed into the office by Dillard.

"Close the door behind you."

"Listen man...."

"I don't want to hear it, Marcus."

"You don't understand...."

"I understand all too well."

"Just let me...."

"Marcus," Vaughn calmly stated. "If you don't sit down, you're going to make me very angry."

The slugger sat down.

Jack took a slow sip of coffee.

"I don't know what you were expecting," Jack said, as he leaned back in his chair, "but this isn't going to be the Marcus Dillard show. If you had any ideas that you could just waltz in here and do as you please, let me be the first to tell you that isn't going to happen."

The manager slowly sipped his coffee.

"As for your spot in the lineup...."

"I had better be hitting cleanup," Dillard interrupted. "Marcus only hits cleanup."

"You will hit where I tell you to hit," Vaughn responded sternly. "You're in no position to dictate things to me, son. You show up two weeks late and then pick a fight in your first ten minutes. To make matters worse, I hear you sucker punched him."

"Marcus Dillard don't take no shit from nobody."

"I don't think you realize how dumb you sound. What do you think your teammates think of you?"

"I don't know what they think of me," Dillard stood up aggressively. "But I personally don't give a shit. I led the league in home-runs last season and I intend to do the same this season while batting cleanup. Got it?"

Vaughn sat motionless for a moment. He took another sip from his cup of coffee.

"I don't want to tell you one more time to sit down."

The slugger sat down.

"Marcus, I'm not here to baby sit you," Jack raised his voice. "If you want to make a fool out of yourself, so be it. But I will not allow your candyass attitude to interfere with our success. You will hit where the coaching staff tells you to hit and you will learn to show a little goddamn respect for your teammates! Am I understood?"

"Sure skip," Marcus responded half-heartedly.

"Ok then, get outta here."

Dillard opened the door and walked into the crowded clubhouse. A few moments later, Trent Blair came strolling into the office looking worried.

"Did I miss something?" Blair asked. "I heard there was a fight."

Vaughn got up and walked passed him disgustedly.

"Hell of a pick up you made, Trent. He's a real quality individual."

The first few games of spring training went by with mixed results. For veteran teams, the spring games were usually more about giving the rookies a chance to show their stuff and some grace time for the veterans to clear out the off-season rust.

Despite being forced to sit out three games under orders from the manager, Marcus Dillard was given a standing ovation by the few thousand die-hard Pioneer fans on hand to watch the proceedings in Jacksonville. He did not disappoint, slugging a double to left-centre on the very first pitch and continuing to tear the cover off the ball throughout spring. His play did little to squelch the controversy over who was going to bat fourth.

First baseman Eddie Griffin was still the unquestioned leader on the team. He always had a quick smile and a sunny attitude that served him well for the ups and downs of regular season. Now 39 years of age, Griffin's breadth of knowledge was a valued commodity. Eddie had a larger-than-life persona, being very active in the inner-city black community and so popular with members of the media that they voted him New York State's "Athlete of High Moral Character." With a family of wife and kids, he seemed to represent the true all-American athlete.

When pressed numerous times over spring training for a response about possibly losing his spot batting cleanup, Griffin demonstrated his adeptness at avoiding controversy.

He would say: "This is something Jack will handle." Or the token "I'm just here doing my business, I'll play anywhere they want" speech.

Scott Harper wanted no part of the dispute either. In contrast to Eddie Griffin's irrepressible penchant for self-promotion or the bombastic rants of Marcus Dillard, the rube from Oklahoma had always been a man of few words. Suddenly, Harper was thrown into the spotlight. Not only did he have to deal with questions about his impending free-agent status, but also inquiries into how he was getting along with Dillard.

As Harper and one of the minor leaguers were doing squats in the weight room one day, Dillard interrupted to shake Harper's hand.

"What's up white boy?"

"I'm busy," Harper replied unimpressed.

"I'm just here to tell you that while you may have been the man on this team before, I'm the man now."

'Excuse me?"

"You heard me, white boy."

It had the makings of a classic testosterone fuelled weight room confrontation. Marcus tried to stare him down, but he had miscalculated. Harper was a simple farm boy with little time for ego games.

"Get out my face," Harper brushed him off. "I've got work to do."

Marcus grabbed Harper's shirt.

"Nobody brushes Marcus Dillard off! You got that?"

The shouting could be heard from across the weight room. Just as things looked as if they might escalate, Eddie Griffin came in to settle things down.

"Give it a rest, Marcus," Eddie insisted.

Marcus released Harper's shirt.

"Don't touch me, old man!" Dillard slapped Eddie's arm away. "This is for you too. Marcus is going to steal your precious clean-up spot right under your nose!"

"You think so, huh?" Eddie scoffed

"That's what I said, isn't it? What you boys fail to realize is that Marcus Dillard is the straw that stirs the drink on this team. You think you can stir it Griffin, but you can only stir it bad!"

If Marcus had said it to anyone else, fists might have been exchanged. Instead, Eddie let out a huge laugh. He had a way of diffusing otherwise sticky situations.

"Man, Reggie Jackson retired twenty years ago. Stop pretending."

"I'm the real deal, Griffin. I'm the fittest, finest and fastest ballplayer that ever lived!"

Griffin laughed thunderously before fanning himself.

"Is that hot air I feel?" Eddie joked. "Oh yeah, I definitely feel a breeze!"

The two men continued clowning around. Marcus even managed to crack a smile.

"I've got a hundred bucks here that says I can bench press more than you can."

Griffin shook his head.

"You kids just love throwing your money away. I'll see your hundred and raise you another hundred."

Dillard threw the extra hundred back in his face.

"We ain't playing poker here, old man. The bet is a hundred. I'm not in to taking money from senior citizens."

Eddie let out yet another thunderous laugh.

"Ok, fair enough. But we might as well put the money in my pocket right away because that's where it's ending up."

"You just made a big mistake, old man," Dillard shook his head. "I've spent the entire off-season training to have the biggest chest in baseball. Back home they call me 'El Caballo'. That's Spanish for 'the horse'. You can call me that too if you like."

Griffin let out another monstrous laugh.

"El Caballo! What a load of shit."

After he regained his composure, Eddie began lifting.

"Remember," Marcus reminded him. "I've got the first-aid kit ready in case your ancient body falls apart on us."

The two went at it for a few minutes, constantly one upping one another. With the bar at well over 350 pounds, neither man showed signs of breaking until finally Marcus crumbled. Much to the elder Griffin's delight, 'El Caballo' was finished at 375 pounds. Griffin began flexing in front of the mirror.

"Mm...mm...mm," Griffin boasted. "They just don't make 'em like they used to!"

Dillard reached into his pocket and reluctantly handed over a bill.

Griffin grabbed the cash, ran it across his nose, and sniffed it. Then to rub it in further, he picked up a Kleenex box off the shelf and handed it to Marcus.

"You might be a little broken over this," Eddie boasted sarcastically.

The burly slugger stormed out of the room without responding.

"I guess it's that time of the month," Eddie joked.

During the last few weeks of spring training, the Pioneers began picking up the intensity. Everything was going according to plan on the field and even in the clubhouse. After their initial blow-up, Marcus Dillard patched things up with Conan O'Shea and brought him out to some of the best Florida nightclubs. The two became close friends.

Not much else had changed though. Dillard was proving to be incapable of containing his indignation about not batting in the cleanup spot.

"It's bullshit man, plain and simple." He told the media horde. "People on this team feel obviously feel threatened by Marcus Dillard's presence."

The reporters soon scurried to Jack Vaughn for his thoughts on the matter. The manager was in a particularly surly mood that morning.

"How do you respond to the sultan of sulk?" Vaughn grunted. "I don't have a goddamn thing to say about it."

As much as the controversy simmered in public, there were some very definite opinions among the coaching staff and management when it came to the batting order.

Eddie Griffin had been the cleanup hitter since he arrived in Buffalo three years prior and had performed quite admirably. Whenever a big hit was needed, in the playoffs or otherwise, Eddie Griffin was the man Pioneer fans most wanted to see at the plate. Still, some people in the organization believed the arrival of Dillard should displace him.

"I can't believe you're even considering not doing this!" Norm Watkins shouted at a meeting. "Marcus has tremendous power, he should hit fourth."

Jack continued to listen to the opposing positions with great patience, as he sat slumped in his chair sipping coffee

"Don't let pride get in the way, Jack," assistant G.M. Al Ferreira said. "We all know you don't like the guy, but that's no reason to bat him fifth."

There was something about Ferreira that deeply irritated Vaughn. His thin moustache was certainly not something that inspired his trust, but it was more than that. Al Ferreira's meek looking physique seemed to tell one story while hiding another. He always seemed to have an ulterior motive.

"I don't think I understand your reasoning either," Trent rhymed in.

Jack sipped his full cup of coffee.

"The guy is selfish, which will manifest itself on the field. Marcus may hit five or ten more homers than Eddie, he may be faster, he may be eight years younger, but Eddie is a team guy. Eddie will make sacrifices. I'm not convinced that Marcus would do that."

"Eddie only tries hard when you're watching," shouted Watkins, "but when you go to your office and I start running drills on the field, he looks slow."

Vaughn raised his eyebrows.

"The man is 39 years old, what the hell do you expect?"

"I expect a top effort all the time! If he can't run it out, sit him out! That's how it's done in the army."

Vaughn leaned over his desk and gave Norm a sharp look.

"This isn't boot camp Watkins, so why don't you just relax. Dillard ain't exactly winning any awards for hard work. I have yet to see him run out a groundball."

"Ok guys, enough is enough," Blair intervened. "We'll go with Jack on this one."

The meeting ended on less than collegial terms.

The following morning, the team boarded its plane back to Buffalo. The title defence was set to begin.

CHAPTER 5

On opening day, a deep sense of anticipation was building in the city. The downtown skyscrapers had huge signs strewn down the sides of them with the inscription, 'Go for Four!' Expectations are high after any championship, and even higher after three, but this went beyond mere expectation.

After years of winning, the fans almost felt as if the World Series had become their divine right. Buffalo had become a northern baseball paradise; the way the sun rose early that morning and the crystal waters of Lake Erie emitted a warm breeze throughout the city. On the day when Buffalo fans would finally be able to taste Marcus Dillard's forbidden fruits, everything was sweet.

"Welcome to BSN Baseball, I'm Chuck Smith with my colleague Terry Davis, glad to have you with us for the opening day of the 2004 season."

"You know Chuck, this is the best time of year because Opening Day is synonymous with hope. It's the day everybody is in first place and there's really nothing like it."

"Absolutely Terry, but I think once this Pioneer squad starts rolling, there's only gonna be one team ruling the A.L East this season."

"I think you're right and it appears as if Vince D'Antoni's New York Yankees will have to shoot for a wild-card berth if they hope to make the playoffs this season."

Chuck Smith laughs.

"The Yankees have really fallen off the face of the earth the last couple of years."

"They really have, but if slugger Benny Rios and some of their high-priced talent could stay healthy, they have a definite shot at the wild card."

"Plus lead-off hitter LaTroy LaRocque finally has his hamstring at 100%."

"The Yankees really missed LaRocque. They've been criticized in recent years for not having enough speed and playing a station to station offence. LaTroy's speed gives them that new dimension. He gets on base and is an 80-steal guy when healthy. He'll help the top of their order."

"Let's talk a little more about the Pioneers, who will be playing in our feature game."

"Well Chuck, at the end of last season I said that the Buffalo Pioneers would be hard pressed to go for an encore after three straight World Series championships, but I think they've done it. Trent Blair acted boldly in signing Marcus Dillard from Florida. This guy makes the middle of their order that much stronger. You have to consider Buffalo as the early World Series favourite for 2004."

"And about his promise to hit eighty homers this season?"

Terry laughs.

"Well I don't know about that, but he makes the team look scary to opposing pitchers."

"What about Scott Harper? This is the final year of his contract and there are rumblings he may leave at the end of the season as a free-agent."

"Rumblings Chuck, that's the key word...rumblings. There is no truth to them whatsoever and if I know Trent Blair, I'd be very surprised if he didn't already have a verbal agreement in place. I mean, can you imagine Scott Harper playing anywhere but Buffalo?"

Both men laugh.

"What do you think of manager Jack Vaughn's decision to bat 39-year-old Eddie Griffin at cleanup? I know a lot of people felt that Marcus Dillard was ticketed for that spot, but instead he will bat fifth."

"Well Chuck, I think there's one thing you can never underestimate and that is Jack Vaughn's loyalty to his players. Eddie Griffin has done all that has been asked of him since coming over to Buffalo three years ago. He's been the captain of this team on the field and in the locker room and those are things that Vaughn really values in a player."

"We'll be back with the national anthem after this break."

Down in the clubhouse, a sense of calm permeated the dressing room. On such a veteran laden squad, any hint of the opening day nerves were conspicuously missing.

Conan O'Shea walked out of the training room with his shirt off when team accountant Paula Lombardi suddenly strolled into the clubhouse. She had the cunning mix of professionalism, stunningly good looks and a mischievous smile.

"Hey there Barbarian," Paula cooed, as she rubbed his large biceps.

He flexed his arm for her.

"There's more where that came from."

The Irishman grabbed her behind with the strength he gripped his searing fastball. Her eyes twirled with the curious mixture of surprise and pleasure.

"Oh I bet there is," she said in her velvet voice. "Now, I know what *Musclemax* saw in you."

Suddenly, the door of Jack Vaughn's office opened.

"Shit, Jack's coming. You'd better go. You know how the old man is."

The accountant looked over her shoulder and gingerly walked out of the room.

"See you around, sexy."

As soon as Jack entered the clubhouse, Eddie Griffin dutifully called on everyone to be quiet.

"Okay guys, skip's got something to say."

The manager commanded such a great deal of respect that the room fell silent.

"Nothing special tonight, boys. I just want to remind you about the importance of getting a good start. We're playing a good team tonight. Texas won the A.L West last year. Every ground ball you run out, every diving catch you make will set the tone for our season."

He paused for a moment and slowly sipped his coffee.

"You may have heard that we are the so-called favourites to win it all this season. People are saying that all the pressure is on us to keep our title, but I don't agree with that for a minute. In fact, I think it's the other way around. I think the pressure is on everyone else to keep up with us. If each and every one of you goes out and plays his game, nobody will touch us."

Vaughn paused to sip his coffee.

"None of you should be feeling any extra burden. If Scott Harper is in a hitting slump, we've got Pete Sampson and Eddie Griffin to pick up the slack. If Frank Ringler gets his ass kicked tonight...."

The whole room laughed.

"....we know that we've got Chris Norton and Conan O'Shea backing him up. We've got some depth and if you all just go out there and play your games, we're fine. Right now the pressure is on everyone else to catch up with us, so let's keep it on them. Let's keep 'em sweating. Just play your game and everything else will take care of itself."

The clubhouse erupted in cheers as the team stormed down the hall and onto the field.

For the 221st consecutive game, Pioneer Stadium was sold-out. There was nothing particularly nice about the old stadium, but put a full crowd of rabid fans in it and the place looked like a jewel. Looking around at the frenzied crowd and the plentiful World Series banners hanging over centre field, it was almost impossible to imagine the city without baseball. Only the large bank tower hovering across the street cast a shadow on that early afternoon.

The parkas were out in full effect on that cold April day, but the chill seemed only to be affecting Texas.

In the top of the first inning, Frank Ringler retired the first two batters on groundballs before getting two quick strikes on defending American League MVP Jeff Hudson. The crowd was already on their feet.

"Nobody throws a heater quite like Frank Ringler. He sets....the pitch....swing and a miss strike three!"

"YEAH!!!" The crowd collectively erupted.

"Three up three down! And the Pioneers are coming to bat right after this."

When Benjy Alvarez led off the bottom of the inning, excitement built up throughout the stadium. This was a lineup of hitters who made things happen and there was a feeling that something special would happen very shortly. On the very first pitch, Alvarez singled up the middle.

"YEAH!!" The crowd roared.

"That is so typical of Alvarez, he just gets some wood on the ball and he has the first hit of this young season. Catcher Terry Miller is up next."

"Look for him to take here and allow Alvarez to steal the base. Benjy is a very good first pitch stealer."

"He checks the runner....the pitch....Alvarez takes off.....Miller takes a strike and Alvarez is in there with his first steal of the season!"

The crowd roared its approval. The catcher later grounded out, advancing Alvarez to third.

Scott Harper and Eddie Griffin were up next. Each man received a hearty reception from the crowd before showing the poise and patience at the plate that had made the Pioneers so successful. After a combined twenty-pitch battle, both of them drew walks.

The bases were juiced, the pitcher was tired and the focus now shifted to the man swinging lumber in the on-deck circle. The previous cheers paled compared to the tidal wave to come.

"These fans have been waiting for this moment for four months and here it is!"

A roar engulfed Pioneer Stadium as Marcus Dillard's name was announced over the public address system.

One huge sign hanging from the upper deck read: 'With Marcus In Tow, Make it 4 in a Row.' Countless fans were wearing Dillard jerseys. The slugger took it all in stride, strutting up to the plate and taking his time to get into the batters box. If the fans had waited months for this moment, he was going to take every delight in making them wait just a few moments longer. His shirt was unbuttoned halfway, partly revealing the gold chains and swelled chest that lay beneath.

"This is absolute bedlam! In his first American League at-bat, the Buffalo fans are giving him a standing ovation!"

"Marcus steps in....the pitcher sets....delivers....swing and a miss strike one!"

The crowd gasped.

"From my vantage point, that looked like it was going to bounce. Bad pitch to swing at."

"Marcus steps back in. The pitcher sets....he delivers....big swing and miss!"

The crowd gasped even louder.

"I don't think there's any doubt what's on Dillard's mind. He's hacking."

The crowd started cheering loudly again.

"The pitcher sets.....the pitch....hit hard!....No doubt about it! Opening Day Grand Slam! What a way to say hello!"

It was a towering blast. The ball sailed over the left-field bleachers and onto Oak Street, where a group of delirious fans scrambled after it.

As soon as he made contact, Marcus knew it was gone. He threw his bat twenty feet in the air, slowly sauntered out of the batters box ten feet, made three side steps to the right of the baseline, did a little shake with his head and broke into a painstakingly slow homerun trot. After rounding second base, he stopped and held up his arms in a raise-the-roof motion, provoking an even larger ovation from the masses.

"Just round the goddamn bases!" barked Vaughn, embarrassed by Dillard's blatant showing up of the other team.

"Marcus was a little free swinging in that at-bat, but he jacked that one. My oh my, 4-0 Pioneers after only five batters!"

The burly slugger was greeted at the dugout by several teammates, who he perfunctorily ignored before taking his seat on the bench.

The game quickly turned into a cakewalk. Despite giving up a run late in the game, Jack Vaughn left Frank Ringler in for the complete game 9-1 victory.

"The Pioneers racked up nine runs here tonight and lived up to their billing as baseball's top dog."

"They really did Chuck, and a win like this, especially on opening day against a good squad like Texas, will reverberate around the league."

"That it will. Just to remind you that the Pioneers will return to BSN tomorrow against Texas at 4:05 eastern. So until next time, this is Chuck Smith and Terry Davis saying so long from Buffalo."

Up in his private box, Blair wore the smug look of self-satisfaction that comes from the belief in one's infallibility. He had always been so incredibly scrupulous about detail and everything had gone according to plan thus far.

"Not even God himself could beat this team," Blair boldly declared to Ferreira after the game.

The assistant general manager thought the comment ludicrous when it was first uttered, but after a few weeks he began to take it more seriously.

As the month of April wore on, the Buffalo Pioneers won their first twelve games to open the season. The team was a juggernaut. While the New York Yankees plodded along at the breakeven point, everyone on the Pioneers was clicking from the hitters, the pitchers and the bullpen.

In the clubhouse, Marcus Dillard was quickly establishing his presence. His rage still simmered just beneath the surface and he was just as likely to snap at an umpire's bad call as completely ignore a teammate's friendly greeting. But despite their spring training blow-up, he had befriended both Conan O'Shea and Pete Sampson. Marcus saw a similar edge in their personalities to his own.

As April gave to May, the New York state elections were starting to gear up.

"Governor Tom Murdoch launched his re-election campaign this afternoon in Albany. Blessed with a 76% approval rating in the latest New York Times poll, he looks to be cruising towards a fourth term in office."

The Republican Governor's only major competitor was retired Columbia University professor Prentice H. Wulloughby III. There was no denying that Wulloughby was a remarkable academic. He had authored or co-authored several award-winning books in sociology while gaining a well-deserved reputation as one of the most highly regarded social scientists in the country. Unfortunately, the professor did not have anything resembling an exciting public persona.

He suffered from the same problem many eggheads face, the tendency to make such a bad public impression that aides and colleagues felt the need to feverishly insist that "the private man, if only you got to know him, is very down to earth." Old college acquaintances gave testimony to his "sense of humour." Anybody who sat through a Wulloughby speech must have found that hard to believe. He meandered in and out of Latin, all the while using words so complicated that their very usage seemed solely motivated by an arrogant power trip to make his listeners consult a thesaurus.

While the erudite Wulloughby may have been brilliant and had an air of complete honesty, he was given little chance at mounting anything other than a principled, losing campaign. Up against the powerful Tom Murdoch political machine, the Democratic Party knew the gubernatorial elections were hopeless and focused their energies elsewhere. Although he might have been better suited in an ambassadorial role at the United Nations, Wulloughby was thrust into action as the sacrificial lamb.

As April gave way to May, the Pioneers cruised at a 27-6 clip. Frank Ringler and Chris Norton were blowing away hitters, Conan O'Shea hadn't allowed a run all year, Benjy Alvarez was leading the league in steals and the big four of Harper, Griffin, Dillard and Sampson were all up among the leaders in home-runs.

Everyone was on fire heading into Miami for the first inter-league series of the year against the last place Florida Marlins, a game that marked Marcus Dillard's return to Florida.

In a pre-game interview, Dillard shrugged off his impending boo birds.

"They boo Marcus because they love Marcus and fear Marcus's greatness."

Despite the constant jeering he endured throughout the game, the Pioneers blew out the lowly Marlins 13-2 and swept the series.

"Another convincing win for the Pioneers this afternoon, Chuck."

"Convincing indeed. These guys are playing in a league of their own."

With two straight off-days following the three-game series, Jack Vaughn decided to scrap curfew. That night, Marcus Dillard, Pete Sampson and Conan O'Shea were seen at the Havana Club, Dillard's old Miami stomping grounds. The three of them didn't return to the hotel until ten the next morning.

Back in New York, Trent Blair and Al Ferreira were at the NCAA Regional Championships scouting for the upcoming amateur draft. As Blair walked around the park with Ferreira at his side, more than a few people noticed him strutting around with his chest held unusually high.

"Look at that jackass," an opposing scout remarked to his colleague. "He walks around like he's the fucking Pope."

"You would too if you had won three championships by age 35."

"If he's not careful," the sage old scout proclaimed. "He'll be out of the game by 40. Once you burn your bridges in this game, you're finished."

As Blair and Ferreira watched the Ohio State-LSU game from the stands, they began to ponder the future.

"You heard anything about the new stadium recently?"

"From what Jenkins tells me," Blair said. "The Governor is only waiting for the election to push this thing through."

"Is it a done deal?" Ferreira asked.

"About as done as done can be."

Unbeknownst to either of them, a beat writer for the *New York Times* was sitting just three rows back.

CHAPTER 6

"I find it appalling and disconcerting that a deal of this magnitude could be kept secret from the very taxpayers who are privy to its knowledge, but are obligated to be informed! If anything, this promulgates all of our worst suspicions that this state is being controlled by Republican special interest groups."

The crowd cheered vociferously as a bespectacled Prentice H. Wulloughby III delivered a fiery speech at the Niagara Falls Convention Hall.

"As the old Latin phrase goes, 'Falsus in uno, falsus in omnibus.' If Governor Murdoch cannot be trusted, he no longer deserves the spoils of office. For Mr. Murdoch and his ubiquitous cronies, twelve years in power has been exceedingly long!"

Wulloughby shouted and pumped his fists awkwardly, eliciting increasingly enthusiastic cheers from the crowd. Few people understood the meaning of his ostentatious speeches, but they seemed to be there for no other reason than to ride the tidal wave of public opinion sweeping the state. It was a political fire fuelled by nothing other than pure emotion. As the days went by, it became increasingly apparent it would be hard to stop.

"The time has come to make a change, Mr. Murdoch. Resign!"

Ever since the *New York Times* obtained a state government memo from an anonymous source laying out the details of the backroom stadium deal, it quickly became a huge political scandal. The revelations were not that shocking, but taken in the context of the controversies the Governor's office had become embroiled in recent weeks, it broke the dam of public mistrust in an administration that many felt had been in power too long.

Only days earlier, the Governor's chief of staff Rod Menta was forced to resign after it was revealed that he held a significant stake in Delaware Falls, a telecommunications company that was repeatedly given undue advantage in securing government contracts despite a bid that was three times as expensive as the competition. When it was later revealed that Delaware Falls was also a leading contributor to the state Republican Party the scandal only deepened. It could not have come at worse possible time for Murdoch, who was otherwise coasting to a fourth term in office.

Doug Henrich, a political analyst for the *Times*, seemed to understand the essence of the scandal.

The stench from the backroom is unbearable

By: Doug Heinrich (New York Times)

The secret stadium agreement between Governor Tom Murdoch and Pioneers owner Jonathan Jenkins, which no doubt was negotiated in some reclusive countryside mansion, is not what so irritates everyone. It is only symbolic of the larger problems with an administration that has grown arrogant and unaccountable, what with Rod Menta and his band of bandits at Delaware Falls. It's the slick and furtive way in which it was handled that has made the people in this state reconsider who they are voting for. It's the nonchalant attitude from Tom Murdoch that the taxpaying public is not privy to how he handles our money. We are led to presume that, unlike in every other state, Mr. Murdoch planned on pushing this stadium deal through without a referendum. What does Joe Schmoe, who likely works for a pittance in one of Jonathan Jenkins' many supermarkets, think? What is he to believe, when his hard earned tax dollars are being directed to a sport he may not even like and without his approval? What is he to think when multi-millionaires are handed hundreds of millions of dollars for a baseball stadium when he is having trouble paying rent? Is it necessary to know one of Murdoch's cronies or significantly contribute to the Republican Party as a pre-requisite for doing business in this state? This is a slap in the face that will not be forgotten. The people will speak, and they will speak in great numbers.

Amidst all the pre-election talk, the Pioneers kept buzzing. While slowing down from their gaudy pace of April, the team was firmly entrenched in first, a full ten games ahead of the second place Yankees.

Grabbing the stat sheet after a game, Marcus made a grimacing look. He was in a dead heat for the American League lead in home runs:

American League Home-Run Leaders (June 10th)

Player	Team	Home-Runs
Scott Harper	Buffalo	18
Eddie Griffin	Buffalo	18
Marcus Dillard	Buffalo	18
Benny Rios	New York	17
Pete Sampson	Buffalo	15

Over by his stall, Eddie Griffin smiled profusely as he buttoned up his shirt.

"Hey El Caballo!" He barked across the room. "What happened to your eighty home-runs! You gonna let an old guy like myself beat you?"

"It's a long season, old man."

"Hey, don't be mad at me," Eddie laughed. "With all those gold chains, you might have a better future in the jewellery business."

A few snickers engulfed the room, although nobody was bold enough to laugh out loud.

"Funny Griffin, real funny," he replied before storming into the shower.

Most of the team had already dressed and were headed out onto the bus, but after getting a couple of base running wounds treated in the trainer's room, Pete Sampson hobbled out to a nearby locker.

"What's wrong with you?" Marcus said.

"Just getting my leg treated. It's all scarred up from that double play ball I broke up in the seventh."

Sampson had a homerun hitter's build with long powerful arms and a strong upper body. He was a big man with explosive strength, but he always seemed to have a disoriented look on his face. Pete played the role of disciple better than leader.

"I don't understand you guys," Dillard shook his head.

"What's not to understand?" Pete asked

"I don't understand why you try so damn hard. Just take your money and play."

"I just want to win," Pete answered, shrugging his shoulders.

"You don't have to do that shit to win," Dillard pointed at his leg. "Just play for yourself."

"I take pride in sacrificing my body for the team."

Dillard shook his head again.

"Fuck the team! You gotta look out for yourself in this world. All they want to see are stats. Do you think they give a damn about sacrifices come contract time?"

"I just want to win," Pete shrugged. "I know Jack cares...."

"Please! Jack Vaughn isn't the one who gives people money around here. Trent Blair is in charge and I've got that cat all figured out. He just wants to see the homeruns."

Dillard glanced appraisingly at Sampson before continuing.

"Look at you! You're a great hitter and you're the fifth wheel around here. But if you want to become a real star like me, start swinging for the fences."

"You make me sick," Sampson stammered.

Dillard grabbed his bag and began walking towards the door.

"You don't have to listen to me. It's your choice, man. You can have the fans eating out of your hands."

Pete appeared upset, but looked more confused than anything.

The following day in Albany, the phone rang in the Governor's office.

"Hello, Governor Murdoch's office," the receptionist answered.

"Could I speak to Tom please? It's Jonathan."

"I'll transfer you right away, Mr. Jenkins."

The phone was on hold for five seconds before a familiar voice came on the other side.

"Jonathan?" The Governor asked

"Tom, how are you doing?"

"What the hell is going on?"

"Don't ask me," Jenkins responded reservedly.

"Who leaked this thing?" The Governor barked. "It sure as hell wasn't from my end."

Jenkins sighed.

"I wish I knew what was going on. The only person I've told is Trent Blair."

The Governor thought to himself for a moment.

"I bet it was that Jew, Dingleman. I've been screwed by that little swine before."

"Don't be ridiculous," Jenkins replied.

"I need answers, Johnny. I'm getting bombarded from all sides here."

Jenkins sighed heavily.

"That's what I called you about. Let's just call this thing off."

"Now you're the one being ridiculous."

"I'm telling you Tom, it's not worth it. It's not worth undoing twelve years of public service over a baseball stadium."

Murdoch would have none of it. For him, promises were agreements of honour between gentlemen. He considered them to be as solid as oak.

"Your team needs that stadium. I made you a promise and I intend to keep it. I don't go back on my word, especially with an old friend like you."

"Think of the consequences first," Jenkins pleaded.

"We can ride this thing out," Murdoch said. "We've been friends for forty years, Johnny. Forty years! I'm not selling you out over something like this."

"I don't want you ruined," Jenkins said desperately.

"Give the people of this state some credit. The Berlin Wall fell fifteen years ago. They ain't gonna elect some closet communist."

The Governor looked through his schedule.

"I'll be in town next week to do some campaigning. We'll catch a game."

"Leave a message with my secretary," Jenkins said

"I will and in the meantime, see if you can't talk to Dingleman. See where he is on all of this. The little bastard isn't answering my calls."

"I'll look into it," Jenkins responded.

"I appreciate it, Johnny. Say hi to Rose for me."

For the baseball club, troubles were beginning to brew behind the scenes despite their 45-19 start to the season. Marcus Dillard was livid at being left off the all-star roster by Jack Vaughn despite being among the league leaders in home-runs. His agent, Rodrigue Salazar, called Blair on three occasions to indicate his client's dissatisfaction. Now the slugger decided to pay a visit to the general manager in person.

"I didn't sign in this damn city to get shafted!" screamed Dillard. "Do something about Jack Vaughn or I'm outta here!"

Trent Blair sat behind his desk with Al Ferreira at his side.

"What exactly are you mad about?"

"I should be on the damn all-star team!" He shouted.

"Marcus," Blair replied in a patronizing tone. "Is that what this is all about?"

"I'm sick of Jack Vaughn. I want him fired. Fire him or trade me!"

Blair shrugged.

"You know I can't just do that."

"You'd better do something!"

"I'll talk to Jack. That's all I can do at this point. You're my number one priority."

"Marcus better see some progress," Dillard shouted. "And it better be soon!"

"Marcus will see progress," Blair responded patronizingly, "I promise you."

"All right then," Dillard ruffled his collar.

Soothed by the stroking of his ego, Dillard calmly walked out of the office.

Ferreira looked at the general manager with a subtle smirk on his face.

"You appeased him pretty fast. I thought we were going to be in here all day listening to him."

I just tell him what he wants to hear," Blair shrugged. "You think I give a damn what that monkey has to say? He signed a contract for four years. He's here whether he likes it or not."

"You have to admit that Jack Vaughn is becoming a problem," Ferreira insisted. "He runs a one-man show."

"Yeah well, I hired him four years ago to give us some credibility and now that we have that....."

Blair stopped himself.

"I say you talk to him," Ferreira said. "Him and Dillard are headed for a major fight."

"Whatever," Blair shrugged. "I've got bigger things to worry about right now."

"Like what?"

Blair checked to make sure the door to his office was closed. The matter was sensitive.

"Paula Lombardi's been sniffing around in accounting a little too much lately. She's getting close and I don't like it one bit."

"What do you care?" Ferreira asked.

"Never mind why I care!" Blair yelled. "We need to get rid of her."

"What are you gonna do?"

"The only thing I can do," Blair shrugged. "Find a reason to fire her. If she digs up any more, it'll be my ass."

"I'll find some dirt on her," Ferreira promised. "She'll be gone by August."

CHAPTER 7

At the annual All-Star Game, the American League squad managed by Jack Vaughn blew away the National League 8-2. Six Pioneers were on the American League side, but the controversy surrounding Marcus Dillard's all-start snub overshadowed it all. Just when the issue seemed to have passed, a new crisis was ignited in the first week back.

After a relatively easy victory over the sad sack Tigers, the threesome of Dillard, Pete Sampson and Conan O'Shea had gone out for a night in Marcus' hometown of Detroit. None of them could be found in their rooms at midnight.

For Dillard, a notorious curfew buster dating back to his days in Florida, this was fairly regular. What concerned Vaughn most, was that the straight shooting Sampson and O'Shea were starting to get into the habit. Even more distressing was the fact that none of them were in their rooms by morning, or at noon for that matter. When everybody got on the bus headed for the stadium at 1:00 p.m., the three men were nowhere to be seen.

"Where the hell are these guys?" Blair asked panicky.

"Yeah I thought you were supposed to be on top of these things Jack?" Ferreira harped.

Vaughn, sitting calmly in the front seat of the bus with his cup of coffee, turned to the two men seated next to him.

"Would you two relax? I'll take care of it."

"You should have dealt with it already," Ferreira refused to let up.

Enough was enough. Jack handed his cup of coffee to Grant Robinson, stepped across the aisle in front of Ferreira, lowered his head and stared the assistant general manager directly in the eye. He resented everything about this man; his squirmy face, his antagonizing voice. He spoke to him in such a quiet and calm tone that only Blair, seated next to Ferreira, could hear what was said.

"Look Al, I'm not the fucking babysitter on this team. If I hear one more word, I'm going to grab you, drag you outside this bus beat the living shit out of you. Got it?"

All the assistant G.M could do was gulp and remain silent.

As the bus pulled into the stadium it was greeted by a Detroit police cruiser.

Vaughn and Blair stepped out to speak with the officer.

"Well well well," the officer replied with a large smirk. "I was hoping I'd be able to find you. There was a little incident last night at a downtown strip-club and your three boys were right in the thick of it."

"Where are they now?" Blair asked.

"Back at the station, we detained them overnight and were just in the midst of questioning them right now."

"What happened?"

"I'd rather not discuss it here," the cop answered, "but if you two would hop in, I'll take you downtown."

The cop drove them to the station.

It turned out that the players were involved in a strip-club fracas that left several people hospitalised and led to several arrests. Many of Marcus's childhood friends, from his days growing up in the Detroit, were at the club and it only took a few inciting comments by him to plunge the three into a full-fledged brawl. All told, there were 49 arrests that night with several people rushed to the local hospital, but that didn't even begin to cover the Pioneers' troubles. Aside from the inevitable assault charges and community service that each of the players would face, there was some bodily harm caused that would force them to miss some action.

O'Shea was the worst. According to a few eyewitness accounts that surfaced in the newspaper the next day, "he was like Rambo in there." He pounded on every person who dared challenge him, but there was a cost. He broke his wrist. At best, he would miss three to four weeks and another week or two rehabilitating on the AAA team in Windsor. He was gone until September. Then there was Pete Sampson and Marcus Dillard. Neither one had sustained any serious damage but both their faces were heavily scarred and would miss a couple of games.

The worst damage of all for the club was from a public relations standpoint. Every newscast and newspaper in North America had the strip club blow-up featured prominently. The *Buffalo News* was first and foremost in this regard, with the caustic Chet Thomas leading the way. True to form, he put most of the blame on Jack Vaughn's shoulders in his morning column:

Vaughn asleep at the wheel

By: Chet Thomas (Buffalo News)

There are several questions that go unanswered when a disaster of this magnitude hits a professional sports team. The first one of course is why Monsieurs Dillard, O'Shea and Sampson were at a strip club late at night the day before a game. In answering that, one is led to a more intricate and inevitable question. What was Jack Vaughn doing? Where was he? More importantly, why wasn't he on top of this? Is it not the manager's job to make sure his players are ready to play? If so, why was he caught holding the bag once again? There are no credible answers but one. Jack Vaughn is no longer fit to manage the Buffalo Pioneers. In the past he has shown his on field negligence, whether it be leaving in the pitcher too long or starting a player after he is no longer useful. In this instance, he has shown himself to be a neanderthal off the field as well. It is the manager's responsibility to look after his players' interests and quite simply Jack Vaughn has failed. There is only one question remaining, how much more damage can his incompetence inflict?

The depleted Pioneers dropped the remaining two games to the Tigers, before returning home to lose another game against Anaheim. The club was suddenly embroiled in a storm of controversy and Trent Blair decided he needed Jack Vaughn to help clear things up.

As he entered the manager's office, Blair stepped on one of the clubhouse towels lying around. Noticing a trainer nearby, he summoned him over to pick the errant towel up and dispose of it before entering.

Vaughn was sitting in his chair with a young woman on his lap.

"Jack, we need to talk."

The woman couldn't have been older than twenty-five.

"Hey sweety, do you mind waiting outside for a minute?"

"Anything you say Jack," the girl replied before kissing him on the forehead.

As she left the room, Trent looked at her indifferently.

"A little young for you, huh, Jack?"

"We all need some fresh meat once in a while," Jack shrugged, while checking out every curve on her young body. "So what's up?"

"I'm here because our organization needs to make a public gesture," Blair said emphatically. "We can't let this thing play itself out in the press. Its making us all look bad."

Vaughn sipped his coffee.

"What do you want me to do about it?"

"I want you to make a public apology for the team," Blair told him.

Vaughn leaned over his desk and stared at the general manager sharply.

"Are you shitting me? You want me to apologize? Me? I gave you the goods on Dillard last November."

"Come on Jack, we gotta do something. We can't just let this fester."

"You have to do something, not me. I'm just the manager. Remember you told me to do my job, while you do yours? I'm only following orders."

Blair sighed and thought to himself for a moment

"You can be so damn unreasonable sometimes, you know that? At least make some public statement condemning the players' actions. Anything that will take the heat off us."

"I don't criticise my players in public," Vaughn shook his head. "If you want me to have a talk with them, I'd be more than happy to. But I don't....."

"You know what? Just forget it," Blair interrupted. "I ask you to do something small for me and you refuse. Forget I even asked."

Vaughn lay back in his chair with his arms tucked behind his head.

"Consider it forgotten," he shrugged.

The two parted company with superficial politeness.

There was something about Trent Blair that rubbed Jack the wrong way. He couldn't quite put his finger on it, although he sometimes wondered about the flair with which Trent wore his flashy designer clothes. The general manager seemed too slick, too suave and too conniving for Jack's sensibilities.

The following week, Jonathan Jenkins paid a visit to Art Dingleman's office to rally support for the beleaguered stadium proposal. With politicians of all stripes attacking the Governor, the stadium deal needed the Mayor's active support if it was to survive.

"Art, we need you to fight for this thing like never before."

"I hate to disappoint you," Dingleman said slyly. "But the situation has changed since November."

"Nothing's changed," Jenkins replied. "You made me a commitment and I have no reason to expect you not to honour it."

"I pledged the city's financial capital, not my own political capital. Once this thing became public, my involvement went out the window."

Jenkins shook his head.

"You know," the old man said. "There was a time in my life when public officials stood for something other than saving their own skins."

Dingleman smiled vainly.

"I guess times have changed."

"You pompous son of a bitch," Jenkins bristled.

"The political winds are blowing against the stadium deal right now," the Mayor said. "And it looks like the Governor might go down. Don't expect me to join him."

The gentle old man became upset.

"And don't expect an ounce of support for your re-election campaign next year!"

The Mayor laughed arrogantly.

"The Jenkins name is not what it once was."

Jenkins shook his head.

"You're a real swine....you know that?"

"Thanks for coming," the Mayor responded sarcastically. "It's always a pleasure talking with you, Mr. Jenkins."

"Don't thank me for anything."

Dingleman smiled politely and paged his secretary.

"Laura, please show Mr. Jenkins to his car."

The old man walked out of the room without a word.

Later that day, Trent Blair was confronted with a phone call in his office.

"Mr. Blair," the secretary paged him, "Commissioner Richard Smalls is on line one."

"Dick?" Blair answered synthetically. "What a pleasant surprise!"

"Good afternoon Mr. Blair," the Commissioner said in his slow southern drawl, "and a good day to you, sir. I'm just callin' to talk to you about some damaging allegations I've been hearing about yourself and your organization."

The Commissioner's raspy old voice had a way of sneaking up on people.

Prior to his hiring by Major League Baseball, Smalls sat on the Louisiana Supreme Court for ten years, making a name for himself based on the ambiguity of his

54

opinions. The old judge certainly knew when a deal was to be made. Despite a change in locale to the league offices in New York, there was still plenty of Cajun left in this southern good ole boy.

"Oh," Blair acted surprised. "What allegations?"

"Well Mr. Blair, we've been hearin' some nasty rumours about Benjy Alvarez, and in this business rumours have a funny way of becomin' facts. Catch my drift?"

"Why yes...of course," Blair responded.

"Since I'm certain you are so eager to vindicate yourself, perhaps you would agree to co-operate with a full-scale investigation by Major League Baseball."

"There's nothing to investigate."

"Well Mr. Blair, that would be for us to decide."

Blair paused nervously.

"There's nothing to decide, there's nothing to investigate. I can't help you."

"I must say Mr. Blair, you don't sound as eager as I would have hoped."

"Check your ears Dick, but I have more important things to do than cooperate with a useless investigation. Is that all?"

Commissioner Smalls sighed deeply.

"You'll never understand how this league works, my friend," he said in a not-so friendly fashion. "And a good day to you, sir."

Click.

It didn't take long for the league to take action

"...moving to baseball now, the Commissioner's Office has announced they will be conducting a full scale investigation into the Buffalo Pioneers loophole signing of short-stop Benjy Alvarez in 1997. Alvarez has since gone on to become one of the best shortstops in baseball, winning five gold gloves and leading the league in steals. There is no definite time frame on the investigation, but it will most likely conclude at the end of the season."

Most people in the know had few doubts about what the investigation would turn up, especially since the case against the Pioneers was considered fairly solid.

It was the last thing the club needed, especially with the constant speculation about Scott Harper's future. Harper's agent Eli Ginsberg made no secret that negotiations were not going well, putting more pressure on the outfielder to maintain a brave face.

"I want to stay in Buffalo," Harper kept telling reporters. "Hopefully Trent and Eli can work something out."

Despite all the external dilemmas, Trent Blair's main concern these days was internal. An anonymous source within the organization leaked information to Chet Thomas of the *Buffalo News* that team accountant Paula Lombardi was engaging in a romantic affair with Conan O'Shea. For O'Shea, a bachelor and a most eligible one at that, the information was not so damaging or shocking. Ballplayers frequently played around. It was, however, grounds for dismissal as far as employees of the organization were concerned.

One Friday afternoon, Blair summoned Mrs. Lombardi into his office.

"It pains me to say this," Blair said, with insincerity dripping from his voice, "but we're gonna have to let you go."

"This is absolutely ridiculous," Paula argued. "We were consenting adults. I don't even know why this stuff makes it into the news."

"Rules are rules. You can't violate them."

The accountant was wearing an irresistible short skirt that revealed her leggy features. The general manager paid it little heed.

"I don't see what the big deal is," she defended herself. "If you'd let me stay on another week or so, we'd be able to trace whoever is taking all the money."

"It's out of my hands," Blair said unemotionally. "Nothing I can do."

The accountant thought to herself for a moment. Her professional duty was to make sure things added up and something here did not.

"I'm being screwed by someone in this organization," she insisted. "You haven't seen the last of me, Mr. Blair."

"I wish you the best of luck in your future endeavours," Blair said unemotionally.

The accountant grabbed her purse and left the room.

On the field, the Pioneers' once insurmountable stranglehold on the division was slowly being frittered away. Just weeks earlier, they had enjoyed an 11½ game lead on the second place Yankees, but the month of July was especially cruel for the team, losing sixteen of twenty-seven games and watching their lead shrivel to only five games.

The only bright light in midst of the swirling controversies was first baseman Eddie Griffin, who made a public relations coup for himself by establishing the 'Eddie Griffin Foundation' in conjunction with several prominent businessmen.

"This is a charity aimed at helping the black inner city youth," Eddie said as he triumphantly held up an orphaned black child. "I think I owe it to this city and to the good Lord Jesus Christ, my saviour, to give something back."

Griffin was extensively praised for his efforts both on the radio and in the newspapers. One radio host was verbose in his praise for the philanthropic first baseman.

"Eddie Griffin is a man who has never lacked in charity. In this age of greedy athletes, he's almost too good to be true."

Not everyone was in such a charitable mood. With everything that was going on with the team and his personal life, these were not heady times for Jack Vaughn. On the professional side, there was the strip club controversy, the Harper situation, the Alvarez investigation and the team's prolonged slump. On the personal side, he was still fighting an alimony suit from his ex-wife and dealing with the break-up of his family. Although he always acted calm and collected in front of others, Jack Vaughn was a man under siege.

In the midst of a five-game losing streak, Jack brought a flask of whiskey into the dugout with him on a hot Saturday afternoon at Fenway Park. The worse the team played, the more he drank, and the more irate he became. By the fifth inning with the Pioneers losing 6-0, Vaughn finally blew his top.

After first-base umpire Dickie Scott missed a double play call that would have allowed Buffalo to escape the inning unscathed, the manager charged out to first-base.

Over the years, Vaughn and Scott had had some classic confrontations and the Boston crowd knew they were in for something special.

"Are you fucking blind?" Vaughn screamed.

"Cool it, Vaughn."

"Well you're obviously dumb...."

"I said cool it," The umpire insisted.

"Your mother must have been a real whore...."

"I'm only gonna warn you one more time," the umpire threatened.

"....to beget a piece of shit like you!"

"All right, 'yer outta here!"

With one wave of the umpire's arm, the Fenway faithful erupted.

"You might as well throw me out!" Vaughn barked back. "You've been killing us all day with your calls anyway!"

As the manager walked to the dugout, the rotund umpire fired one last salvo.

"Hey Vaughn, maybe you should give alcohol rehab another try! It doesn't seem to be working!"

Vaughn turned to walk back as the crowd roared.

"That high-fat diet you're on doesn't seem to be working either! When was the last time you missed a meal?"

The two of them jawed at each other for a few more minutes with no signs of abating until pitching coach Grant Robinson corralled Vaughn back into the dugout.

"Come on now Jack, we ain't doing anyone any good out here."

Vaughn kicked dirt at the umpire repeatedly. The crowd ate it up.

"You're bush league, Dickie. Fucking bush league! Always have been, always will be!"

Up in the press box, Trent Blair shook his head appraisingly.

"How much do you want to bet Jack's been drinking again?"

"He's out of control," Ferreira agreed. "And if we let this go on, he'll take the team down with him."

"I can't say anything to that man," Blair replied. "He never listens to anyone."

The Pioneers could not get out of Boston soon enough. Following a disastrous road trip, the team returned to Buffalo for a much-needed win against lowly Kansas City.

After the game, Vaughn headed over to the Duke of York with Grant Robinson to unwind. The little tavern benefited greatly from the post-game baseball crowd that came in after home games. It was Jack's place of refuge from whatever was troubling him and today was one of those days when there was a lot on his mind.

The bar was littered with sports memorabilia from the Sabres, Bills and Pioneers scattered along the wall. The two men came so regularly that they were on a first name basis with the bartender, Gus. Even without saying a word, Gus prepared Jack's favourite scotch just the way he liked it. The manager quickly downed two shots as he and Robinson sat in silence.

"What's troubling you Jack?" The pitching coach asked.

Vaughn had a glum look on his face as he sat dejectedly on the barstool with his face looking down. The liquor was already taking control.

"Everything feels like it's out of control. Things used to be so simple...this game used to be so simple...."

Robinson wouldn't let him finish.

"Ah, don't be starting on that tired old story Jack. The past ain't any better or worse than it is now, it was just different."

Vaughn continued rambling.

".....real baseball people were in charge and frauds like Trent Blair had to pay for a ticket to get in."

He smiled absently.

"There's always been a few pricks around," Grant quietly disagreed. "The difference is that they had a lot more power back then. I don't know about you, but my memories of when we were playing aren't all good. When I was comin' up in the minors, I dreaded them road trips into the southern states. All of them rowdies would get up and be calling me nigger and be throwing things at me. It wasn't all peaches and sunshine, ya' know."

Robinson spoke with such quiet tranquillity that his words flowed like a waterfall.

"Besides, what's so wrong with today?" Grant continued. "Sure there have been some troubles lately, but the team's doing great. We're in first place and three straight titles is hard to argue with."

Jack stared at the television catatonically as a girl in her early twenties came by to ask him for his autograph.

"Sure honey," he smiled, "who do I make it out to?"

"Cindy."

"Ok Cindy," he answered, as he wrote in marker just above her chest, "A..L...L......T...H...E.....B...E...S...T.........J....A.....C....K.........V."

"Thanks."

"Anytime, sweety."

He deliriously slapped her backside.

"This club is headed the wrong way," Vaughn muttered. "I can see it happening before my very eyes. Trent Blair is wrecking this team....the bastard."

"Come on now, Jack."

"You heard me, HE'S A FUCKIN' BASTARD!"

People from across the bar turned around to see what all of the commotion was about.

"I gotta get you outta here," Robinson said quietly, putting his arm around him.

"I'm okay," Vaughn insisted.

"You're making a fool out of yourself."

As Grant put his arm around him, Jack finally relented. The two men left a generous tip for the bartender and slowly made their way out of the pub.

Just as they were about to step into a cab, Vaughn turned to his confidante affectionately.

"What would I do without you," he mumbled incoherently.

The pitching coach smiled.

"Ah, Jack. You're just a little drunk, that's all."

CHAPTER 8

On a sunny afternoon at City Hall, Mayor Art Dingleman called a press conference to distance himself from the growing uproar over the proposed stadium deal.

"The city of Buffalo has formed the opinion that the actions of Governor Tom Murdoch in conjunction with the Buffalo Pioneers are ludicrous and detrimental to the public good and hereby distances itself from the proposed stadium deal."

The Mayor looked around the room gleefully.

"I want to clear the air once and for all," the Mayor continued. "Contrary to some reports, the city of Buffalo was never a part of this travesty that would see public funds going to a millionaire owner who pays his millionaire athletes. Our state and our city can't afford to subsidize a sports team when there are hospitals and schools that need the money. There's just no way."

Although seen through by some analysts as political opportunism, the press conference was another spear in the side of Tom Murdoch's election campaign. With just a few months until the election, the Governor's once sizeable approval rating had shrunk down to 46%, neck and neck with the surging Prentice Wulloughby campaign.

As Ferreira and Blair watched the press conference on a television in the office, the general manager sounded off.

"When was the last time that asshole actually built a hospital with public funds? A new stadium would be the best thing that happened to this town."

"Didn't they just close a ward in Cheektowaga last month?" Ferreira replied.

Blair shook his head.

"That's why I don't trust politicians."

"He's just protecting his own interest," Ferreira remarked. "You can't really blame him for trying to survive."

"Yeah, well if we don't get that stadium we're in big trouble. There's no way we'll be able to afford Harper...."

Blair put his hands over his face agonizingly.

"....gawd....if we don't find a way to keep Harper, Vaughn will never let me hear the end of it."

"Jack Vaughn's opinion is irrelevant."

The look on Blair's face told another story.

"He never gives me the credit I deserve," Blair agonized. "Things always have to be done his way."

Ferreira looked on in surprise. He disliked Vaughn more than anyone, but was still surprised at what was coming out of the general manager's mouth. He had rarely seen such trivial hurt and thin skin. It seemed that beneath Trent's cold, steely demeanour lurked an inner mush of emotional frailty. The apprentice took notice.

The team's tailspin continued into the month of August. Not only was Conan 'The Barbarian' missing in action with his wrist injury, but several other key members were not playing up to their usual performances.

Frank Ringler, long the anchor of the rotation, was beginning to show his age. Last year's Cy Young Award Winner might have been blowing away opponents in April and May, but as the season wore on he began to struggle like no other time in his storied career. His strikeouts were down, he was getting hit hard, and for the first time in ten seasons his earned run average climbed above 4.00 runs a game. Other parts were starting to come unglued as well.

Pete Sampson was in a free fall. Although he was still hitting the home runs at a frequent rate, his average had fallen from .280 to .235 since June while he had struck out in 50 of his last 150 at bats. Even more disconcerting to the manager was the fact that he was no longer advancing runners or running out ground balls with the same zeal he once did.

Had it not been for the steady starting pitching from Chris Norton and the offensive production out of Scott Harper, Eddie Griffin and Marcus Dillard, the team might have fallen out of first place entirely.

During the first week of September, Jonathan Jenkins hosted the annual Pioneer barbecue at his mansion. The get-together had always been a joyous occasion for everyone associated with the organization to intermingle, but this year was just a little different. While there were the familiar sights of smiling faces, cold beer and juicy hamburgers, there was an underlying negativity to the proceedings. The petty squabbles, the team's recent struggles and the brushes with the law had all added up.

Still, some people managed to have a good time. Marcus Dillard and Conan O'Shea spent most of the afternoon hitting on the team cheerleaders, otherwise known as the 'Pioneer Girls.'

On the other side of the estate yard, Eddie Griffin and Frank Ringler grabbed some lawn chairs and cold beers. The two greybeards spent most of the night reminiscing about the past.

"I tell you Eddie, it gets harder and harder to get the old arm ready for each start," Ringler said, while rotating his ailing arm several times. "The years have taken their toll."

Griffin laughed knowingly.

"I know what you're saying, man. We're gonna be collecting our pension cheques soon."

"Seriously though," Ringler asked. "Where do you see yourself in a couple of years?"

"Anywhere and everywhere," Griffin said confidently. "I've smiled for enough cameras to assure my future somewhere."

"All I want," Ringler continued, "is to retire on my own terms. I think I deserve it.....I can't believe I'm even talking about retirement."

Griffin nodded in agreement.

"Remember the '84 Olympic Team?" Griffin asked, harkening back to their early days together in college.

"That was the best time of my life," Frank smiled, before pausing and putting his hand in his face.

"Oh man we can't do this. I'm starting to get misty eyed."

"Yeah, I'm getting a bit of that too," Eddie laughed.

Up by the pool deck, Blair was having an animated discussion with some of the scouts. It was more of a one way conversation. He was busy telling them exactly what he thought of the Benjy Alvarez investigation.

"Those morons in New York won't find a damn thing!" Blair stated brashly, as he sipped on a martini.

His diatribe was cut short when the 'Pioneer Girls' came over to stoke up friendly relations. They were buzzing around both Blair and Ferreira like bees on honey, but it was no matter. After half an hour of general disinterest, the girls quietly and disappointedly moved on to other things.

Over by the open bar, Jack Vaughn sat on a stool with Rose Jenkins. She was a wine drinker while Jack was a liquor man, but together they downed beers. Rose was only a few years younger than her husband, but seemed so much more.

"Oh, you devil," Rose laughed and slapped his intruding hand away.

"I know a good woman when I see one," the inebriated manager replied.

"And what would that be?" She played along.

"Someone with class and dignity like you."

"Well if it means anything to you at all," she said, while placing one arm on his shoulder. "You're just my kind of old fashioned man."

Jack grabbed the other arm and pretended to bite it off. There was little doubt he had passed his level of intoxication.

"I'm not a man, I'm an animal."

As she laughed and pulled away there was a regal elegance about her. Not the kind of haughty snootiness that many woman of her class exuded. She was blessed with the rare combination of an upright, dignified demeanour without the nasal inclination that quite often accompanies it. There was something in Rose Jenkins' ageless face that was easy to like.

"You're a pill, Jack. What's the story with you and Beth?"

The smile quickly left his face at the thought of his ex-wife.

"You trying to cheer me up?" He replied slightly annoyed.

"No I was just wondering," Rose placed her hand on his arm tenderly. "I wonder about you sometimes."

"Don't ask," he answered, while scratching his head. "We ain't never getting back together. She says I don't understand her feminine feelings....whatever the fuck that means."

Rose smiled sympathetically

"How old are you? 60?"

"64," he answered awkwardly.

"You're 64....some of these girls I see going into your office have to be at least two or three times younger than you."

"What are you doing to me?" he replied defensively. "Is this the sexual inquisition or what?"

Rose smiled.

"You know I don't judge."

"The girls serve their purpose," Vaughn said, "quickly and with little aggravation. I don't have time for a complex relationship. I have enough stress as it is. I don't need to deal with some neurotic woman on top of that."

Rose smiled in such a way that showed both disapproval and deep sense of understanding.

"What about your kids? You still see them?"

Her questions were posited out of curiosity, but with each subsequent one he looked more and more uncomfortable.

"They're all grown up now," he answered shamefully, "but I can't say I'm any closer to them than I am to my ex."

"That's too bad," she replied with genuine sorrow.

He shrugged with a glum look on his face.

"Yeah, a real fucking shame. What can I say? I'm not the family type, I'm a bad father....but what the hell are we talking about this for? You sure know how to spoil a good mood."

"Sorry Jack," she smiled and held out her hand. "Come on, let's dance. My favourite song is playing."

After grudgingly consenting, the manager quickly returned to his good humoured mood, tossing and turning the owner's wife with a few of his patented and overly romantic dance numbers. With every new twist she laughed a little more. Then he started singing.

"*The lady in red......she's dancing with me......cheek to cheek......*"

"Ah Jack, cut it out," she blushed.

He ignored her plea and continued.

"*There's nobody here......it's just you and me....where I wanna be. But I hardly know....this beauty by my side!....it's just you a-a-and me....the la-dy in the red.*"

As the song ended, Jonathan Jenkins walked by to get a beer.

"Well look at you two," the owner chuckled heartily. "I leave you alone for a minute and you've already run away with another man!"

"Now now, Jonathan," she leaped into her husband's arms. "Jack and I were just talking."

"Oh I'm sure of that," Jenkins laughed again.

The manager looked at his watch.

"Well, I think I need to go pass out somewhere," Vaughn said. "Madame, it has been a pleasure."

He kissed the ring on Rose Jenkins' finger.

"Likewise, Jack. It's always a pleasure."

As he said goodbye to the couple, an equally intoxicated Conan O'Shea walked by the bar.

"Well, I'll be damned if it's none other than Conan the Barbarian!"

The two men slapped hands. Jack grabbed the young pitcher to keep his balance.

"How's my injured closer feeling today?" he asked.

"Ah don't worry about me," Conan said. "You look like you need some help."

"Worry?" Vaughn said, while struggling to maintain his balance. "Who said I was worried? The only thing I'm worried about right now is getting home intact....(belch)...matter of fact why don't you grab me another cold one to go."

The two of them grabbed more beer before jumping into a waiting taxi.

Everyone seemed to have a good time with the exception of Benjy Alvarez. The young Dominican was never a big talker, but the allegations surrounding his contract made him retreat further into silence. Jack Vaughn tried speaking with him earlier in the day, but the sullen young man was impenetrable.

"You know, Benjy. You're one of our leaders on the field. It would be a shame for us to lose someone like you."

"I no want to leave, skeep," Benjy replied. "But my agent tell me I have many option if the commissar make me free-agent."

Jack put his hands on the young man's shoulder.

"I've always looked out for you, Benjy. And I always will."

"I respect you, Jack Vaughn. I always respect you. It's just business."

Jack Vaughn hated to hear those words. For him, the game had never been nor ever would be about business. But with Rodrigue Salazar as his agent, Jack knew what the club was up against. If ever there was blood to squeeze out of a rock, Salazar squeezed it dry. If and when Alvarez was eventually set free by the Commissioner's Office, Jack knew the Pioneers could expect no hometown discount. Salazar constantly reminded Alvarez of how much the club had wronged him.

On the field, the team limped into the month of September only two games ahead of the hard charging Yankees. With a three-game series against the Bronx Bombers at home during the first weekend in September, the pennant race was starting to heat up.

CHAPTER 9

"Welcome to BSN Baseball, I'm Chuck Smith with my colleague Terry Davis, glad to have you with us on this cool September night in Buffalo."

"Well Chuck, there's a lot on the line tonight and we couldn't have asked for a better pitching match-up than Frank Ringler against Yankee ace Erik Anderson."

"You said it. I know a lot of people have been wondering how much gas Frank Ringler has left in the tank, but I tell you, he's the reigning Cy Young Award winner and I expect to see a tremendous pitching duel tonight. Other news to tell you about, the Pioneers called up closer Conan O'Shea from AAA Windsor yesterday and presumably he's ready to pitch."

"I saw him throw a few days ago during his rehab assignment and he didn't look too sharp, but I expect that he has gotten rid of the rust and is ready to go. This man has some nasty stuff."

"What about the playoff picture?"

"All of the division leaders pretty much have it locked up except for here in the AL East. The Yankees have firm control of the wild-card but the division title is up for grabs. There is a huge intra-state rivalry between these clubs and I expect to see a hard-fought series."

"Okay we're all set to go here. We'll be back for the national anthem after this commercial break."

As had been the case all season, Pioneer Stadium was packed to capacity as the series took on the frenzy of a playoff game. Pennant fever was fast becoming a September tradition in Buffalo. Combined with the inferiority complex many Buffalo fans harbour towards New York, the series held an importance of epic proportions.

Adding to the whole crazed atmosphere were the 8" x 11" inch posters distributed in the *Buffalo News* that morning with the words in big, bold print: "SPANK THE YANKS". Several thousand of the placards made their way to the stadium that evening.

Even Vince D'Antoni was not spared from several rambunctious fans jeering him as he stepped off the team bus. A cadre of a few hundred fans vociferously jeered the Yankees owner the moment his gold sandals hit the pavement. More than anyone else, he was the man Pioneer fans loved to hate.

As Jack Vaughn and Yankee manager Tommy Bedowes walked to home plate to submit their line-up cards, each man barely acknowledged the other.

"Jack," Bedowes nodded. "It's been awhile."

"Not long enough," Jack retorted.

"You've always been honest," the Yankee manager replied. "That's probably your only virtue."

Bedowes was a short man, who wore glasses and chewed his gum with a fast pretentiousness. Known around baseball as 'the guru' for his reputation as a strategic mastermind, he sometimes commanded more spotlight than his players. For a hands-off manager like Jack Vaughn this was heresy, but the hatred went deeper. Bedowes was a long-time Yankee and Jack's days as a Dodger had not dissipated the natural antipathy. Vaughn couldn't stand Bedowes and it was safe to say that the feeling was mutual.

With all of the semantics and stare downs out of the way, the game finally proceeded. It was left up to the fans to provide a hearty Buffalo welcome for the visiting New York Yankees.

"BOOOOOOOO!!!"

"I can feel the electricity in the air! Here we go, LaTroy LaRocque is leading off here in the top of the first."

"LaTroy has just been phenomenal this season stealing 71 bases while hitting .335. It looks like he has completely recovered from his hamstring problems of the last few years."

"Ringler sets...he deals...strike one!"

The crowd cheers.

"Caught the outside corner. I wonder what he comes back with here."

Ringler stared into the batter's eyes. The old heater was on its way.

"Ringler toes the rubber....he sets...deals...oh...this one is hit a ton."

The crowd lets out a collective sigh.

"...over the head of Dillard and off the wall! LaRocque is running hard for third and he's in there with a lead-off triple!"

"Not the start the veteran pitcher wanted, but we'll see how he responds."

The next two batters reached base on consecutive singles

"....LaRocque's coming in to score and its 1-0 New York!"

"Ringler is in a whole lot of trouble here. Two men on and the dangerous Benny Rios is up to bat with nobody out."

"The Yankees have been riding this man's bat all season. Not the person you want to see with runners already on base if you're a Pioneers fan."

Ringler quickly got two strikes on the Yankee slugger.

"He needs this out, Chuck. You don't want to put your team in a deficit early. Look for him to come back with his heater."

"He sets...the pitch..."

The veteran pitcher threw as hard as he could. It was the same fastball he had used countless times to strike batters out, but this one was just a couple miles per hour too slow.

"....uh oh.....its deep and I don't think it's playable!"

The crowd was hushed.

"4-0 Yankees! Has the air ever been sucked out of this place. With one swing of the bat, Benny Rios has silenced 32 000 people."

The pounding continued as Ringler gave up two more solo homers without recording an out. The crowd began booing vehemently.

".....6-0 Yankees after only six batters!"

"Frank Ringler just doesn't have it here tonight and you'd have to think Jack Vaughn is going to make a move here."

Vaughn sat in the dugout sipping his coffee. As the battered pitcher looked to his calm, composed manager in the dugout, he knew this was his game until the end. A few pitches later, Ringler settled down and got out of the inning.

"After that first inning, Frank Ringler has really shut the Yankees down this afternoon."

"That's the sign of a great pitcher, Chuck. When he doesn't bring his best stuff to the ballpark, he's able to regroup and fight to keep his team in the ballgame."

Run by run, the Pioneer offence slowly clawed its way back. By the bottom of the eighth, they had cut the lead to 6-5 and chased Yankees starter Erik Anderson out of the game after loading the bases with nobody out.

Suddenly the Yankees were in trouble. Manager Tommy Bedowes brought in hard throwing right-handed reliever Dan Wiggins, who induced Terry Miller into a home-to-first double play. There were men on second and third with two outs and Scott Harper coming to bat.

"Two outs, men on second and third and left fielder Scott Harper steps in. The crowd is on their feet...and I think there is going to be a pitching change. Yankee manager Tommy Bedowes is making his way to the mound. He wants the lefty...."

Left-handed reliever John Miller trotted in from the bullpen.

"A very interesting move on the part of Bedowes to change his reliever. Obviously he is playing the percentages here with the lefty Scott Harper coming to bat, but you gotta wonder about the logic of taking this guy out, especially after how sharp he looked."

"Interesting move indeed, we'll be back after this break."

After the commercial break, the camera panned the crowd standing on their feet and the players in both dugouts tensely leaning over the railing. The nervousness ran up and down their faces. Over in the corner of the dugout, Jack Vaughn sat calmly and sipped his coffee.

"You can cut the tension in this place with a knife. The pitcher is ready.....he checks the runners...he deals.....hit to the right side and through!"

"YEAH!!!" The crowd erupted.

"One run is in! Alvarez gets the go ahead at third and there's a play at the plate.....he's in! 7-6 Pioneers!"

The crowd went berserk.

"My oh my, what timely hitting on the part of Scott Harper!"

Vaughn sat in the dugout snickering.

"Looks like old Tommy out-managed himself again," he remarked snidely. "What a putz."

In the top of the ninth, Conan 'The Barbarian' did his best to let the air out of the balloon by loading the bases before retiring the final Yankee on a fly-ball to the warning track. He looked nothing like he had before the wrist injury.

"What a game we have seen here this evening! There is a reason these Buffalo Pioneers are the three-time defending World Champions."

"This is a real statement game for Buffalo. They showed a lot of heart tonight and sent a message to New York. The road to the division title goes through Buffalo."

The Pioneers swept the series and followed that up with a sweep of Baltimore and Boston. After a mid-summer swoon, the team seemed to be peaking for the Fall Classic once again. Despite a couple of blown saves by the suddenly shaky Conan O'Shea during the month of September, Buffalo cruised to the division title and the best record in baseball at 103-59, while New York sputtered down the stretch and made the playoffs only by virtue of the wild card. It was just the kind of momentum Buffalo needed to finish the regular season.

2004 American League East Standings

Team	W-L	GB
Buffalo	103-59	-
New York	96-66	7
Boston	85-77	18
Toronto	82-80	21
Baltimore	70-92	33
Tampa Bay	65-97	38

2004 Buffalo Pioneers Statistics

Player		Average	HR	RBI	SB
SS	Benjy Alvarez	.323	8	66	76
C	Terry Miller	.305	2	75	0
LF	Scott Harper	.356	43	135	25
1B	Eddie Griffin	.298	38	122	0
RF	Marcus Dillard	.273	41	105	8
CF	Pete Sampson	.231	26	79	6
DH	Orlando Mateo	.285	17	75	8
3B	Dave Kelton	.263	12	67	0
2B	Esteban Pena	.245	2	41	12

Pitcher		W-L	E.R.A.	Saves
SP	Frank Ringler	14-11	4.08	-
SP	Chris Norton	23-8	2.88	-
SP	Johnny Turner	14-10	4.34	-
SP	Rich Lopez	13-12	4.56	-
SP	Dave Rivers	10-7	4.87	-
RP	Conan O'Shea	1-3	3.97	39

"Another regular season in the books," Griffin hollered while buttoning up his shirt. "Time to gear up for the playoffs."

Dillard sat in his locker with an unexcited look on his face.

"Gear up? Man, the playoffs won't be nothing. I've already designated my ring finger."

"What do you know about the playoffs, El Caballo?" The wily first baseman fired back, smiling profusely and hoping to elicit a response. "You've never been on a team that didn't finish in last-place."

"I can count to 103 and that's how many wins we got."

"Yeah it is," Griffin replied with a touch of sarcasm. "I'm surprised you can count that high."

Dillard held up both of his middle fingers.

"Oh I'll give you something to count," Dillard shot back. "Can you count this? How many fingers am I holding up? What is that? 1....2?"

The two men laughed.

"It looks like two fingers to me," Pete Sampson chimed in.

Dillard fired back at the dim witted outfielder.

"Listen here dumb ass. Hurry up and get dressed. We've got some bitches to pimp tonight. Tell Conan to move his ass."

"Okay," Sampson obliged subserviently.

Marcus turned back to Griffin.

"You coming with us old man?"

"Naw, got the wife and kids waiting at home," Eddie responded.

"Man, forget your wife and kids! Come out with us."

"What and get caught in a strip club melee with you guys?" Eddie scoffed smugly, as he fixed the cuffs on his shirt. "I wouldn't be caught dead. I've got a reputation to uphold."

Marcus laughed.

"And what would that be? As a tight-ass family man?"

"No it wouldn't," Eddie replied matter-of-factly. "It would be as a distinguished African-American who gives back to the community and takes care of his family. You might want to try it sometime. I'll show you how to make a living doing this shit."

"Whatever," Marcus blew him off. "I don't care what no damn people think about me. I'm just a dumb nigger to all them anyway."

Griffin grabbed his bag and bolted out the door.

"It's nice to see you have such a good attitude about these things."

Eddie left the clubhouse and was greeted outside by a gorgeous blonde white woman in her early twenties. It was definitely not his wife or his daughter. After kissing for a few seconds, he looked over his shoulder to make sure nobody was watching and rushed into a waiting cab.

The Pioneers faced the Cleveland Indians in the first round of the playoffs. The three game series was over before it began. The only real blemish was a blown save by O'Shea in Game 2, but even that was rectified by a game-winning double by Eddie Griffin in extra innings. The Indians were simply overmatched.

The American League Championship Series did not prove any more difficult. Buffalo rolled over New York in four games while limiting Benny Rios and company to only five runs throughout the series. Pitching may win playoff games, but it was not as if the Pioneers offence slacked any. They had racked up 27 runs in the four game series.

It was left to Chris Norton to put the finishing touches on the series in Game Four. As Norton walked out onto the mound in the ninth inning to finish his complete-game shutout, the crowd gave him a standing ovation. The Yankees were finished and the Buffalo fans were enjoying every minute of it.

"NA-NA-NA-NA.....HEY-HEY-HEY.....GOODBYE!!" The crowd chanted.

Many in the crowd were swinging brooms and white towels wildly. The stadium was engulfed in collective playoff frenzy.

"5-0 Buffalo...Norton sets...the pitch....fly ball left field...Harper's under it!....The Buffalo Pioneers are going back to the World Series!"

Down in the dugout the players ran onto the field, but not with the same spontaneous revelry or reckless abandon as years past. After three seasons of winning the big prize, their eyes were clearly set on doing it again; anything less would be unacceptable.

The crowd was a different story. As the dejected New York players walked off the field, many fans stood and cheered as the scoreboard flashed, "SO LONG YANKEES!"

There was an indescribable feeling of jubilation in the stadium. It was almost too easy. The way the team played in the regular season and still managed to win the division, the way they floated through the first two rounds of the playoffs, the way the Yankees self-destructed, and the manner in which D'Antoni subsequently and predictably blew up in anger. Beneath it all, there was a hollow feeling. Surely it could not be so effortless.

CHAPTER 10

"Welcome to Game One of the 2004 World Series here on BSN. In a rematch of last year's lopsided World Series, we have the Buffalo Pioneers taking on the Atlanta Braves."

"Well Chuck, I don't think the Pioneers will sweep the Braves like they did last season, but the way they've played of late you gotta think they're the favourites."

"Who would you say are the key players in this World Series?"

"On Atlanta it's definitely Troy Timmons. After Conan O'Shea struck him out in the final at-bat last season, he's wanted revenge. They need him if they hope to win."

"And for the Pioneers?"

"I'm going to go with a less obvious choice for the Pioneers. The key for them is Conan O'Shea. For five or six years this guy has been untouchable, but 'The Barbarian' has looked shaky in the past month: a few blown saves here and a few near misses there. The World Series usually has a lot of tight games and you need a reliable closer."

"What factor do you think will sway this series?"

"The Pioneers need their power hitters to come out and play. More than in years past, Buffalo has relied heavily on home-runs this season. It's easy to win like that in the regular season, but pitching generally tightens up in the playoffs. That's a big key for them."

"Okay we'll be back after this commercial break."

The locker room was remarkably quiet. The players sat in their stalls with weary faces and not saying anything, while others either waxed their bats or fixed their gloves. There were a lot of veterans on this team and just about everyone, with the exception of Marcus Dillard and a few rookies had been here before.

The World Series was a sacred event. Players work so hard over 162 regular season games: the grind, the sweat and the time on the road. When they finally get to the big show, they're hit with the stark realization that absolutely everything is on the line. The entire room was silent in anticipation of what was to come.

The only person who did not seem nervous was Jack Vaughn. Whenever he walked around the clubhouse he absolutely reeked of self-assurance. It wasn't arrogance or cockiness, but confidence, the type of quiet condition that comes with success, experience and the right personality. Jack had all of the above. He seemed to personify grace under pressure and was equally adept at radiating his own soothing nature onto others.

"Loosen up boys, I feel like I'm at my mother-in-laws."

The clubhouse erupted in laughter.

Before Game One even started, the Buffalo crowd was already stirring. Scalpers outside were demanding outrageous sums of money for a chance to see the Pioneers win another championship and for the sacred hours on that chilly Saturday evening in mid-October, it seemed as if the city stood still. The bank tower across the street was dark, but the spotlight still shone brightly at Pioneer Stadium.

With the upcoming state elections in full swing, Jonathan Jenkins invited Governor Tom Murdoch to throw out the first pitch. The Governor tossed a strike to catcher Terry Miller.

The game started as any World Series should: scoreless. Frank Ringler threw five shutout innings, while Atlanta also held Buffalo scoreless through five.

That all changed when Troy Timmons came up in the sixth inning with a man on first.

"Ringler sets......delivers......Timmons crushes it!"

The crowd hushed.

"It's gone!......2-0 Atlanta here in the sixth inning!"

For the next few innings, the Braves managed to keep the Pioneers off the board, barely escaping with the bases loaded in the seventh when Pete Sampson struck out to end the inning. The Pioneers came up in the bottom of the ninth for one last gasp.

"Here we go. Bottom of the ninth, 2-0 Braves and Benjy Alvarez is leading things off."

"Benjy has gone 1 for 3 today and is always a dangerous player."

"Mason sets...the pitch...ball one."

"A tough one to lay off of, but Benjy's got a good eye up there."

"Mason sets....and deals...hit up the middle....base hit! The leadoff batter is aboard!"

The home crowd started to stir.

"Not the man you want running the bases. Alvarez has terrorised opposing catchers this season, stealing seventy-six bases."

"Miller is up, he's gone 1 for 3 tonight."

"Look for Terry to take a few pitches here. There's no doubt in my mind that Alvarez is going to steal. He likes to run."

"I wouldn't be at all surprised if the Braves elect to do a pitch-out here. This whole stadium knows that Alvarez is going to steal"

"Mason is set....checks the runner....and deals....Alvarez is running....it's a pitchout!.....The throw is in and......Alvarez is safe!"

The crowd erupted.

After three years of gutsy comebacks and majestic triumphs, it looked as if another glorious victory was on its way. The white towels began to twirl faster and faster at the sniff of victory.

"Benjy Alvarez has just showed 32 000 people here and millions of viewers world-wide how talented he truly is! The Braves pitchout and still can't nail him at second!"

After working the pitcher to a full-count, Miller grounded out to the right side, advancing Alvarez to third.

"That is perfect execution by Terry Miller. He really knows how to handle a bat out there and he moves the runner over."

"Scott Harper is up, he's 1 for 3 tonight."

Harper came to the plate. There was nothing superfluous about him, just a few dirt marks on his pants and the competitive fire in his eyes. After fouling off several pitchers, Harper worked the count full.

"I tell you," Jack Vaughn turned to the pitching coach. "There's an old-time ballplayer if I've ever seen one."

"....the pitch....lined through the right side!.......Alvarez is coming in to score! What a patient at-bat by Scott Harper and the Pioneers have cut the Atlanta lead in half to 2-1."

First baseman Eddie Griffin was up next. He worked a full count on Mason, fouling off pitch after pitch and making the closer earn every strike.

"....Eddie fouls off another one. Griffin and Harper have really made this pitcher work."

"The pitcher sets....he winds...works...."

The first baseman's face was zeroed in. The trademark smile was nowhere to be seen. Eddie was all business.

"Griffin smacks it down the line!"

"YEAH!!!" The crowd went berserk.

"Harper is on his way to third....he's being held up and the Griffin is on second base representing the winning run!"

"This Pioneer team is so crafty. That was a quintessential Eddie Griffin at-bat, he picked his spots, tired out the pitcher and smacked a double down the line."

"All they need is a fly-ball to tie this game up or a single to win it!"

The crowd pumped up the decibel level as Marcus Dillard stepped up to the plate.

"Dillard comes to the plate with men on second and third and one out. Marcus has gone 0 for 3 tonight, with two strikeouts and a long fly-ball."

"This crowd is on their feet, Chuck. They smell blood!"

"Mason checks the runners and deals......swing and a miss strike one!"

The crowd sighs.

"Mason threw the slider down and away and he got Dillard to chase."

"Dillard had an impressive first season moving to the American League, hitting .273 with 41 home runs, but they paid him the big bucks to come through in situations like this."

"He steps into the box.....Mason sets.......fires......and this one is well hit! Hooking.....hooking.....foul."

The crowd lets out another gigantic sigh.

"I don't think there is any doubt what Marcus' intentions were there. He was pulling all the way, trying to end this ball-game with one swing of the bat."

"He doesn't need a home-run. All they need is a single to win this game."

"Dillard steps back in....Mason gets the sign.....he deals....swing and a miss strike three!"

The crowd let out a collective sigh. Down in the dugout, Jack Vaughn shook his head.

"I don't know what Marcus was thinking there, but you don't swing at pitches in the dirt when the pitcher is on the ropes like this."

"Two down and Pete Sampson is coming to bat. He struck out to end a bases loaded rally in the seventh but hopefully he can redeem himself here."

"Pete ended the season poorly. He's been swinging at a lot of bad pitches and his batting average plummeted to .231 because of it."

"Sampson steps in....Mason sets....the pitch.....swing and a miss strike one."

The crowd sighs.

"Buffalo still needs a single to win this game! Mason is set....he deals....swing and a miss strike two!"

The crowd sighs again, this time letting out a few boos.

"Pete's gotta be patient or he's going to strikeout for the fourth time tonight."

The moment of truth came upon the stadium as television cameras panned the nervous crowd biting their nails, the players overhanging the dugout steps and both owners anxiously standing up in their private boxes. Finally, it settled on Jack Vaughn, who was slumped in the dugout with his legs crossed and a collected look on his face.

"Here we go....the Pioneers are trying to stay alive here in the bottom of the ninth."

"Sampson steps back in....Mason sets...the pitch....swing and a miss strike three!"

The crowd sighed.

"The Atlanta Braves have taken Game One of the 2004 World Series here in Buffalo!"

A hush overcame Pioneer Stadium. After putting all the chips into play this wasn't supposed to happen. The Buffalo Pioneers had built a reputation for coming through in the clutch; making sacrifice bunts, being patient at the plate and pouncing when the opponent was down. None of that had occurred, leaving the fans feeling jilted and bewildered at the absence of such characteristics they had come to know and expect.

"Well Chuck, Buffalo had its chances to score and uncharacteristically failed to capitalise. That was the only difference tonight. They out-hit the Braves nine to two, but one of those two hits was a two-run bomb by Atlanta's Troy Timmons. That was the difference tonight."

The team filed dejectedly into the dressing room. Dillard kicked the water cooler and others threw gloves into their lockers.

A few minutes later, Vaughn strolled in and gave the perfunctory "we'll get 'em next time" speech. It turned out he was right.

In Game Two, the Pioneers won 11-1 off a strong pitching performance by Chris Norton that was capped with by a titanic eighth-inning solo homerun from Marcus Dillard that travelled well over 550 feet.

As the camera panned Jack Vaughn's reaction in the dugout, the manager looked far from pleased.

"That fucking guy," Vaughn muttered to Grant Robinson. "Where the hell was that last night when we needed it?"

As the series shifted to Atlanta, the Braves took the next two games in extra innings. The clutch hitting and timely pitching, a Pioneer staple for so long had vanished. Marcus Dillard and Pete Sampson went a combined 0 for 11 with nine strikeouts. For the first time in years, the team was in the precarious position of being down 3-1 in the series. It was do-or-die.

"*Welcome to Game Five of the 2004 World Series here on BSN. The Braves have a 3-1 stranglehold on this series, with the Pioneers needing a win tonight to stay alive and force a Game Six in Buffalo.*"

"*Well Chuck, the Pioneers come in needing a victory here to keep this series and their three year title-run alive. It's been an exciting series thus far with each game, excluding Game Two, coming down to key hits.*"

"*Young Chris Norton takes the mound tonight in hopes of turning things around.*"

"*You know, Chuck, this very well could be a changing of the guard for the Pioneers. Traditionally Frank Ringler has been the lynchpin of the rotation, but he slowed down in the second half of the season and hasn't won either of his starts this series. On the other hand young Chris Norton, 27 years of age, had a great season and pitched brilliantly in Game Two. Is he the new ace of this staff? Some people think so. How he pitches tonight will give us a good indication of that.*"

Before the game, Vaughn held a meeting in his office with the coaching staff.

"Desperate times call for desperate measures," hitting coach Norm Watkins said. "We gotta shake up this lineup."

Jack looked at him disgustedly.

"Are you shitting me? That would be the dumbest possible thing to do right now. What kind of message does that send?"

"It might wake a few guys up," the hitting coach barked.

"No Norm," Jack said emphatically. "Managers don't win ball games, players do. This is in their hands and I have every reason to believe they're gonna do it, without us meddling."

"Well Jack, you gotta do something. If you're not gonna change the lineup, at least lay into them. Break a few bats or something!"

Jack shook his head before standing up to leave the room.

"I hope to God you never manage a ball-club, Norm. I say that with all sincerity. You have absolutely no concept of dealing with people."

As Jack walked into the clubhouse, Griffin was the first person to get everyone's attention.

"Ok guys, skip's got something to say."

The manager grabbed a stool and sat in the middle of the locker room waiting to get everyone's attention. It never took long.

"Well guys, I don't think I have to tell you the importance of tonight's game. Our season is on the line tonight and there's no way to sugar coat it. But that doesn't mean we have to play like our season is on the line. This game is just like the 103 that we won during the regular season. We can't erase a 3-1 lead overnight, but we can make a start."

He paused to sip his coffee.

"I'm not asking anyone in this room to do the impossible. We've been in holes in the past and gotten out of them."

The manager smiled at his veterans.

"I remember a few years ago being down 5-2 to Los Angeles in Game 6 of the World Series before Eddie Griffin hit us a grand slam to win it. Then Frank Ringler went out in Game 7 and pitched us a complete game shutout."

Both veterans smiled back.

"The point is, boys, we're capable of great things in this room. We beat this same team four straight times last year. We've had three eight-game winning streaks this season."

He took another sip of coffee.

"I look around this dressing room and I'm in awe.....absolute awe. There's a lot of talent here and I'll be damned if we just roll over and die. That World Series trophy belongs in Buffalo and I believe you guys have it in you to make sure that it stays there. That's our trophy, goddamn it and nobody's going to take it from us!"

The speech ignited a sense of pride throughout the room. The players shouted and ran out of the clubhouse.

The roar of the Atlanta crowd was overpowering as the Braves took the field. Americana playoff banners adorned the upper deck and a dizzying array of tomahawks seemed to be attacking the field at once. It had been a long time since the Pioneers had played in such a hostile environment. Game 5 was shaping up to be quite a battle.

The first three innings were scoreless.

"......the bases are loaded here in the top of the fourth and Eddie Griffin is at the plate with no outs!"

"I know Pioneer fans are praying for Griffin to go deep here and break this scoreless tie, but my gut feeling is that Jack Vaughn would be happy with even a single. He has seen his hitters bat just .125 in this series with runners in scoring position."

"The way Chris Norton is pitching and has pitched these entire playoffs, a couple of runs may be all they need. Lewis gets the sign....he sets........delivers.......ball one."

"That was a very, very close call. Griffin has a good eye up there and is content to look for his pitch."

"Lewis is set.....the pitch......punched into right field for a base hit! Alvarez scores!.....Miller gets the wave and is heading home....its close.....he's in there! 2-0 Buffalo!"

The visiting dugout erupted in celebration.

"Eddie Griffin is a true pro. He's got the power to hit one out, but he goes up there, looks for his pitch and doesn't try to do too much.....that's all you can ask."

"Marcus Dillard is up next with no out and runners on first and third."

The slugger sauntered up to the plate.

"Aside from his home-run in Game Two, Marcus has been hitless and Pioneer fans can only hope he snaps out of it before it is too late."

"Lewis is ready.....he sets.....the pitch.....Dillard pops up behind home plate!"

Vaughn threw his full cup of coffee onto the dugout steps in disgust.

"Jesus Christ!" He yelled.

"Lopez is under it and there is one away!"

The crowd cheers.

"I've given up trying to figure out Mr. Dillard. There's a pitcher battling with his control, so he swings at a fastball out of the zone and pop up. Go figure."

"Pete Sampson is up next and he's been even worse than Dillard this series. He's hitless with eight strikeouts."

"Pathetic."

"Lewis toes the rubber.....the pitch....grounded to the short....flipped to second for one....to first for two...double play!"

"Well Chuck, I don't know what to say. You just saw two very impatient hitters. Buffalo got two runs but if these guys don't start producing, the Pioneers are dead in the water."

Vaughn shook his head in the dugout.

"Hey Norm," Jack barked over to the hitting coach. "Don't these guys know how to take a fucking pitch?"

The game remained deadlocked until the Braves scored a run off Norton in the seventh to cut the Buffalo lead to 2-1. It would all come down to the bottom of the ninth inning. Conan O'Shea hadn't looked like much of a 'Barbarian' the past month, but Vaughn still went to his closer with the season on the line.

"Here we go! The Pioneers are three outs away from sending this series back to Buffalo for Game Six and Conan O'Shea is in trying to shut the door."

"O'Shea has had only one appearance in this series, but it wasn't in a save situation. He pitched 1 1/3 innings giving up a run and two hits, but like I've said many times these past few weeks, Conan 'The Barbarian' is not pitching with the same effectiveness."

"Juan Ramirez comes to the plate. Conan needs to make some big pitches here because he's right in the heart of the order."

"O'Shea gets the sign and sets...the pitch...belted to left field for a base hit!"

The crowd stirred.

"Ramirez is on and look who is coming to bat!"

"Coming to the plate," the public address announcer proclaimed, "Troy Timmons!"

The stadium exploded in ovation. The hopes and dreams of Braves fans were resting on Troy Timmons' powerful bat. After being struck out by O'Shea to end the previous World Series, Timmons was looking for redemption.

"The World Series champion is dangling on the ropes! One big punch and this thing could be over!"

"Troy Timmons comes to the plate representing the winning run."

"O'Shea is lucky he got away with the last pitch with only a single. If he throws that garbage to Timmons, he'll park it."

"Timmons steps in as O'Shea gets the sign."

With the importance of the moment, the camera panned both dugouts before focussing on Jack Vaughn. He was grace personified, a man with a firm grip on his emotions, even when things seemed to be spiralling out of control.

"O'Shea is ready to go.....he deals....hit hard!....GONE!"

"YEAH!!!" The crowd erupted.

"The Atlanta Braves are the 2004 World Champions!"

The announcers wisely remained silent for a minute as they let the viewers take in the dramatic victory. A champion had been dethroned.

If a picture tells a thousand words, there were more than enough compelling images and sounds to tell this story: the Braves players deliriously scurrying off the bench to mob Timmons, a few hundred rowdy fans skirting security and running onto the field, and reliever Conan O'Shea slowly walking off the mound with his head down. Most of the Pioneers glumly walked into the visiting clubhouse.

Down in the dugout, Jack Vaughn sat still with a blank stare on his face, slowly sipped his coffee and watched the festivities unfold.

Up in a private suite, Trent Blair and Al Ferreira looked on in astonishment. Sweat cascaded down the general manager's clean face. His act of God had indeed happened.

"At a time like this there are so many people to be happy for. First and foremost are the Atlanta Braves. But you have to tip your cap to the Buffalo Pioneers. It was a wonderful run and I can only think if they're able to keep Scott Harper and get the Benjy Alvarez situation resolved they'll be right back here next season. So on behalf of BSN, I'd like to congratulate the Buffalo Pioneers on a great run. You guys provided a lot of exciting moments these last few years. But this is a night of celebration for the Atlanta Braves."

As the pall from the disturbing loss sunk in all over Western New York, Chet Thomas was armed and ready with a post mortem the following morning:

The greatest Pioneer team ever?
By: Chet Thomas (Buffalo News)

2004 was supposed to represent so many things. Words like dominant and dynasty come to mind. In the aftermath of it all there is only one word to describe the truth of what actually took place: failure. It started in spring training and continued throughout the season. Failure to put Marcus Dillard in the cleanup spot, failure to control the late night escapades of his most valuable players, failure to wrap up the division as early as usual, failure for the manager not to look asleep in the dugout and most damning of all: failure to win a fourth consecutive World Series Championship. Remember that this was supposed to be the best Pioneer team ever. It was a team that won the World Series thrice and then added Marcus Dillard as icing on the cake. It didn't turn out the way it should have. Not only were the Pioneers life and death to win the division, but looked badly overmatched against the Atlanta Braves, the team they easily swept the year before. Something simply doesn't add up here and when the math is wrong, blame the mathematician. Surprise, surprise, but that is none other than Jack Vaughn. It is the manager's turn to go. In the meantime, with even more bad news hovering on the horizon, one must ask the question: Has the sun finally set on Buffalo's dynasty?"

CHAPTER 11

"After months of investigation and deliberation on the part of the league," Commissioner Richard Smalls explained to the assembled media, "we have reached a firm consensus regarding the Benjy Alvarez situation."

The Commissioner pronounced his words with a strong Louisiana accent. His tone was not reassuring.

"Citing section 120, part F, paragraph 34 of the MLB Code of Conduct, any player signed under false pretences unknowingly, must be granted his immediate and unequivocal free-agency. Furthermore, any club which has acted purposefully in this manner is responsible for compensation towards the player involved at an amount determined by the office of the Commissioner. We have discovered that the Buffalo Pioneers have violated this rule."

He took a sip of water as the press gallery waited breathlessly.

"Therefore the league has no choice but to grant Benjy Alvarez his immediate free-agency. The Buffalo Pioneers baseball organization is also responsible for a payment of $1.7 million dollars towards the player in question to compensate for any lost wages incurred."

The off-season was only a day old, but already the bad news had begun.

Things did not improve a few nights later when the state election results were announced. By the time most of the polls closed at 7:30 p.m., the voice of the television news anchor came in loud and clear.

"The people have spoken and after twelve years in office, Governor Tom Murdoch has been ousted by Democrat candidate Prentice H. Wulloughby III in one of the closest races in recent memory!"

"According to the results that are just coming in from most of the counties, Wulloughby has captured 47% of the popular vote, while Governor Murdoch took 46%. The percentage of people who voted was also up significantly."

"Very interesting numbers. Wulloughby was able to draw people who don't usually vote because of their disgust for Governor Murdoch's stadium proposal and the fallout over Delaware Falls. If anything, that deal is now dead in the water. What we have seen tonight, ladies and gentleman, is one of the biggest election day shockers in modern political history."

"Let's now go live to the Democrat headquarters in New York."

"You people know what you want and you know how to get it!" Wulloughby awkwardly pumped his arms in the air.

The new Governor looked like a nerd on prom night. His demeanour was out of synch and he needed to repeatedly adjust his glasses from slipping off his sweaty face. For that shining night in New York City it didn't matter how obtuse he appeared. The people supported him for nothing other than the base idealism of change.

As the television camera panned the convention floor, it caught glimpses of several Broadway stars and influential executives.

"'Fax mentis incedium gloriae,' the power of glory is the torch of the mind. You have all demonstrated today the innate glory of the democratic system when educated citizenry take a stand against corruption."

The crowd cheered softly, although many seemed confused by the frequent Latin references.

"We have fought this campaign on the issues people care about and sent a message to the special interest groups that have been leaching off the state of New York for years. Your time has seen its nadir!"

Wulloughby stepped away from the podium and raised his arms distortedly to the cheers from the contented multitude. Even with the burden of unattainable promises hanging over his head, this was Wulloughby's night to celebrate.

A few days later, the ex-Governor sat dejectedly in his office as his staff was packing up most of their belongings. A knock came at the door.

"Jonathan, good to see you!"

The two men shook hands.

"I just thought I'd stop by," Jenkins said glumly.

"You didn't have to do this."

"The least I could do is buy you lunch."

Murdoch put his arm on Jenkins consolingly

"You didn't lose me the election. That piece of shit Dingleman...."

Murdoch caught himself raising his voice, before he calmed himself.

"....but I won't get into that. Let's go eat. I need to get out of this place."

It was a hard two weeks for Jonathan Jenkins. That weekend, he and Rose travelled to their ski chalet in Ellicottville, New York to escape from the distractions of the city. Still, his wife could see that all the bad news was wearing her husband down.

"Oh Johnny, let it go."

"Sorry, honey. I can't get it off my mind."

She looked at him understandingly and massaged his head.

"You don't have to apologize. You're going through a lot right now, sweetheart."

"Yeah," he responded glumly. "I just don't know how much longer this can go on. Doctor Rosenblatt keeps telling me the stress is bad for my heart. Maybe I should sell the team."

She continued massaging his head.

"Oh Johnny, it'll probably cause you more heartache to sell the team than it will to keep it. You love that team, you love baseball. Throwing all of that out the window will dwarf any stress you might have right now."

"That's a nice thing for you to say, but I know you've always hated it."

"I don't hate it," she denied, "I've come to tolerate baseball because I know how much it means to you."

He smiled contentedly.

"But," she said coyly. "I really think you should make some changes."

The old man's ear perked up.

"Like what?"

"I know nothing about baseball, but I know people. And that Trent Blair is about as rotten as they come. Something about that man just rubs me the wrong way."

"Trent?" The old man raised his head out of her lap in surprise. "What's not to like about him? He's sharp minded, he's quick and he's decisive. He's the person most responsible for our success."

"He's a son of a bitch Johnny and I can't believe you don't see it."

The old man frowned.

"I have nothing but great things to say about that boy."

"You don't seem to know him very well," Rose insisted. "He's a manipulator, him and that gimp of his, Ferreira."

The old man sighed in a fit of astonishment.

"He just happens to be one of the best young, baseball minds in the business. He was the Executive of the Year for crying out loud! I can't believe what you're telling me."

"Believe what you want," she replied. "Sooner or later you'll find out for yourself. The only person I can tolerate in that entire front office is Jack Vaughn."

"Jack's a good man," Jonathan agreed.

"Sure he's a bit of a chauvinist," she smiled, "but he is what he is. A man like that I can respect."

The old man thought to himself.

"I don't know what to say, Rose. I'm glad you've taken such a sudden interest in the ballclub, but I can't believe what you're saying about Trent Blair."

"Believe what you want," Rose replied. "Just don't say I didn't warn you."

The old man kissed his wife.

"Let's not fight, honey. I'm getting tired."

"You're right. Go to sleep, pumpkin."

The old man fell fast asleep in her lap.

A few days later, Scott Harper won the AL MVP Award after leading the league with 43 homeruns and 135 runs batted in, while finishing second with a .356 batting average. Combined with his 25 stolen bases and great attitude, it was easy to see why he was not just the American League MVP but the best player in baseball.

Unfortunately the focus wasn't on his gaudy season when he took to the podium. All the reporters kept asking about were his plans for next season.

"For the last time," he answered, looking visibly annoyed. "That's not why I'm here today. I know as little as you about where I'm going to be playing baseball next season. I will say this though. I want to stay in Buffalo."

With each passing day, that was looking less and less likely. At Harper's urging, Eli Ginsberg swallowed his pride and reluctantly made a telephone call to Trent Blair in a last ditch effort for a deal.

"I can't believe I'm even doing this Trent, but I'm giving you another chance to sign Scotty. He wants to stay here, but if we don't get an answer from you we'll have to move in another direction."

The general manager looked outside as the rain poured down upon the city.

"Go right ahead," Blair responded nonchalantly.

"Excuse me?" Ginsberg replied incredulously.

"You heard me. If there is so much interest, go somewhere else."

"Quite frankly Trent, as I've already outlined to you, he doesn't want to go somewhere else. He wants to stay here and he's willing to do defer a good portion of his contract to do so."

Blair shrugged his shoulders.

"Good for him. You know my position already. If you don't lower your demands, there is no money to satisfy you. It doesn't matter how much money you defer."

"Trent, I know we've had our differences, but the feelings I'm experiencing right now go way beyond simple anger. Frankly, I'm baffled. Why are you playing hardball? We've already told you we'll sign here for cheaper than anywhere else."

"$70 fucking million! Yeah, you guys are real humanitarians."

"He'll get more on the open market."

"I told you our price already. We won't go above it."

"Don't be so childish. You know as well as I do that this is part of the business. Don't let something as trivial as money end Scott Harper's career as a Pioneer."

"It's up to you to make this happen, not me."

"Let me get this straight. I'm calling and begging you to sign my client for cheaper than he could get on the open market. He also happens to be the best player in baseball. You win. Is that what you want?"

"I want him to sign at my price!" Blair yelled imperiously. "Not yours!"

The agent huffed.

"I didn't want to make this call in the first place. You think I like begging you, of all people? You think I like sacrificing millions in commissions because my client wants to stay in Buffalo? Of course not! I did because Scotty wanted me to."

"What do you want....a cookie?"

"You know what?"

"What!" Trent fired back.

"Fuck you and fuck your two-bit organization! Scotty is gonna sign somewhere else and he is going to stuff it down your throat every time he comes into town!"

Click.

A momentous sound of thunder and lightning emanated from outside as Trent Blair put the receiver down. The heart of the Buffalo Pioneers batting order had just been torn out.

Given the law of economics and the vanity of Vince D'Antoni, it was only a matter of time until the inevitable happened. That December day would soon go down as one of the worst in Buffalo Pioneers history.

In the Yankee Stadium dressing room, the media quickly assembled themselves at the hastily called press conference. Try as he might, Vince D'Antoni could not wipe the huge Grinch-like smile off of his face; he had just stolen Buffalo's Christmas. As the club executives and coaches finally arrived, the owner addressed the media.

"We are absolutely thrilled to announce," D'Antoni began with his face beaming, "that Scott Harper has signed with the New York Yankees to a 5-year deal totalling $75 million dollars. It took a lot of doing and it's gonna take a bit of a mental adjustment on Scott's part...."

The press gallery laughed.

".....but I have a feeling he's gonna look just great in pinstripes. Matter of fact, why don't we find out."

As Harper stood up, manager Tommy Bedowes helped him put on a Yankees jersey to the applause of the New York scribes. There was a minute of rapid picture taking from the media before Harper took to the microphone to answer questions. The first one was from a magazine reporter.

"Any predictions for this season?" he asked.

Scott scratched his head.

"I'm not really one to make predictions...."

"I am," D'Antoni brashly interrupted. "We're going to the World Series!"

The assembled media laughed again.

"Where do you see yourself fitting into the lineup?" The reporter asked.

Harper paused for a moment before answering.

"Wherever they put me," he said humbly. "I mean, that's totally up to them."

The questions continued for another ten minutes before a Buffalo reporter asked one final question.

"Are you gonna miss anyone back in Buffalo?"

Harper had to have known it was coming, but the question still blindsided him. He had managed to go the entire press conference without talking about Buffalo, but it was out in the open now and it was all he could do to avoid breaking down in tears.

"Oh God," his voice quivered. "I loved that town. I.....ah....I'm going to miss all of the guys, especially Jack Vaughn. He was like a father to me. It's a shame things turned out the way they did in Buffalo. Who knows what we could have accomplished there. I never wanted to leave."

At a subsequent press conference in Buffalo, Blair had his own version of events.

"Absolutely, categorically untrue," the general manager denied Harper's claim. "We made an offer to them that was more than fair, but they wouldn't take it. Somebody has to take a stand against inflated salaries because the money they were asking for was absolutely astronomical. You know, it's kind of sad that in this day and age, loyalty means nothing to these players. I always liked Scotty, but he turned his back on Buffalo. I hope he's happy, I genuinely do, but quite obviously the money meant more to him than anything else."

The Buffalo media wholeheartedly accepted Blair's facade of damage control as Gospel truth. In the Saturday edition of the *Buffalo News*, the front page had a large picture of Scott Harper at the press conference wearing a Yankee uniform, with the headline above that read: '$ELLOUT.'

It was a bitter pill to swallow for baseball fans in Western New York. Their home-grown star had seemingly sold them out and fled down state to the hated Yankees. Many columnists, including *Buffalo News'* Chet Thomas, bemoaned the lack of loyalty and did the predictable thing by ripping him.

Not everyone in the Pioneer organization was totally convinced about the general manager's version of events however. The annual team meetings took place the following week and all of the organization's baseball personnel, except Jonathan Jenkins, were in attendance. For the first time, several scouts were openly questioning Blair's judgement.

"There are several free agents out there we can go after," Trent assured everyone. "Barry Jackson from Pittsburgh and Stan Milluck from Oakland to name just a few. These guys are powerful homerun hitters."

"None of them replaces Scott Harper," Luis Toca, the Dominican scouting director complained. "They no have five tools like Scotty. They no field, they no steal, they no hit for high average."

"You don't need five tool players to win ball games," Blair countered. "You need someone to get on base and hit a homerun, nothing more, nothing less."

"I seen Stan Milluck play in Baltimore last summer," Luis continued. "He did nothing to impress me that day."

Al Ferreira laughed haughtily from across the room.

"In all due respect to your scouting report," Ferreira said arrogantly. "Trent and I use a more scientific basis for our statistical analysis of players. We're moving forward the way we see fit."

"Moving forward?" The scout wondered. "You call losing our best player moving forward?"

"The bottom line," Trent defended, "we need to get someone to replace Harper's homerun and on-base production."

Vaughn had mostly kept to himself, but he couldn't take it anymore. The blunt truth needed to be said.

"I don't know what just came out of your mouth, but Luis is right. You can't replace Scotty Harper and I damn well told you that a year ago."

The general manager wiped his forehead. The sweat was starting to trickle down.

"Look," Blair reasoned, "once we get Benjy Alvarez signed under wraps and pick up one of these free-agents we're right back in it."

Jack wasn't buying it.

"And you think you're going to do that with a $55 million payroll? You're dreaming."

The general manager was now becoming visibly annoyed.

"Let me worry about that. Jonathan Jenkins has always been flexible with the payroll. The plan is in place and we will move forward with it."

"Some plan," Jack sniped back. "If you really think Benjy wants to sign here after what happened, you're probably the most short-sighted son of a bitch I ever met."

"You've got one year left on your contract, Jack. I'd be careful how you talk to me."

The room sat in stunned silence.

"Is that a threat?" Vaughn asked.

The manager stared him right in the eye.

"You can interpret it any way you please," Blair shot back.

Many of the scouts looked on nervously. The tension could be cut with a knife.

"Do whatever you want, Trent. You never listen to anyone anyway."

Vaughn threw his coffee cup in the garbage and walked out, leaving an awkward silence to descend upon the room.

After a brief silence, the Dominican scout voiced his opinion.

"You two have no right to talk to Jack Vaughn in this way," Luis Toca piped up once again. "He's done more than either of you two clowns put together."

Blair banged his fist into the table.

"Damn it, Luis! Get your priorities straight! You work for me and as long as you want to continue working for me, you'd better shut your mouth!"

The scout sat down.

"That goes for all of you," Blair looking around the room imperiously. "There's only one person who makes decisions around here and that's me. I will not hesitate to give anyone their walking papers. Understood?"

"Yes," the room replied half-heartedly.

"We're gonna be cutting back the scouting department in a few weeks. Most of you are useless anyway and believe me when I say it: I will be getting rid of many of you."

A few minutes later, the meeting adjourned. It could not have ended on more poisoned terms.

Eleven of the team's amateur scouts handed in their resignation papers later that evening rather than continue to work in such an odious environment. Scouting director Luis Toca was one of the few scouts who decided to stay until the bitter end. Two days before Christmas, Trent Blair fired him by e-mail. Little mention of it was made in the local media, but the scouting purge sent shockwaves throughout baseball circles.

Aside from cutting costs in the scouting staff, the general manager's off-season plan was two-fold: re-sign Benjy Alvarez and acquire an outfielder to replace Scott Harper. He soon found out that was much easier said than done. There were certainly budget limitations, but that was only one of the many obstacles facing the team.

Once he became a free-agent, retaining Benjy Alvarez would prove to be nearly impossible. There just weren't that many quality short-stops around of his calibre. Not only did Benjy play Gold Glove defence, but he could hit for a high average and steal bases. In short, he was the apple of any contending team's eye. There was no way the small-market Pioneers could hope to match the massive offers Alvarez would receive.

To make matters worse, the pain-in-the-ass agent otherwise known as Rodrigue Salazar had played his client like a harmonica. Whatever thoughts Benjy might have entertained about returning to Buffalo for a discounted price were dashed when his agent constantly reminded him of how much the Pioneers organization had wronged him. It did not take long for the impressionable 26-year-old to become bitter towards the Pioneers front-office.

Ultimately it came down to Benjy's personal mistrust for Trent Blair and the persistent, aggressive nature of Vince D'Antoni that cemented his decision.

"I......happy to be New York Yankee," he proclaimed at a press conference to a room of stunned reporters. "This is.....this.....life long dream."

The Yankee owner sat next to him with a smile that was so big and so wide that it threatened to break his cheekbones.

"Did you ever consider going back to Buffalo?" A reporter asked.

"I no want to go back there....no after what happen. They no treat people with respect....they no treat Latino with respect."

The terms of the contract were enormous: 6 years for $65 million. The sheer size and scope of the deal underscored an important point. When Vince D'Antoni had his sights set on something or someone, he would not allow anything to get in the way. For a man who had clawed his way through the New York City construction jungle, cost and caution were simply thrown to the wind. There had been other suitors after Alvarez and Harper, but once D'Antoni got involved, the consensus was clear; they were both going to the Yankees.

Stealing these two superstars from Buffalo not only tilted the balance of power in the American League East division to their favour, but made New York the odds on favourite to win the World Series. This team had everything; flash, dash and a whole lot of panache. Not since the late 1970's with Reggie Jackson and Jim 'Catfish' Hunter had the Yankees made a bigger splash in the free agent derby and had a greater amount of star-power in one dressing room.

The projected line-up would boast of LaTroy LaRocque and Benjy Alvarez hitting at the top of the batting order. Alone, each was a great table-setter for the top of a team's lineup. Together, they were a run producing machine that could double as an Olympic track team. The people hitting behind them made the offensive potential all the more awe-inspiring. Scott Harper and Benny Rios had two of the most powerful bats in the game. Basically, the line-up made you want to throw up, especially if you were an opposing pitcher.

Any attempts by Trent Blair to match these moves quickly went for nought. Making a trade was nearly impossible since most general managers refused to deal with Blair anymore based on past experiences. The general manager's relationship with most player agents wasn't much better. It seemed that each free-agent he approached promptly signed elsewhere with barely a response.

"It's an interesting offer," they would say, "but we'd like to explore other avenues."

Barry Jackson resigned with Pittsburgh, while Stan Milluck signed with Texas. Not only did neither player show the remotest interest in coming to Buffalo, but the money Trent Blair offered was nowhere near their asking price.

After striking out on the marquee players, Blair was forced to go bargain hunting. The Pioneers desperately needed a short-stop to replace Benjy Alvarez and signed journeyman Tom DeVellieres to a modest two-year contract. DeVellieres was a good defensive shortstop, but hardly struck fear into the hearts of opposing pitchers. He posted a career .232 batting average and had recently been released by Detroit.

On top of all the financial difficulties the Pioneers were facing, the club's television deal was up for renegotiation and the networks weren't biting.

"I'm sorry Mr. Blair," the BSN executive said, "but we're not thinking along the same wavelength here."

Blair was stunned at what he was hearing.

"What wavelength? We're defending American League Champs for crying out loud, you're telling me we're unmarketable?"

"That's exactly what I'm telling you. Your best players are gone and the ones remaining are either old or in bar fights. Do you expect me to sell that to the public?"

"We've got a good team and we'll show you when we take the field."

"You guys will be lucky to make the playoffs," the network executive differed. "The best I can offer you is 10% lower than our last deal. The Pioneers aren't a feel-good story anymore. I hate to say it, but nobody wants to see a loser."

"A loser?" Blair shouted. "If you think you can hold us ransom, then you've got another thing coming. BSN isn't the only network out there."

As most things went that winter, it turned out Blair was dead wrong. A few days later the Pioneers reluctantly accepted the BSN offer after the other networks rebuffed them. They were no longer a hot television property, no longer a team on the way up burgeoning with young talent that provided glimpses of a bright future. Rather they had been dotted with controversy and the perception existed that the aging Pioneers were on the decline.

Frank Ringler had slowed down in the second half of the season, leading many to ask whether his days as a dominant starter were almost over. Even Eddie Griffin was a question mark. His production had not yet declined, but at 40 years of age how much did he have left? Was this to be the year it fell apart on him?

The two players who caused even more concern were Pete Sampson and Conan O'Shea. Aside from the occasional home-run, Sampson had been horrendous in the second half, striking out over 170 times. Conan O'Shea was equally horrendous in the final month of the season. Some said his wrist hadn't completely healed, but others felt he was simply out of shape. He had been seen less and less in the weight room and more often in bars and strip clubs with Marcus Dillard and Pete Sampson. At the very least, his future as a dominating closer was in question.

Even Trent Blair was coming under scrutiny for the first time. Hailed for so long as a baseball genius, his reputation had taken some hits. The Marcus Dillard signing was not a bust on a statistical level, had hurt the team in other areas. The Pioneer clubhouse had once been so balanced and sanguine, but once Dillard was thrown into the mix the whole chemistry was destroyed. Marcus intimidated teammates he disliked, questionably influenced the ones that he did, and utterly bombed in the playoffs.

Further blackening Blair's spotless resume were comments from Harper and Alvarez themselves. Both gave a perception that this organization didn't treat its players as it should. The team was suddenly being shunned from all over and nobody in the Pioneer front office could comprehend why.

One chilly afternoon in January, Jonathan Jenkins sat down with Al Ferreira and a stone faced Trent Blair at a downtown eatery to discuss what was happening.

"I bet they're turned off by the thought of playing for Jack Vaughn," Ferreira postulated.

Jenkins began choking on his food.

"I find that very hard to believe," the owner disagreed. "Jack's a legend."

"Al might be on to something here," Blair replied. "Jack is getting on with age. Maybe the perception is that he's out of touch with today's player."

The owner looked outside at the snow falling. He couldn't understand what was happening. Everything was changing so fast.

"There's a dry rot in this organization," Jenkins said glumly, "and I'd like to know what on earth it is."

CHAPTER 12

Spring training is always a special time of the year. It offers a brief escape from the harsh realities of this world, a time to forget one's worries and tackle the new season with fresh optimism. For Jack Vaughn, training camp was an especially welcome sight. It was a time when the politics ended and the game itself began. The feeling this year was doubly poignant, coming off a winter when both he and the organization learned that nothing could be taken for granted any longer.

Frank Ringler reported to camp healthy and with the velocity still on his fastball, while Eddie Griffin looked in the best shape of his career at age 40. Even Pete Sampson arrived trim and vowed that the nightmarish end to last season was behind him. Unfortunately, there was far more bad news to start camp.

Conan O'Shea did not look at all like he was in shape to pitch. He arrived in Jacksonville roughly twenty pounds heavier than he had ended the last season, with a large gut to accentuate his new roundness. Word out of Georgia was that he hadn't been seen in a weight room all winter.

Further complicating the pitching situation, Chris Norton was making noises about wanting a new contract. Although not eligible to become a free-agent for another three years, Norton was vastly underpaid at $375 000 and his agent wanted to rectify that situation sooner rather than later. With the payroll budget already tight at $55 million, Trent Blair was not going along with that line of thinking.

"The kid signed a contract. He has to honour it."

"Pardon me," the agent replied, "but this kid you are talking about won 23 games last year. He's the ace of your staff."

"Frank Ringler is our number one starter," Blair said dismissively.

"Frank is past his prime. Chris is the future of this team. All he's done since he arrived in the big leagues is pitch effectively, but he's buried behind Frank. You either show him that you can change that or he'll go somewhere else."

"Where are you gonna go?" Blair shrugged. "He has three years left on his contract. I'm the one who controls his destiny, not you."

"You want to act unreasonably? Fine!" The agent shouted. "You'll see how unreasonable I can be when his contract comes up for renewal!"

"That was a very unprofessional statement," Blair said

"You're the only one who's unprofessional around here," the agent shot back.

"I'm unprofessional?" Blair laughed pretentiously. "That's a good one, but Chris Norton has a little ways to go before he can justify your demands."

"The word is out on you, Blair. You can't operate the way you do and expect to get away with it."

"Is that supposed to mean something to me?" Blair laughed.

"It means you have a verbal invitation to go fuck yourself."

Click.

A few days later, the circus came to town. Marcus Dillard arrived at camp only two days late this year, but armed with his controversial autobiography that hit shelves across North America just days before the start of training camp. It was called: 'The Gospel According to Marcus'. At first glance it appeared to be nothing more than the memoirs of a major leaguer, but for anyone who actually read it, they knew that it was much, much more.

The book, which was written entirely in the third person, was laced with racial undertones with much of Marcus' resentment directed towards a vague person or group whom he referred to only as *"the man."* While he never wrote who *"the man"* really was, it was fairly obvious he was fingering the entire white race *"who for centuries put Marcus' people down and are now trying to do everything in their power to keep Marcus down."* Among other things, he charged *"the man"* with *"preventing Marcus from getting the recognition he deserves"* to *"keeping Marcus out of the cleanup spot."*

The book wasn't completely reserved to comments about perceived racism. In fact, Marcus devoted many pages to ripping other people. Among them were: Scott Harper *"who ran away to New York because he couldn't take the realization that the spotlight was meant for Marcus alone,"* Trent Blair *"who has done little to satisfy Marcus' appetites,"* the New York Yankees *"who wasted their time buying gutless players like Scott Harper and Benjy Alvarez,"* and New York fans *"who are bandwagon hopping fools."* Even the fans of Buffalo didn't escape Marcus' wrath, referred to as people *"who have failed to embrace Marcus to the extent his prodigious talent demands."*

When all was said and done, Marcus let very few people off of the hook. But lest anyone be concerned that he wasn't still focused on baseball, he was equally adamant to the reporters on hand that he was arriving at camp in peak physical condition.

"Marcus is fit of body and mind," he proclaimed, "and I am ready to terrorize American League pitching once more."

The next morning, Jack Vaughn could only shake his head in dismay as he read the slugger's bombastic comments in the Florida newspaper.

"I'm glad we got that cleared up. God forbid he's not fit of body and mind."

Coming into spring training, there were a few unfamiliar faces on the roster. Journeyman Tom DeVellieres was pencilled in to take over for Benjy Alvarez at short, but was looking far from impressive. As Jack Vaughn watched his new shortstop take a few cracks in the batting cage, he groaned.

"He bats like he has a fucking millstone around his neck," Vaughn barked.

"But you should see him turn the double play," Norm Watkins replied.

Vaughn shook his head disgustedly and walked away.

"Oh I have no doubt he'll be involved in a lot of double plays," he muttered sarcastically.

The replacement for Scott Harper in left-field was less obvious. Since Trent Blair had come away empty on the free-agent front, the replacement would have to come from within the organization. Unfortunately, the Pioneers farm system was not what it once was. With the exception of E.J. Winters, a skinny base stealing outfielder who played the previous season at AAA Windsor, nobody was even close to the major league level.

Many in the organization even had their doubts about Winters. He was good defensively, could get on base, and ran extraordinarily well, but some wondered about his slap-hitting style and childish attitude. He had earned a reputation for himself as a troubled kid; either by fighting with teammates, inciting bench clearing brawls or talking back to coaches. In his first day at training camp, he did little to correct that reputation.

"Give it here," he hollered out to the pitcher throwing batting practice. "I want to take this one deep."

He hit the first pitch high in the air, landing in the middle of the outfield.

"I don't want to see you going deep!" Hitting coach Norm Watkins barked impatiently.

The rookie ignored Watkins and swaggered back into the batter's box. Aside from a quickness of feet, the skinny outfielder had no great physical attributes. There was something very raw and natural about him, he possessed a childish cockiness and petulance of undisciplined adolescence. He sent the next pitch into the palm trees just over the right-field fence.

"Did you hear me, goddamn it!" Watkins yelled again.

"Yeah I heard you! That doesn't mean I care."

After swaggering back into the box, E.J. hit another looping fly-ball that barely left the infield. Had it not been for Jack Vaughn stepping in to handle the situation, Watkins might have strangled the rookie.

"I'll take care of it, Norm," Jack reassured Watkins.

As soon as Vaughn stepped into the cage, the rebellious stare in the kid's eye was gone. It was replaced with a look of awe, the look of a boy meeting a legend for the first time.

"Listen to me kid," Vaughn said with a calm authority, "I don't know you too well but I'd have to say, when I see you blow off a coach like that, you're not exactly endearing yourself."

"Yes sir," he gulped.

"In fact you're pissing me off."

"Yes sir."

The manager put his arm around the rookie.

"I'll only say this once. If I see one more pop fly out of you in these next ten minutes, you might as well book your bus ticket to Windsor because that's where you'll be spending the season. For that matter, if I ever see you blow off a coach again, the same thing applies. Understand?"

"Yes sir," E.J. responded, slightly trembling this time.

"Good," Jack patted him in the back of the head. "Now listen to everything that Norm tells you."

Once he overcame his anger, Norm Watkins signalled for the batting practise pitcher to resume throwing. Winters slapped the next ball down the line.

At four-o-clock, everyone proceeded into the clubhouse to call it a day. The disaffected youngster sat quietly in his locker. In the next stall, Frank Ringler and Eddie Griffin chatted away. A few minutes passed until Vaughn walked by.

"How's the arm feeling, Frank?" Vaughn asked.

"It's feeling good," Ringler answered.

The veteran pitcher wore a pained expression as his right arm was immersed in a bucket of ice. Jack looked at him sharply.

"Don't be holding back from me," Jack said.

"Honest to God, Jack. I'd tell you if something was wrong."

"That's good to hear," Jack replied, before pointing to Winters, "because I need the two of you to look after young E.J. here.. He needs vets like you to show him how things are done."

"E.J.?" Griffin wrapped his arms around the skinny rookie. "I'm all over him."

"Good," Jack said sternly. "He needs some guidance."

Vaughn slowly walked away.

"Hey kid," Frank asked, as he continued icing his arm. "What the hell did you do to get Jack on your case like that?"

"Nothing man," he shrugged defiantly, "absolutely nothing. That hitting coach be trying to bust my styles."

The two veterans laughed.

"Be trying to bust your styles?" Griffin smirked. "Look kid, just cause you're black doesn't mean you have to talk stupid. What did Norm say to you?"

"I hit one over that fence and the man starts trippin' on me. I don't take that shit from nobody."

"So what happened?" Ringler asked.

"Jack came over and I gave him a piece of my mind."

The two veterans laughed again.

"Bullshit!" Griffin hollered. "Jack Vaughn would eat you for breakfast!"

"For real kid," Ringler concurred. "Don't screw around with Jack. With Watkins....okay....nobody listens to Watkins.....but don't mess around with Jack."

"Nobody be busting my styles. E.J. plays by his own rules."

"Are you some kind of special needs case?" Griffin joked. "I've already heard enough Ebonics from you than I wish to hear in my lifetime!"

"Whatever," Winters shrugged, before walking off.

The two veterans shook their heads.

"That kid is bad news," Ringler said.

"You're telling me," Griffin mused. "It looks like we got another Marcus Dillard on our hands."

On the field, most of the team was rounding into shape except for Conan O'Shea. The once sculpted reliever had turned portly and was continuing to have problems on the mound.

"I don't know what we're gonna do with him. He's overweight and he's pitching like he belongs in single A," Grant Robinson told the room.

Jack sipped his coffee as the others leafed through their note pads.

"We'll keep him in the closer's role for now," Jack said.

"Are you sure about that?" Blair asked. "He's been absolutely dreadful all spring."

Jack glared at the general manager sharply.

"What would you like me to do about it, Trent? He's the only one down there with any experience."

Blair threw up his hands in agitation.

"Nothing Jack, absolutely nothing. Let's move on. The starting rotation is pretty well set, correct?"

"Ringler's starting opening day," Jack responded.

A few eyebrows were raised around the room.

"What about the starting lineup? Have we made a decision on the Winters kid?"

"I don't want him on the team," Jack replied sternly.

"Why not?" Blair wondered. "He's played pretty well and he's our left-fielder of future. We need a lead-off hitter."

"No," Jack differed, "we need a lead-off hitter with some maturity and that kid doesn't have any. He's a child."

"We're not looking for maturity, Jack. The question is whether he can get on base for our power hitters."

The hitting coach jumped into the conversation.

"I agree with Trent on this one," Norm Watkins said. "E.J.'s got a good head on his shoulders and a bright future ahead of him."

Vaughn sensed something untoward. He had been around the game long enough to know when something was going on behind his back.

"Oh really Norm," he said snidely. "I guess we're talking about the same player who blew you off on the first day of camp?"

"What are you implying Jack?" Watkins asked worriedly.

"You know God damn well what I'm implying," Vaughn shot back.

The general manager tried to tone things down.

"Look guys, let's not let things get out of hand."

Al Ferreira decided to add fuel to Vaughn's fire. The assistant general manager seemed to take great delight in opposing the manager.

"I like the kid," Ferreira interjected. "I think he's a real find."

The whole conversation was so planned, so staged and such a charade that Vaughn knew right away what he was up against. Before he could say anything, the clubhouse attendant came bursting in.

"Can't you see we're doing something?" Blair shouted at the boy. "What is it?"

"I apologize for bursting in like this," the attendant said anxiously. "I was sent here to deliver some bad news."

"Well what is it?" Blair demanded.

"The cops just busted Marcus Dillard, Pete Sampson and Conan O'Shea in a local motel with two convicted drug pushers! It's all over the news. Apparently there were massive amounts of narcotics. Cocaine, ecstasy.....you name it."

"Holy mother of God," Blair exclaimed. "Where are they?"

"Down at the precinct, that's all I know," the attendant said before leaving.

Jack banged his fist into the table and made a strangling motion.

"Jesus Christ! That Marcus....I could kill him!"

The three players spent the night in jail, but were eventually released on bond. Since the charge was not a more serious felony of dealing, but rather simple possession, their trials were quick and expedient. Each one received several hundred hours of community service and some form of probation due to previous assault convictions in Michigan.

The harshest penalty of all came from the Commissioner's Office. Each player was suspended thirty games for violating the league drug policy and fined $25 000. The most backbreaking loss of the three was Marcus Dillard, especially the way he was being relied upon to compensate for the departure of Scott Harper.

The fans and the numerous media outlets that had welcomed Marcus Dillard with open arms upon his arrival were now tired of his act. Callers flooded the phone lines on radio talk shows to express their indignation, while several columnists criticized him. Even players such as Eddie Griffin expressed their disapproval when pressed for comment.

None of it compared to the torment of rage emanating from Jack Vaughn. On the final day of spring training, he ordered Dillard into his office for a stern talk.

"Marcus, I've had it up to here with your dog and pony show."

"Listen skip...."

"Just sit there and shut up!" Jack interrupted. "I have no use for you Marcus, absolutely none."

"I wasn't the only one there!" Marcus pleaded.

Vaughn threw his full coffee mug against the office door in unrestrained anger. The sound of shattering glass could be heard across the clubhouse.

"You just don't get it you thick son of a bitch!"

"Get what?" Marcus pleaded.

"I don't care!" Jack yelled back. "And you want to know why? Because none of this shit ever happened before you arrived! YOU HEAR ME?!! NONE OF IT!!!!"

The yelling penetrated the office doors and could be heard across the dressing room as the startled players listened in silence.

"Damn," Griffin commented from his stall. "I've never heard Jack yell that loud."

Ten seconds later Dillard came out of the office, gathered his belongings and barged out of the room without saying a word to anyone.

A few days before the season started, the Los Angeles Dodgers staged a 40th anniversary reunion for their 1965 World Championship team. It was a chance for the retirees to renew acquaintances and see old faces for the first time in years. For most of the evening, Vaughn chatted at the bar with ex-Dodger teammate Casey Warren. The two men maintained a good relationship over the years that had no dissipated any since Warren took the Boston managing job a year earlier. The amicability was evident on their faces and from the welcoming tone in their voices.

"I'll have a scotch," Vaughn said to the bartender.

"Same here," said Casey.

The bartender quickly handed them their drinks.

"Good to see you Case," Jack smiled.

"Likewise," Casey replied.

"How's life?"

"Same old, same old. Scrapping a lineup together.....looking for the next Jack Vaughn."

Jack blushed.

"Nobody can blow smoke up my ass like you, Case."

"I respect what you've done," Casey insisted. "And that's not a word of lie."

"How was your first year in Beantown anyway?" Jack asked.

"Things were rough at first," Casey replied. "But we had a good second half. Hell, we might even be able to take you guys down this year."

Both men laughed.

"You've got a good young team there, Case. And you're the right man to lead them."

Casey took another shot of liquor.

"We'll see after this year. This managing gig is killer on the family. What about you? You and Beth gettin' back together anytime soon?"

Jack threw back a shot of scotch.

"Fat chance of that happening," Jack replied. "We're beyond the point of reconciliation. When it came down to it, I had to make a choice and I tell you, I prefer it this way. I love baseball and I love managing."

"Managing definitely puts a strain on things," Casey agreed, "and the pressure is insane."

"Ah Case," Jack smiled. "That's the best part. Aside from one shit-head with the Buffalo News, it's been pretty good here."

"A lot of controversy though," Casey noticed. "I heard about your players getting busted."

Jack's face suddenly darkened.

"That's Marcus Dillard for you," Jack said angrily. "I knew he was bad news the minute I saw him."

"Be easy on him," Casey sympathized.

"Be easy on him?" Jack responded bitterly. "Why should I? First it was the strip-club, then it was that stupid book and now this drug bust. Both O'Shea and Sampson were straight shooters 'til he came gallivanting along."

"He's not a bad person, Jack. I got to know him pretty well when I was managing him in AAA a few years ago. When you get beneath the surface with him, he's a good person. He just had a rough childhood...."

"Cut the sob story," Jack interrupted. "It's no excuse. You and I both came from the wrong side of the tracks. You remember how it was back in Jersey. We practically had to fight our way to play ball everyday."

"Would you just listen for once," Casey argued.

Vaughn put his drink down.

"Go ahead," he nodded reluctantly.

"This kid grew up in the Detroit ghetto. I mean we're talking East Detroit here, the project of all projects. He didn't have an easy childhood to begin with, but then he saw his father gunned down in front of him when he was only five, his two brothers were murdered right next to him on the way to school, and then his mother took off on him. He was alone, completely abandoned by the age of eight. That's a lot to deal with when you're a child, especially in that city. They don't call Detroit the 'Murder City' for nothing, you know. Marcus grew up in all that and he did it without any family."

Jack listened sombrely. He had always found Marcus so completely despicable, but what he was hearing from Casey Warren made him think.

"When I managed him in AAA," Casey continued, "we used to have a lot of long chats. Usually about baseball, but sometimes we'd hit on his childhood. I'm no psychiatrist Jack, but I came away with the impression that this guy has a low self-esteem. He feels like the world gave up on him. He often displays a brash attitude to hide it, but it's just a shell. He once told me that the only person who ever cared about him was his agent and even then, he said, the agent was only doing it for money. Think about how sad that is. I feel for the kid, I really do."

"I didn't know that," Jack replied sombrely

"Don't think I'm making excuses for him, because I'm not. He was a handful when I had him and I'm sure he's a handful now, but you should get to know the kid. You'd be surprised what you find."

Jack was at a loss for words. Within a few minutes, his image of someone had been so utterly altered.

"Anyways, Jack. I think they're calling us over for a photo."

The manager slowly dismounted the barstool.

"Yeah, all right. Let's go."

CHAPTER 13

"Welcome to BSN Baseball. I'm Chuck Smith with my colleague Terry Davis, glad to have you with us for this chilly afternoon here in Buffalo for the 2005 Opening Day. Today's game features the defending American League Champion Buffalo Pioneers taking on the Detroit Tigers."

"This should be a good momentum builder for the Pioneers. They're coming off a rough winter and have a lot of new faces in the line-up. Playing a last-place team like Detroit should get them off on the right foot."

"The Pioneers definitely have an uphill battle to win the division because the Yankees have really beefed up, but this is still a good team and if they can survive this first month without Marcus Dillard, Pete Sampson and Conan O'Shea, I think they'll do just fine."

"A few new faces."

"Yes there are. Foremost among them is young left-fielder E.J. Winters. This kid doesn't quite have the average to replace Benjy Alvarez in the lead-off spot nor the power to replace Harper in left-field, but he has the speed and defence. He is very small and also very skinny for that matter, but I don't think it hurts him. He's always been a slap-hitter who can leg out infield singles."

"What about today's starter, Frank Ringler. What do you expect from him?"

"Frank had a good spring and hopefully he can bring it into the season with him. He just turned 39 and really slowed down last year, but along with Chris Norton should anchor the top of the rotation. Jack Vaughn gave Frank the opening day start out of loyalty."

"We'll be back with the first pitch from New York Governor Prentice H. Wulloughby."

The Governor emerged onto the field to a smattering of boos from the capacity crowd. In only his first five months in office, Wulloughby had already proven himself to be completely out of touch. He seemed to govern with a bumbling sincerity; a willingness to do what is right but a clueless disposition as to what that might be.

With the introduction of tough state labour laws and a hefty tax increase to pay for his extensive social platform, unemployment levels had soared. Several demonstrations had already taken place outside the state capitol building in Albany, while newspaper editorials lambasted the new Governor's economic policy. It had been a rough year politically for Wulloughby.

The Governor didn't fare any better at pitching. His ceremonial first pitch to catcher Terry Miller bounced four times before reaching home plate.

"Here we go, Frank Ringler takes the hill and is set to face the first batter of the 2005 season."

"Frank went 14-11 with a 4.08 era in 2004, a very un-Ringler like season. Was it a fluke or a trend? We're about to find out."

Ringler cruised through the first three innings and was given early support by an Eddie Griffin two-run homer. Heading into the fourth inning all looked promising, but everyone in attendance was about to find out a lot had changed.

"Ringler's offering is crushed to left field for a base-clearing triple!....The game is tied!"

"Crushed to left field! Three-run home run!.....and its 5-2 Detroit......."

".......double down the line......two runs will score....... The Pioneers are down 7-2....."

"......line drive......off the wall........9-2 Detroit!"

The crowd booed lustily and began filing out of the stadium.

"You'd have to think that Jack Vaughn will make a change here. This is getting ridiculous."

Vaughn sat in the dugout sipping coffee. There was nobody warming up.

"I tell you Chuck, opening day is supposed to be a festive occasion, but there is such a stale atmosphere in Pioneer Stadium right now. I don't think anyone, save a Detroit fan, could take joy out of this."

The final score was an ugly 15-3 shellacking. With 5-1 and 6-2 losses the following two days, a sweep at the hands of the lowly Tigers did not bode well for the season ahead. Aside from Ringler's opening day massacre, the combination of a bad bullpen and absolutely no offensive support outside of Eddie Griffin proved disastrous.

The trend would continue throughout April.

"......the Royals absolutely throttled the Pioneers tonight, 8-2."

"......Ringler was bombed this afternoon for nine runs as Buffalo takes the loss, 12-5."

"......being shutout 6-0 here today, the Pioneer losing streak reaches eight games........"

".....another dreadful performance by the bullpen, coughing up a late inning lead. The Pioneers lost 8-6."

After one particularly hard loss, Jack Vaughn and pitching coach Grant Robinson walked over to the Duke of York to drown their early season sorrows. The Pioneers may have been short-handed, but nobody expected the team to get off to the worst start in franchise history at 7-19. As glum as things looked, Jack remained fairly confident they would eventually come out of it.

"What are we gonna do about these guys?" Robinson asked

"We're just off to a slow start," Jack responded calmly, "and a little undermanned right now. The boys will come out of it."

Not everyone was so sure. As the two coaches chatted away in the local watering hole, Trent Blair and Al Ferreira held a meeting of the minds up in the general manager's office.

"This is a bloody disaster," Al Ferreira said disgustedly, "and if you don't remove Jack Vaughn soon, the blood will be on your hands."

The general manager's normally clean cut face had gone days without a shave.

"We haven't reached that point yet," Trent replied shrewdly.

Ferreira was flabbergasted.

"If you wait any longer, this season will be over before it begins!"

"Look Al," Trent calmly stated. "As much as I'd like to fire Vaughn, now is not the time. Not when three of our best players are suspended."

The assistant G.M. refused to let the subject drop.

"The man is living in the past," Ferreira complained. "He's still treating Frank Ringler like he's a Cy Young Winner."

"Frank's an icon."

"Frank is finished! I don't know why we don't just release him."

"We'd look cold hearted if we did it in the middle of the season. And we both know we're not cold hearted people, right?"

"Right," Ferreira laughed impishly.

The general manager put his hand on Ferreira's shoulder.

"As for Jack, just let things play out by themselves."

"What if Jenkins steps in?" Ferreira wondered.

"Jenkins is the least of our worries," Trent laughed arrogantly. "I got that old man in the palm of my hand. The bottom line is, if things don't turn around by July, we have an excuse to can Vaughn."

A few days later, the three suspensions finally ended. After a brief minor league rehab stint in Windsor, all three men returned for a west coast swing in Anaheim. With the team finally intact, it looked like things might return to normal.

In the first game back, the Pioneers looked like the team of old. Chris Norton pitched eight shutout innings, while Marcus Dillard and Eddie Griffin both went deep. Even Conan 'The Barbarian' managed to close it out, despite giving up a run in the ninth inning. It was a relatively tidy 3-1 victory, the type of win that boosts morale.

It all unravelled the next night.

"*Eddie Griffin is up now, trying to cash in another runner.*"

"*What a season it has been thus far for the 40-year old. AL Player of the Month for April, 13 home-runs, 32 runs batted in. Where would the Pioneers be without him?*"

"*They'd be winless!*"

The two commentators laugh.

"*The pitcher is set....he delivers.....hit to the right side.....flip to first, one away.*"

Eddie fell to the ground and grabbed his hamstring in obvious pain.

"*Oh no. Oh no! It looks like Eddie is pulling up lame here. I hope it's nothing serious.*"

"*The Pioneers aren't taking any chances. They're taking him out.*"

There was more heartache to follow in the bottom of the ninth.

"*The Pioneers are clinging to a slim 2-1 lead here.....Conan O'Shea has walked the first batter and is now facing the power-hitting Milton Veras.*"

O'Shea was sporting an earring for the first time in his left lobe.

"*We saw a wonderful pitching performance put on tonight by Johnny Turner, it would be a shame to see that go to waste.*"

"*O'Shea is set....the pitch.....belted to right field!*"

The sparse crowd in Anaheim rose to their feet.

"*No doubt about it! Henry Veras has just ended this ball-game! 3-2 Anaheim!*"

The carnage only continued the next night in Minnesota. Frank Ringler was being hit all over the Metrodome to the tune of eight runs by the third inning.

"*Another lacklustre performance thus far for Frank Ringler.*"

"*This is getting pathetic. For my sake and for the sake of all in attendance tonight, I hope Vaughn takes Ringler out soon. I feel like I'm watching a punch-drunk ex-boxing champion get beat up.*"

"8-0 Minnesota, no outs, bases loaded.....Ringler sets......the pitch......hit to right field.....it's going to go for extra bases!"

The veteran pitcher fell to the ground writhing in pain.

"Oh dear God! Ringler is down and this does not look good."

The manager and team trainer ran onto the field to assist the pitcher.

"Jack Vaughn is making his way out onto the field and I can only hope this isn't what I think it is."

On the following day's sportscast, everyone's worst fears were confirmed.

"Long-time Pioneers starter Frank Ringler has apparently blown his arm out. It happened in last night's game at Minnesota. At this point details are sketchy as to what exactly the injury entails, but Pioneers' doctors are saying he is out for the season. He may never pitch again. Ringler was suffering through the worst season of his career going 0-5 with an 8.85 earned run average."

After the game Jack Vaughn and Grant Robinson walked towards the manager's office,. The manager stepped on an errant towel lying on the ground. Despite seeing the clubhouse attendant nearby, Jack picked up the towel and disposed of it himself.

Frank Ringler was waiting for them inside the office.

"Hey Frank," Jack asked with surprise. "What can I do for you?"

The pitcher looked uneasy.

"Don't give up on me, Jack. I still have something left."

Vaughn took a sip of coffee and ran his hands through his hair.

"I'd like to believe you Frank, but the prognosis doesn't look good. They're saying you'll be lucky to pitch next season, if at all."

"I don't have a next season," Ringler said grimly. "This is it for me."

"Don't be saying that."

"What else am I going to say? This might be it for me. I've never been good at anything but baseball...."

The notion of retirement terrified him. He had been raised with a ball and a glove and knew nothing else.

"You know, its funny," Frank added bitterly. "Five years ago, Trent Blair was practically kissing my ass to stay in Buffalo. Now he won't even say hello in the hallway."

Vaughn shook his head.

"Well, that's pretty much par for the course with Trent Blair."

"All I ever wanted is to retire on my own terms. Could you promise me one thing?"

"What is it?" Vaughn wondered.

"If I prove I'm ready to pitch later this season, will you put me out there?"

Jack sighed heavily. He remembered all of the gutsy performances Frank had provided over the years, how his once scorching fastball always seemed to add a few extra miles-per-hour for the big playoff games. His heart swelled with loyalty.

"As far as I'm concerned, you're still my ace."

As Vaughn shook Ringler's hand, the veteran pitcher affectionately bear hugged the manager off of the ground.

"Jesus!" Jack laughed. "You still have some power in those arms after all."

"You won't regret it," Frank insisted. "I'm going to work my ass off in rehab. I'm going to lay it all on the line for you, Jack!"

As the pitcher walked out of his office, the manager turned to his pitching coach.

"What do you think, Grant? You think he's got a hope in hell?"

"Well," Robinson pondered for a moment, "it does seem impossible, but I wouldn't discount it. Determination goes a long way."

"I hope so," Jack added, "because I have a feeling we're going to eventually turn things around. And when we do, we sure could use him."

The effect of Ringler's injury on team morale was devastating. As poorly as he had been pitching, the wily veteran was still highly regarded by the younger pitchers for his sage advice and impressive accomplishments. Four Cy Young trophies and 274 career wins have a way of doing that.

The next day in the dressing room, nobody said a word. The only conversation was between Marcus Dillard and E.J. Winters, but even that was mostly one-way.

"It looks like you and me are the only stars left on this team," Winters said cockily.

Marcus sat in his locker looking extremely disinterested.

"Yeah....okay," he said carelessly.

"Power and Glory, man."

"What?"

"Power and glory," E.J. repeated. "You're the power, I'm the glory."

"Yeah....whatever," Dillard replied with increasing disinterest.

"That's right man," Winters continued. "It takes a couple of brothers from the ghetto to set this team straight."

Marcus had been content to let the rookie continue rambling on, but he'd had enough of the kid's bravado. He knew that anybody from the projects understood it was nothing to gloat about.

"Man, you ain't from no ghetto."

"What you sayin'?" Winters defended.

"I'm sayin' you're full of it."

"You just playin' wit' me. You know how it is."

Winters slapped Marcus's shoulder affectionately.

"Don't touch me kid," Marcus growled. "You ain't from no fuckin' projects. I bet you grew up with all them crackers in Auburn Hills."

Winters face turned red.

"Ah man, don't be sayin' that," he defended himself.

"Just stay away from me," Marcus ordered him. "Kids like you I can't stand. You remind me of myself when I was your age."

Marcus walked towards the door of the dressing room.

"I'll take that as a compliment," Winters responded ingratiatingly. "You're the man Marcus....you've always been the man."

The burly slugger shook his head and continued walking.

"If only you knew that wasn't a compliment," he muttered under his breath.

The team's horrendous slide continued into June. Young left-fielder E.J. Winters was certainly not to blame. He had put himself into consideration for Rookie-of-the-Year honours by getting on base and stealing enough bases to put him in the league's top-five. Veteran catcher Terry Miller was also hitting well and playing defence at his usual Gold Glove level. Unfortunately neither player was the type capable of carrying a stagnant offence.

First Baseman Eddie Griffin was at least a few weeks from returning. Pete Sampson looked lost at the plate, and Marcus Dillard had been in a prolonged slump since returning to the lineup. The fickle fans took notice.

"Here comes Marcus Dillard, with a man on second and two outs."

"BOOOOOO!!" Jeers rained down from crowd.

"And the Buffalo fans are really letting him have it!"

For the first time in several seasons, there were a few thousand empty seats seen at the top of the upper deck. It had all became so painfully frustrating; the mounting losses and the daily humiliation. Throughout the turmoil, it was Marcus Dillard who became the lightning rod for all of the club's troubles. As he entered the batters box, he was showered with peanuts that were tossed from rambunctious fans.

"Compare this to the standing ovation he received in his first home at-bat last year. It really is like night and day isn't it?"

"Marcus steps in....the pitch....swing and a miss strike one!"

The booing continued.

"Marcus is in a rut right now. With Griffin gone, he's trying to do too much and as a result he's swinging at bad pitches."

"Javier sets....the pitch....swing and a miss strike two!"

The persistent booing continued as Dillard stepped out of the batter's box. His face looked helpless and vulnerable.

"There's a man on second, this is a big situation. Marcus really needs to start hitting with runners in scoring position."

"Javier gets the sign......he's set.....fires.....swing and a miss strike three!"

The booing reached a fever pitch.

"BOOOOOO!!!"

"Dillard you bum!"

"Go write another book, jerk off!"

Up in the owner's box, a frail looking Jonathan Jenkins watched on in dismay.

"I don't know if this can get any worse," Jenkins said grimly. "I really don't."

The team truly hit rock-bottom during a three game road trip to Yankee Stadium the following weekend. New York was already eighteen games ahead of Buffalo in the standings, but the media's attention was more fixed upon the story surrounding Scott Harper and Benjy Alvarez's first game against their old club.

When neither player seemed willing to feed the controversy, the media turned its glare to Marcus Dillard. Nobody had forgotten the things he had said in his recently published book and the New York fans were spoiling to let him know just how they felt about it.

"Two down and Marcus Dillard is coming to the plate."

"BOOOOOO!!" The crowd thundered.

"And look at this! All 45 000 in attendance here at Yankee Stadium have risen to their feet."

"Yeah, they're giving him the old fashioned Bronx cheer!"

As Dillard tried to concentrate, the fans carried on with a ceaseless bevy of taunting.

"MARR....CUSS!.......MARR....CUSS!.......MARR....CUSS!"

He looked rattled as he swung and missed the first two pitches he saw.

"Anderson sets........the pitch.......called strike three! Three up, three down! Marcus goes down on three pitches and we'll be back right after this."

The taunting continued all night long.

"MARR...CUSS!.....MARR...CUSS!.....MARR...CUSS!"

Each time Marcus swung harder in attempt to silence the masses. He struck out three times on the afternoon.

The Yankees held a commanding 8-0 lead heading into the ninth inning. Scott Harper and Benny Rios had both gone deep. Benjy Alvarez stole two bases and scored three runs.

With the listless Pioneer offence unlikely to stage a wild comeback, Jack Vaughn brought in a minor-league pitcher to mop up the rest of the game. For all intents and purposes this one was in the books. In the top of the ninth inning, E.J. Winters changed all of that.

"Anderson deals.....whoa....and this one is high and inside."

The pitch whizzed by Winters' head. The pitcher tipped his cap in deference.

"A little chin music! Probably an honest mistake on Anderson's part."

"E.J. Winters doesn't seem to think so! He's walking out towards the mound."

"What are you trying to do?" Winters demanded.

"Go back to the batters box, rookie," Anderson shook him off.

"I'll kill you white boy!" Winters screamed and pointed towards the mound.

E.J. charged towards the Yankees pitcher, breaking all hell loose. Conan O'Shea sprinted in from the bullpen before most of the other relievers had even gotten up from their seats. Marcus Dillard and Pete Sampson jumped right into the fray immediately, taking on several players at once. Only Eddie Griffin was playing the role of peacemaker. Both benches cleared.

Jack Vaughn remained above the fray until he saw Yankees manager Tommy Bedowes punch E.J. Winters in the back of the head. The manager's blood pressure rose and a shot of adrenaline rushed through his body.

"Take your hands off my players!" Vaughn shouted angrily.

"Stay out of it, Jack!" Bedowes yelled. "He had it coming!"

Jack calmly waved his fist.

"You don't understand how long I've wanted to do this."

With deadly accurate precision, Vaughn slugged Bedowes with an upper cut that bloodied the other manager's nose and sent him down onto the field. The titanic blow was witnessed by an entire coliseum of bloodthirsty fans who roared their approval. Before Vaughn could do anything else, security officials restrained him.

"I hope that felt good!" Bedowes yelled back, as he wiped the blood off his nose. "Because that's the only pleasure you're going to be feeling this season! How does it feel to manage a bunch of losers!"

"You'd be the best person to ask about that," Jack responded sarcastically. "When was the last time you won a World Series, Tommy?"

Vaughn tauntingly caressed his World Series rings.

"Okay that's enough, Mr. Vaughn," the security guard said as he escorted him off the field.

Nobody sustained any serious injuries in the brawl, but Winters' aggression had deeper consequences. Six players including Jack Vaughn received five game suspensions. In the interim, Norm Watkins took over the managing duties as the Yankees easily swept the series to pull twenty-one games ahead of the Pioneers. It had been such a humiliating ordeal. In three days, the Pioneers had been out-pitched, out-hit and out-classed.

As Jack Vaughn and Grant Robinson made their way down the tunnel to the visiting dressing room following Sunday's finale, all the two men could hear was shouting.

"You guys are playing like bullshit! BULLSHIT! If you think you can just go through the motions, then you've got another thing coming!"

The sound of shattered wood could be heard down the hall.

"YOU GUYS NEED A FUCKING WAKE UP CALL AND I'M THE PERSON TO GIVE IT TO YOU!!"

CRACK!!!

As soon as Vaughn and Robinson heard the loud blast, both men hurried into the clubhouse. The first thing they saw was the sickening image of Norm Watkins standing over a shattered water cooler with a bat in his hand. Most of the players had their heads down in shame.

Vaughn looked around and assessed the situation.

"Norm, come into my office for a minute," Jack said calmly.

"In a minute," Norm responded.

"Now," Jack answered tersely.

Once inside, any hint of civility in the manager's tone quickly disappeared.

"DON"T YOU EVER, EVER DO THAT AGAIN! YOU AREN'T THE FUCKING MANAGER ON THIS TEAM!! YOU GOT THAT?"

"Somebody needs to shake these guys up," Watkins defended. "This clubhouse is a country club."

"You know Watkins, you've always been such an alarmist! You're beating a dead horse here. I don't run my team by chewing out the players!"

"If things keep going the way they're going, you won't be running this team at all!"

Every bone in Jack's body raged with deep pulsation as a bloody rage of terror rippled through him. It would have given him tremendous satisfaction to knock Watkins silly right then and there. He barely kept himself under control.

"Norm," Vaughn said calmly. "Get the fuck out of my office."

"I'm the hitting coach. I have a right to be here."

Vaughn grabbed the table. It was all he could do to prevent himself from assaulting the hitting coach right then and there.

"Norm," Vaughn repeated, this time shaking his fists. "If you don't leave within five seconds, so help me I'll throw you out myself. I no longer consider you a part of this coaching staff. You are not to address the players, you are not to speak with me, and you sure as hell are not allowed to come into this dressing room ever again. Get the fuck out of here."

Watkins quickly left the office. After a few minutes of composing himself, Jack walked into the dressing room. The players' faces looked tired and exhausted. He knew what they were going through and that all they needed was some reassurance.

"Guys, I know we're going through tough times. I know everyone is writing us off but I believe we still have a lot of good baseball left in us."

He took a sip of coffee before continuing

"I want you all to disregard what Norm said today. I don't think you guys are going through the motions, but I think we're all hurting a little bit. We've had some bad luck and some injuries, but I'm gonna ask you to pick yourselves up off the mat and start fresh. These first two and a half months have been worse than anything I could have ever imagined. There is no reason why it has to end this way."

He sipped his coffee again.

"I know everyone is saying we're nothing without Harper and Alvarez, but I don't believe that for a minute. There is still a lot of talent in this room. In a few games we'll be getting Eddie Griffin back. For the first time all season, we'll have a full team. The only guy we're missing is Frank and he's told me that he'll do everything in his power to come back this season. So what I'm asking you guys is to wipe the slate clean starting now."

Many of the players looked visibly relieved.

"What about all the rumours?" Catcher Terry Miller piped up. "I keep reading that Trent Blair is going to gut our team and bring in prospects."

"That will never happen as long as I'm managing. I'm telling you guys, if we start now we can still make something of this season. Our new season starts today."

Coming from Vaughn, the words meant something. The talk loosened up some downtrodden spirits inside the dressing room.

As fruitful as the private discussion might have been, it did little to reassure those outside the dressing room. Not only was the team in the midst of a terrible losing streak, but several players were suspended and Norm Watkins' dismissal as hitting coach had turned into an ugly public spat. The *Buffalo News'* Chet Thomas threw up the white flag in his column the following morning:

Pioneers ship is sinking

By: Chet Thomas (Buffalo News)

Disaster is not a word that should be used lightly. It is a strong word that implies a failing of an enormous magnitude on the part of many people, but in this instance it isn't nearly strong enough to describe the massacre that the Pioneers 2005 campaign has become. Only a year ago the Buffalo Pioneers were coming off three World Series titles and had the best record in baseball. But after a dispirited effort in last fall's World Series and a first-half that has been punctuated by bad pitching, no hitting and decisions from the dugout that leave us all scratching our heads, it has been hard to watch. Here we are on June 16th and the Pioneers remain mired in last in their division, last in the American League and last in all of baseball. In a word, the ship has reached the point of no return. There will be no playoffs and for the first time in almost a decade, no meaningful games in September. So like any ship that is stranded in the middle of nowhere, there remains only one option. Captain Vaughn must be thrown overboard, or else next season may become a wash as well.

Aside from Chet Thomas' predictable, anti-Vaughn rant in the Buffalo News, several other columnists were beginning to take shots at the manager. For the first time since he had taken the job in Buffalo five years earlier, Jack Vaughn was suddenly on the hot seat. For every writer calling for Vaughn's head however, there were many others pinning the blame directly on Marcus Dillard. Paul Jones of the *Buffalo News* was the most caustic.

Jones wrote in his column that: *"Marcus Dillard is an irredeemable virus who is past the point of no return. And it has taken only a year for him to infect this once proud franchise with his selfish, losing mentality. A year ago he demanded Eddie Griffin's cleanup spot. But there is only one problem: Marcus Dillard is the worst go-to guy in baseball."*

The next day, the team despondently boarded the bus back to the airport. Some players decided to sleep and forget about the agonizing weekend while others read the morning paper, which had no shortage of opinions expressed in it.

As the bus pulled away, Trent Blair grabbed the newspaper and began reading the baseball section. The situation on June 17th looked ominous:

American League East Standings (June 17th)

Team	W-L	GB
New York	43-26	-
Boston	37-31	5.5
Toronto	34-34	8.5
Baltimore	31-38	12
Tampa Bay	24-46	19.5
Buffalo	22-47	21

Buffalo Pioneers Statistics (June 17th)

Player		Average	HR	RBI	SB
LF	E.J. Winters	.305	2	24	21
C	Terry Miller	.287	1	26	0
RF	Marcus Dillard	.241	10	28	8
1B	Eddie Griffin	.312	13	32	0
CF	Pete Sampson	.195	6	22	0
DH	Orlando Mateo	.283	8	30	2
3B	Dave Kelton	.250	4	24	0
SS	Tom DeVellieres	.232	0	17	3
2B	Esteban Pena	.238	1	18	8

Pitcher		W-L	E.R.A.	Saves
SP	Frank Ringler	0-5	8.85	-
SP	Chris Norton	6-7	3.01	-
SP	Johnny Turner	5-8	4.72	-
SP	Rich Lopez	3-7	5.48	-
SP	Dave Rivers	2-9	5.95	-
RP	Conan O'Shea	0-8	6.03	7

"How much money are we paying Dillard for him to be hitting .241?" Blair complained. "I just don't understand it."

"Why don't you go talk with him?" Ferreira replied.

"And why would I do that?" Blair asked. "I get dumber just listening to him."

Marcus Dillard sat by himself at the front of the bus. Jack Vaughn knew the slugger could use some encouragement and decided now was the time for a heart-to-heart. After a few minutes, the manager walked up to chat with his struggling outfielder.

"Marcus, lets talk."

"Great," Dillard replied unenthusiastically. "What did I do now?"

The slugger's face looked so emotionally drained and forlorn that Jack felt only sympathy for him.

"Nothing," Vaughn replied. "I'm not mad at you."

"Then what are you here for?"

Jack was a proud man and he was especially proud of his ability to judge character. Since his talk with Casey Warren though, he had come to realize that he might have misjudged Marcus. It was hard to admit and the crusty old manager was even more uneasy expressing it.

"I guess what I'm here for is to....well....I'm partly here to apologize and I.....um.......I'm also here to get to....uh....to get to know you better."

"Apologize?" Marcus said with a great deal of shock.

"Well yeah," the manager continued. "I think that I might have been a little quick to judge you. I was talking with an ex-teammate of mine, Casey Warren......"

"Case," Marcus grinned, "he's a good man."

The slugger's smile appeared so naturally that Jack wondered where it came from. It had been locked up for so long.

"He was telling me about your childhood and it was a bit of an eye opener."

"I don't want to talk about it," Marcus replied coldly.

"That's fine. I'm just trying to get a better understanding of you. If we're going to do anything this season, you and I need to be on the same page. And I think we both have to make a few sacrifices."

"Sacrifice?" Marcus responded, as if it were a late addition to the English language.

"Yes, sacrifice. I'd say that part of the reason I may have misunderstood you was the way you acted. Put yourself in my shoes for a minute. If you saw some player waltz into your clubhouse and predict eighty home-runs, demand to bat cleanup, and get arrested twice in one year, what would you think?"

"I'd probably want to kill him," Marcus grinned.

"I'm glad you see my point of view," Jack smiled. "I may not have done the best job getting to know you, but you didn't exactly make it easy on me."

The slugger sat quietly. It appeared that he was actually listening.

"I'll admit, Mr. Vaughn, I haven't been the best citizen. I always looked up to you and appreciated what you've done in this game....."

The slugger looked out the window.

".....but I never felt like you gave me the time of day."

There was a brief pause.

"I think we can both learn a few things," Jack admitted reluctantly.

As Marcus tried to compose his thoughts, he continued staring out the window towards the urban landscape. He had never been adept at expressing his deepest emotions.

"I think....uh.....I don't know what Casey told you, but sometimes....I....uh.....well basically what I'm saying Mr. Vaughn is that deep down I'm a little insecure."

"Insecure?" Jack said with surprise.

"I think that's the word for it. Sometimes....I....uh....I might do things I know are stupid and might reflect badly on me as....uh....as sort of a mask."

Jack still found it hard to believe. All of that machismo was just for show.

"A mask?" Jack said with equal surprise

The big man nodded his head.

"Yeah, a mask. I grew up in hard times Mr. Vaughn and I had to deal with a lot of hard realities at a young age. And.....I had my heart broken a few times. But in the neighbourhood I grew up, you can't show that. You gotta be strong. So I hid it and I've been hiding it ever since."

"Why did you feel you had to hide it?" Jack asked

"I was always the biggest kid on the block. You know how it is, there's always people looking to bring you down, so I had to act mean and rough....or else I would have been roughed up. I guess I never stopped acting that way."

There was a long silence as each man thought to himself.

"I read your book," Jack smiled. "Or at least I tried to read it. I had to put it down after awhile."

"I don't blame you," Marcus laughed.

"Do you really believe all that shit?"

Marcus was at a loss for words. He was so confused that he turned towards the window to hide any seeping emotion.

"I don't know. Part of me does and part of me doesn't. On one hand, I do hold the white establishment responsible for the position I was born into. Take a quick look around and tell me, on average, who is generally in a worse position, blacks or whites? It's pretty obvious...."

He paused.

".....but on the other hand, I look at the events after my birth and all I have is shame and contempt for my own race. It was a black gunman that killed my father, it was a gang of black vandals that murdered my brothers and......."

He held his hand over his face and covered his eyes.

".....it was my own momma that ran off on me. I don't care how bad things are, there's no excuse for any of that."

The manager was stunned by what he was hearing. He had never known the articulate Marcus, the mature Marcus, the reflective Marcus. The only Marcus he had known was the brooding and arrogant blowhard; the one who seemed to invite disdain. He was floored.

"I don't make excuses Mr. Vaughn," Marcus continued. "I know all the shit I've done and believe me, I ain't proud of any of it. I'm not saying I'm gonna be perfect from now on, but I'll make an effort."

The manager affectionately patted Marcus on the back of the head.

"That's all I can ask," Jack said. "And I'll try to be a little more understanding."

"That's all I can ask," Marcus replied.

The smile on the big man's face seemed to mirror the sun, which was just poking its head out from behind the clouds. Like a comet that only comes along once every few years, it was a sight to behold.

CHAPTER 14

The Yankees came to town the following weekend. Ticket sales may have been slow all year, but a series against New York always brought out the crowds. Not only was Eddie Griffin returning from the disabled list, but it marked the long awaited homecoming of Scott Harper and Benjy Alvarez.

The local media mobbed both players as they arrived in the airport, but neither provided the inflammatory remarks dished out by Yankee owner Vince D'Antoni.

"Stop crying over spilled milk," the Yankee owner snivelled. "The bottom line is that Scott Harper and Benjy Alvarez wanted to play for a real team in a real town."

While the fans mostly let Alvarez off the hook, Harper was booed mercilessly when he stepped to the plate. One group of fans seated in the upper deck, had a huge banner overhanging the balcony that read: "GREETING$ $COTT."

"And here is Scott Harper leading off the fourth inning. For the second time tonight, the fans are giving him a rude reception."

"BOOOOOOO!!"

"Well, it ain't exactly a welcome back party, I'll tell you that much."

"The pitcher gets the sign and sets.....the pitch.....taken for ball one."

"A good eye for Harper. He's really picked up where he left off last season, leading the American League in runs batted in and batting average. We all know that Vince D'Antoni is a hard man to please, but he has to be smelling roses with this deal."

"Harper steps back in.....the pitcher sets....delivers.....hit the other way into the gap and Scott is in with a double to lead-off the fourth!"

After both teams put runs on the board early, the game remained deadlocked at 3-3. Heading into the bottom of the ninth inning, the top of the order was up for Buffalo. After E.J. Winters singled and Terry Miller walked, Marcus Dillard came to the plate.

"Full count on Marcus......lets see if he has the patience to take a walk here."

"The pitch....ball four! Marcus Dillard draws a rare walk....the bases are loaded!"

"The kid's learning," Vaughn beamed to Robinson. "He's learning!"

Eddie Griffin strutted up the plate with the game on the line. Held up to messiah status in the days prior to his return, Griffin was revelling in every minute of the spotlight. The crowd was on their feet.

"What a return this would be for the veteran Griffin."

"Canatella sets.....the pitch.....taken for ball one."

"Eddie is just waiting on his pitch. He's looking for something to drive."

"The pitcher is ready.......sets.....fires........drilled to left field!.....Over Harper's head!.....Pioneers win! Pioneers win!"

The crack of the first baseman's bat had the rare quality of uniting a stadium full of rabid fans in celebration. It seemed like the script had been written beforehand; the 40-year-old veteran returns from the disabled list to bring his club back from the dead. For anyone at Pioneer Stadium that afternoon, they knew this team wasn't dead yet.

Following the game, the clubhouse was in a jovial mood.

"One day at a time, boys!" Jack Vaughn yelled enthusiastically. "We're gonna climb our way back into this thing!"

Any happiness that Jack might have been experiencing was soon tempered when he and Grant Robinson arrived in the manager's office. The smile quickly eased its way off his face.

"Beth," he greeted her unenthusiastically, "what an unpleasant surprise."

"Believe me," his ex-wife responded with a wry smile, "the pleasure is all yours."

She had short brown hair and a face that had been hardened by years of solitude. Her body was short and unnaturally vigilant, complete with a flat chest that seemed to render the burning of bras a redundant task. As she sat down, Jack leaned back into his chair and took a sip of coffee.

"So now that we have the pleasantries out of the way," he said sarcastically, "what are you here for? Are you sniffing around for more money? Or is this one of your feminist humanitarian missions?"

"Ah Jack," she laughed. "I can only take you in small doses."

"What happened to us anyway? When I met you in college you were just the nice and pretty, low-maintenance girl I fell in love with."

"I wonder the same thing myself," she smiled to conceal her annoyance. "When we first met you were wonderful, an incurable romantic and a natural charmer. Then baseball got a hold of you...."

"Okay I think I better get going," Robinson said uneasily.

"....and turned you into the jerk you are today."

"No Grant, stay," Jack insisted. "If you ever want to hear paranoia and bull-shit all rolled into one, listen to this wench babble on for five minutes."

Beth shook her head impatiently.

"Paranoia?" She replied angrily. "Where's your latest bimbo, Jack? Or are you currently in between one-night stands?"

"Her name is Cynthia and she's in Paris doing a photo shoot."

"Some things never change," she scoffed. "I didn't know you gave names to your toys."

"I think I better get going," the pitching coach repeated softly.

Their eyes were fixed on each other with an explosive combination of love and hate as the emotional energy filled the air like shower steam in a bathroom. When Robinson returned an hour later, the two were sitting quietly with bitter looks on their faces.

"I'm sorry to walk in on you two," Robinson said reverently, "but I need to tell Jack something."

"Its okay," Beth said after wiping her face dry. "I was just going."

She got up from the couch and walked out with nary a word to either man. Jack looked beat, almost as if he had just been thrown into a cage with a wild tiger.

"What is it now?" He asked wearily.

There was redness under his eyes.

"You aren't going to believe what I just heard," the pitching coach said.

"After this past hour, I'll believe anything."

The pitching coach prepared himself for the explosion that was sure to come.

"Trent Blair just traded Terry Miller to San Francisco for prospects?"

The manager jumped out of his chair.

"You gotta be kidding me?"

"I couldn't believe it myself," Robinson added.

With an air of expediency and urgency rarely seen in him, Vaughn ran upstairs to the executive floor and barged into the general manager's office. He hardly noticed Jonathan Jenkins and Al Ferreira sitting quietly in the corner.

"What do you think you're doing!" He barked at the general manager

"Haven't you heard of knocking?" Blair sniped. "There are certain human conventions."

"You traded my starting catcher without telling me?" Jack interrupted.

"Frankly, I don't know how this involves you."

"You traded Terry Miller?" Jack demanded an answer.

"Yes I did." Blair answered, as he trimmed his nails. "It still needs approval from the San Francisco owner, but the basic deal has been agreed upon."

Jack ran his hands through his hair to calm himself.

"Call them back, call the deal off."

"Absolutely not," Blair dismissed the idea. "This deal means a lot to this club. We get a premium shortstop prospect in return, and we save on Miller's $3 million salary. We're rebuilding for the future and Miller is not part of it."

"Rebuilding?" Jack turned to him with a sickened look. "Rebuilding!"

The very word ran against his nature. It was an admission of defeat, a sacrifice in the name of hope down the road. Jack wanted no part of it. He ran his hands through his hair a few more times. A few ill looking black marks were percolated over his coarse face.

"Trent," he instructed. "Pick up that phone right now and call off this trade immediately."

"My hands are tied Jack."

"Tied? Who's tying your hands? Jonathan?"

The manager looked over to the owner for answers. Jenkins sat in his chair without saying a word. He grievously stared out the window at the pouring rain.

"What the hell is going on here?" Jack asked with utter confusion.

The manager looked across the street at the bank tower. It seemed that the game was no longer decided on the field, but in the corporate boardrooms. Blair handed Jack a financial statement in hopes of pacifying him.

"We're losing money, we're losing fans, we're losing viewers on the television stations. But most damning of all....we're losing games."

Jack threw the sheet back in his face.

"What are you, a fucking accountant? I thought you were a general manager!"

"Why do you have to be such a dumb jock all the time?" Blair shouted back. "Why do you have to pretend that money isn't part of the game. It's reality, get used to it."

"We're turning this thing around....."

"We're twelve games under .500, nowhere near the Yankees and fourteen games out of the wild card."

Vaughn wouldn't have any of it.

"Frank Ringler is coming back," Jack countered. "You should see him working out early in the morning, getting his arm back. If you leave this team alone we can catch Boston for the wildcard."

"Frank Ringler?" Trent laughed. "Are you out of your fucking mind? The guy was throwing batting practise before he got hurt."

"He's working his ass off and when he gets back I'm giving him a chance."

Trent sighed.

"Even if he does come back, do you think he will actually make a difference or that we'll even be in a position to make the playoffs? This team needs to be rebuilt for its long term health."

Jack paced around the room. He leaned over the general manager's desk and grabbed his tie forcefully.

"Trent," he handed him the phone, "if you don't call San Francisco right now and call off this trade, I'm going to walk out that door and I ain't ever coming back."

The general manager's casual demeanour suddenly stiffened up. Amidst the tension, Al Ferreira walked behind the general manager's desk to lend his support.

"You're running out of ultimatums Jack. It always has to be your way or the highway, doesn't it?"

"Ferreira, why don't you just shut the fuck up! I've never respected anything about you. You were a shitty player, a shitty assistant G.M and an even shittier person."

"Who do you think you are?" Blair said indignantly. "You think you run things around here? You've already pulled this stunt on Watkins."

"Watkins still thinks he's on a goddamn platoon in Vietnam."

"Norm was a fantastic hitting coach!" Blair shouted, "And he'll make a damn fine manager some day!"

Everyone stopped cold. It was clear that the last part had slipped out. Vaughn glared at Blair for several seconds and nodded his head in cognizance.

"So that's how things are? At least I know where I stand."

"Jack, I didn't mean it that way," Blair backtracked.

"If you want to destroy this team, so be it. But it sure as hell ain't happening when I'm here. You've got a choice to make."

The general manager was in a bind. The team had just won four of their last five games, Eddie Griffin was finally off the disabled list and the general manager knew there would be a public outcry if they threw up the white flag just when the team was starting to play well. Blair tried to look bold and resolute in his stature, but the pressure became too heavy to bear.

The general manager grabbed the phone out of Jack's hand and dialled long distance. As he waited for the other side to answer, the rainstorm outside had subsided.

"Elliot," he said into the receiver, "the deal is off."

"You're damn right it's off," Vaughn triumphantly strutted out of the room.

In the ten games before the all-star break, the Pioneers put a lengthy winning streak together. For the first time all season, they were firing on all cylinders for a sustained period of time.

"Buffalo wins 4-1 compliments of an Eddie Griffin three-run homer....."

"Norton throws a complete game shutout to give the Pioneers a 2-0 victory....."

"Despite making it interesting, Conan O'Shea closed it out for the 5-4 victory....."

The biggest morale boost of all came in the final game before the all-star break. With the game tied in the bottom of the ninth and E.J. Winters on third base, Marcus Dillard came to bat.

"If Marcus could get Winters home, what a great way that would be to go into break."

"The pitcher fires....missed the outside corner!"

The ball squirted to the backstop.

"Winters sprints home!.......He's in there! Pioneers Win!"

The players mobbed E.J. Winters at home plate as he broke into his patented foxtrot. The old feeling of Pioneer pride was returning and even Jack Vaughn jogged onto the field with a huge smile on his face.

"Marcus!" he hollered, "that has to be the cheesiest run-batted-in I've ever seen!"

"Hey man, I ain't complaining!" Dillard grinned.

Over by the dugout, several television reporters interviewed Eddie Griffin.

"This team seems to respond to you," the reporter told him. "It seems like your return has lifted these guys up."

"Well," Eddie replied piously. "I'd just like to take this opportunity to thank the good Lord Jesus Christ for giving me the gift to play baseball. Just as the Lord giveth, he can also taketh away. He gave me another chance to come back from this injury and I am eternally grateful for that."

The reporters were blown away by Eddie's eloquence, his verbosity and apparent humility. After finishing the interview, Eddie entered the clubhouse and moseyed on down to his locker stall.

"You're the man, Eddie!" Conan O'Shea bellowed.

"What can I say," Griffin smiled vainly and winked at Dillard. "It's true."

"I plan on spending the next three days drinking," O'Shea gloated.

He looked around and received an absent-minded smile from Pete Sampson. No such signal was forthcoming from Marcus.

"What's wrong?" Conan asked. "We just won. Lighten up."

"Marcus is mad he didn't make the all-star team again," Griffin said antagonistically.

Dillard remained silent. He was busy nursing his ankle, which had swollen up after he tried to break up a double play in the fifth inning.

"Hey Marcus," O'Shea said. "Are you coming out with us or what?"

Marcus grimaced as he ripped the bloodied bandage from his leg.

"All right, call me if you change your mind."

As Conan and Pete took off for the break, Eddie looked at Marcus curiously.

"I'm surprised at you El Caballo," Eddie piped up. "I though you couldn't get enough of the nightclub scene."

"I've got new priorities now," Marcus responded straight-faced.

Eddie laughed thunderously.

"Like what!"

"I don't know," Marcus shrugged, "winning, playing well, being a good citizen."

"You stopped being a good citizen a long time ago, my friend."

"Say what you want, Eddie. Most of it is bullshit anyway."

Eddie smiled vainly. It was one of those smiles that spread so wide it threatened to crack his cheekbones. His teeth were bright white, a little too white for nature.

"And what's wrong with a little bullshit now and again? You see, Marcus, you just have to be a little more discreet about it. I probably pull twice as much ass as you, but the perception is exactly the opposite. It's all media management. You say a few prayers in public and these saps will be all over you."

"Congratulations," Dillard replied disgustedly. "You're the sleaze ball of the year."

He undressed and headed to the shower.

"Come on Marcus," Eddie tried to stop him. "We all have our vanity. You just may not want to admit it."

When the first baseman turned around, Marcus had already disappeared out of sight.

CHAPTER 15

In the All-Star Game, Jack Vaughn once again managed the American League to a rout of the National League. The manager traditionally brings many of his own players with him but after a lacklustre first half, few on the Pioneers were deserving of such an honour. After years of bringing a large Pioneers contingent, only Eddie Griffin and Chris Norton attended the mid-summer classic.

Following the game, the players, general managers, owners and media made their way to the grand hall for the all-star gala dinner. It was rare to see all of the movers and shakers schmoozing in one room.

As the hall began to fill up, Trent Blair and Jack Vaughn strolled in together. Neither spoke a word until Blair saw the seating plan.

"I don't think I could handle sitting next to Vince D'Antoni for three hours," Trent complained. "I'm going to another table."

Vaughn shook his head with grave annoyance.

"You won't be missed," he muttered under his breath.

The moment Jack Vaughn sat down next to the Yankees owner almost everyone stopped talking. Very rarely do the planets come into alignment for two men of such high stature. It was a meeting of two giants, each man having a dynamic presence all his own.

"Jackie Vaughn!" D'Antoni shouted brashly. "How the hell are you?"

At the sound of D'Antoni's voice, Trent Blair darted across the banquet hall.

"Looks like I already sent Blair to the showers," D'Antoni remarked.

Vaughn nodded.

"It doesn't take much."

"How do you work with that piece of shit?" D'Antoni asked boldly.

The manager shrugged. He never badmouthed people, as much as it would have provided tremendous satisfaction.

"I survive," Jack said bluntly.

The Yankees owner wouldn't let up.

"Look at the way he holds himself...."

Over by the drinks table, Blair was standing extremely upright as he spoke to a league official. He almost seemed to be compensating for some unknown deficiency.

".....he takes himself too damn seriously."

"It's funny you say that," Jack smiled, "because I've heard people say the same thing about you."

"Well," D'Antoni shrugged his shoulders. "I want to win and if I gotta step on someone's toes, so be it. Anybody that says differently suffers from the loser syndrome. They aren't strong enough to fight their own battles, so they cry foul. Fuck 'em."

"I hear you," Jack sipped his scotch.

"How was the boxing match with Tommy a couple weeks back?" D'Antoni laughed. "I thought you were gonna kill him!"

Jack shook his head.

"Don't get me started on that guy."

The Yankees owner leaned towards the manager.

"Don't tell anyone this, but I was happy to see you knock that son of a bitch out. If I see him over-manage one more game, I might just walk down there and do it myself. When I'm paying these players over a hundred million dollars, I don't need some manager trying to control the game."

"I feel the same way," Jack agreed.

"I can tell by how you manage," Vince replied. "You let the players do their job, the way it's supposed to be. Not like Tommy. By the way he talks about himself you'd think he was the second coming of Connie Mack....."

The owner placed his fingers flat on the table and bent even closer to Vaughn.

"....but the bottom line is that we haven't won a World Series for a few years. If we don't win it come October, he's gone. Believe me when I say it, I won't be sad to see him go."

"I never liked the man," Jack said bluntly.

"Well, I tell ya'," D'Antoni leaned ever close to the manager's face, "life is too short to put up with petty annoyances."

Jack smiled faintly.

"That's why I'm happily divorced rather than unhappily married."

The two men toasted.

"Amen to that," D'Antoni concurred. "Women are just a different breed, aren't they? They can't understand that none of us feels like being the shoulder to cry on. I can understand the shit you must have gone through; the crying, the non-stop talking. Did you know they average 15 000 words a day?"

"I can believe it," Jack replied.

"It's a scientifically proven fact. 15 000 fucking words! Who the hell wants to listen to that? After awhile I'm not even hearing the words anymore, it's just a non-stop siren!"

As the alcohol kept pouring, the two men became louder and more animated. With their views on life and baseball they seemed to be looking at the world through the same coloured glasses. The two men found a bond, a passion for baseball that consumed them almost to the point of absurdity. And their shared enjoyment of a good yarn became a new beginning for the mutual respect each held for the other.

Across the hall, Jonathan and Rose Jenkins ate at another table.

"Do you need help, Johnny?" Rose asked.

The old man began choking on his food and had difficulty breathing. Grabbing his back, Rose gripped him in a steady and caring way. It was the type of support that grows out of a long-term devotion.

"No....(cough)...I'm fine," he insisted.

"Jesus, you don't sound fine. We need to get you to a hospital."

As she was getting up to call someone, he grabbed her arm.

"Rose, don't make a scene. Not here, not now. We'll call Doctor Rosenblatt in the morning."

"You don't sound like you can wait until the morning."

The old man continued refusing help, forcing the couple to leave the gala early.

When the season resumed a few days later the Pioneers picked up right where they had left off. They won ten of their next twelve games.

"Dillard crushes this offering to left field!....6-1 Buffalo!"

"Norton is here trying for the complete game shutout...the pitch...fly ball left field....Winters is under it...and it's a 4-0 Buffalo victory!"

The Pioneers cruised through the month of July. Nobody was going to catch New York for the division lead, but Boston was starting to fall within reach. It seemed that just as the Pioneers started to play well, the Red Sox hit a mid-season tailspin. By the end of the month, their wild-card lead over Buffalo had narrowed to ten games.

The only problem was that for every few games that the Pioneers won, Conan O'Shea blew another in the ninth inning.

"Tie game, bases loaded.....O'Shea delivers.....ball four! He walks in the winning run! And Kansas City takes this one 4-3!"

Through the end of July, Conan 'The Barbarian' had been raped and pillaged to the tune of a 5.97 earned run average, while converting only 16 of his 25 save opportunities. Things got so ugly that the disc jockey in Oakland played 'Bringing on the Heartache' by Def Leopard over the public address system each time O'Shea made an appearance.

Pete Sampson was going through similar troubles. Not only had he missed curfew at as equally an alarming rate as O'Shea, but was striking out so frequently that Vaughn considered benching the former all-star centre fielder. Before he took extreme measures with either player, the manager decided to sit down and talk with them.

"What's going on guys? You've been playing like shit."

The manager was never one to use soft words, but his concern was genuine. He worried about them like a concerned father.

"What can I say," Conan shrugged. "I'm not making my pitches."

"I'm going through a rough stretch," concurred Sampson.

"That's the understatement of the year," Jack said. "Both of you are playing yourselves off this team."

"What do you want from us?" Conan opened his arms out defensively. "We're trying our best."

"Bullshit you're trying your best," Jack shot back. "You know Conan, its one thing if a guy is having a rough year. I can sympathize with that, but you two are doing this to yourselves."

"What is that supposed to mean?" Conan stood up.

Jack slowly took a sip of coffee.

"Sit down and don't raise your voice at me," he said sternly.

The reliever sat down.

There was pained expression on the manager's face. The players' inadequate performances were certainly hurting the team, but he seemed to be more concerned with their futures. Jack always looked at Conan like a son, while Pete had long been one of his favourite players. He wanted what was best for them.

"I don't know what happened to you, Conan. You used to be one of the hardest working players on this team. I remember the days you were built like a brick shithouse, but it ain't like that anymore. I don't know what it is, maybe the parties, the girls or that stupid earring you're wearing nowadays, but you've changed. And it ain't for the better."

He sipped his coffee once more.

"The same goes for you Pete. I remember when you were a model baseball player. You hit well with runners on base, you sacrificed and played good defence. I never had a problem with you, but everything seems to be falling apart."

As Sampson listened intently, O'Shea's face conveyed a sense of anger. There was something brewing inside of him.

"You two are like different people. I really don't know what else to say."

"I guess you have a point," Sampson concurred.

As Jack looked over to Conan, the reliever stared back blankly. He gave off the impression of disinterest.

"Look Conan, you're drinking yourself out of the league. I've seen cases like you before."

"Oh I see," Conan retorted. "I'm the one with an alcohol problem. Give me a fucking break! You're the guy who had to go to rehab."

Vaughn shook his head.

"I've made some mistakes in my life. I've never hid that. But there is no reason you have to follow down the same path."

"Whatever you say Jack," O'Shea replied half-heartedly.

"You know, Conan, this is your career not mine. I only want what's best for you."

The manager shook his head in dismay as he dismissed both players.

"We should lay low for awhile," Pete said outside the office.

"Fuck him," Conan insisted. "I ain't gonna let some old lush tell me not to drink. I'll do whatever I want."

Inside, Vaughn sat behind his desk with his face buried in his hands. He knew when he was taken seriously and when he was paid lip service.

"In one ear and out the other," he said to himself. "They'll both be out of baseball within two years."

The next day O'Shea blew another save opportunity only to see Eddie Griffin come to the rescue with an 11th inning home run. It was a telling sign of things to come.

As August rolled around, the Pioneers could not lose. Chris Norton was a dynamo on the mound, while both Eddie Griffin and Marcus Dillard were putting together monster second-halves to bring the Pioneers back into contention; a feat even more impressive considering Griffin's age and Marcus' early season troubles both on and off the field. With the Pioneers back in the playoff hunt, fans flocked to Pioneer Stadium in droves. Pennant fever was filling the air.

The most encouraging news of all was the improbable and seemingly impossible return of Frank Ringler. When he blew his arm out in early May, it seemed like Frank was finished. Rather than opt for career ending surgery, the cagey veteran chose an aggressive rehab program and it looked like there was a chance it could pay off.

"I've never seen him work this hard," Al Ferreira told Trent Blair. "I've never seen anyone work this hard. He's on a mission."

His progress was impressive and the medical reports were positive, but the general manager was less than enthusiastic.

"I guess we'll give him a few starts at AAA," Blair said grudgingly. "Who knows? We may even be able to use him."

As the month of August came to a close, the Pioneers continued gaining ground on the slumping Red Sox. Entering September, Buffalo sat only five games out of the wild-card.

"*The Pioneers have won once again this evening by a 5-3 margin.*"

"*You know Chuck, their turnaround has been remarkable, but a lot of it goes back to Jack Vaughn. This man has such a calming influence on this dressing room. He never panicked, even in the darkest days of May and June.*"

At the end of the month, word came down that the annual barbecue at the Jenkins mansion would be cancelled due to the owner's failing health. Jenkins was certainly in no shape to host a huge party. It might not have been such a good idea in any case. Vaughn and Blair weren't even on speaking terms and it seemed everybody in the organization was at each other's throats. Putting them in close proximity would almost be inviting mayhem.

On the field, the early reports on Frank Ringler kept coming back from the AAA team in Windsor and they were all optimistic.

"In his first start back from a debilitating arm injury, Frank Ringler looked impressive, shutting out Syracuse over seven innings."

Five days later, he was even more effective.

"Frank had a no-hitter through six innings today as Windsor shut out Columbus by a 4-0 margin."

There were more impressive starts until on September 2nd, before a sell-out crowd at Pioneer Stadium, Frank Ringler took to the hill. More than anyone, Ringler symbolized the Pioneers extraordinary mid-season turnaround from the depths of baseball hell. Given up for dead, he had resurrected his own career and was now helping bring the team back from oblivion.

"What a miraculous turn of events! Who would have thunk it last May, that we'd see Frank Ringler on the mound ever again, let alone this year."

"It really has been a miracle and it can be attributed to his steely desire to pitch again and the loyalty of Jack Vaughn to give him that chance."

"The fans are giving Ringler a standing ovation I must say he deserves it"

Ringler breezed through his first few innings.

"He gets the sign...he pitches....ground ball to the shortstop....flips to Griffin...and he's now tossed five shutout innings!"

The veteran hurler stroked his moustache and gave catcher Terry Miller the finger-gun salute. Now in the sunset of his career, the old warhorse once again felt the adrenaline rush of a rookie making his major league debut.

For the rest of the night he pitched economically, lasting eight innings and giving up only two runs in a tidy 5-2 victory. The velocity may not have been on his fastball anymore and he could not overpower people like he used to, but Frank Ringler was managing to fool hitters through veteran guile.

Day by day, the Pioneers slowly chipped away at the Red Sox lead until it had shrivelled down to only two games.

With a week left in the season, the fatalist Boston press was in full-blown crisis mode. When things go wrong in Beantown, the Massachusetts media rarely show any qualms about turning their knives inward. It was not long before every columnist in New

England was calling for manager Casey Warren's head if the Red Sox failed to make the playoffs.

Even the editorial page of the *Boston Globe* reserved a column slamming Casey Warren for *"his inability to make the right calls, change the right pitchers and motivate his charges. This is a team that thought it had a playoff spot locked up in July. Their arrogance may cost them that, and Warren's failure to stop the slide should cost him his job."*

By comparison, the Buffalo media was in an absolute tizzy over the Pioneers second half miracle. All the criticisms about Jack Vaughn from earlier in the season had turned into flowery compliments.

Paul Jones of the *Buffalo News* wrote that: *"Jack Vaughn's steadying influence has been the fundamental reason why the Buffalo Pioneers can even think about making the playoffs today."*

A far more telling sign was that Chet Thomas had begun writing about the Buffalo Bills football exploits rather than admit he had erred in prematurely calling for Jack Vaughn's head back in June.

Still, in the heat of a pennant race, Trent Blair and Al Ferreira had more on their minds than winning games. Loyalties needed to be investigated in preparation for next season.

"You called me up here?" Grant Robinson took off his cap.

The elderly pitching coach had an unsophisticated way about him and was somewhat intimidated when he walked into the office.

"Yes we did," Blair responded. "We called to perhaps get a feel for what your plans are next season."

"Well, I'm under contract to you," Robinson responded with innocent bewilderment. "I thought I'd be back coaching the pitchers."

"That's kind of what we wanted to talk about," Blair said, as he put his arm around the old man. "You see, Grant. It's no secret that you and Jack Vaughn are very close. We were just....oh....how do you say it?"

"Conjecturing," Ferreira piped up.

"Yes....we were conjecturing as to what your thoughts might be about returning next season if he isn't here."

Robinson was at an absolute loss for words. He was inexperienced in the politics of the game. All he had been thinking about was making the playoffs, so he was both puzzled and ignorant of such thinking.

"Well....uh," he stumbled. "I guess I'd want to be here with Jack. Why do you want to know?"

"We're just wondering," Blair responded.

"Oh okay," Grant replied, while holding his ball cap in hand

"You can go now," Ferreira instructed him.

The pitching coach left the office not knowing what had just transpired, but with an uneasy feeling inside. He never felt comfortable around those two.

After winning the first two games of their series against Toronto, the Pioneers entered the final game of the season one game back of the elusive wild-card. Early in the afternoon, the Red Sox did their part to help the Pioneer cause by losing to Oakland. All Buffalo needed was a win at home to force a one-game playoff.

Entering the ninth inning with a three-run lead, all looked promising. But nothing was automatic anymore when Conan 'The Barbarian' walked through those bullpen doors.

"O'Shea has already allowed two runs to cross the plate and its 6-5 Buffalo."

The Buffalo crowd began booing the reliever.

"The boo birds are out in full effect. Jack Vaughn must have a lot of faith in Conan O'Shea to leave him out there after the way he has pitched."

After looking like it was locked up minutes earlier, the game had turned into nail-biting affair.

"Two outs and the bases are loaded. O'Shea gets the sign from Miller.....he delivers....belted to left field!....oh no....this could be it!"

The crowd was hushed.

"Winters climbs the wall....what a catch!"

The players jubilantly converged at the mound as the Pioneer Stadium organist played the hymn to 'Hallelujah!' It was a fitting tune given the team's miraculous comeback from the dead.

"I can't believe my eyes! What a play by A.J Winters!"

"Conan O'Shea has earned his 22nd save of the year and the Buffalo Pioneers have forced a one game playoff at Fenway Park in Boston!"

CHAPTER 16

The one game wild-card playoff had all the makings of a classic. What made it special was the sense of poetry surrounding it. The cold autumn rain postponed the game for two hours while the leaves seemed to fall everywhere with reckless abandon. In a city with deep historical roots dating back to the Revolution, Bostonians knew that history was never on their side when it came to baseball in October.

It all began with the Curse. Ever since the trade of Babe Ruth to the New York Yankees nearly a century earlier, the Boston Red Sox had seen their share of October heartache. 1978 and 1986 were already in the pantheon of great collapses in baseball history, but the 2005 season had seen the Red Sox blow an astonishingly large fifteen game lead over the Buffalo Pioneers in only half of a season. A sense of dread permeated New England in the days leading up to the big game. Long suffering Red Sox fans knew that nothing good could come of this.

As the bus pulled out of the Boston airport and headed towards the hotel, E.J. Winters furtively opened up his carry-on bag. A couple rows back, Frank Ringler noticed several vials of an unidentified substance stashed within.

"I ain't no doctor," Ringler said. "But that don't look like medicine."

"I wouldn't be surprised if it isn't," Griffin sneered. "That kid's on something."

Winters definitely looked bigger than the scrawny kid who had come to spring training. Off the field, he spent most of his time juicing up in the weight room before heading out to nightclubs with Sampson and O'Shea.

The two men could only shake their heads in dismay.

"I don't understand kids these days," Ringler said. "I really don't."

The manager walked by.

"Frank," Jack said gruffly. "I want you to start tomorrow."

"Me, skip?"

"I've always gone to you when I needed a big game and you never let me down."

Ringler was speechless. He felt so indebted to Jack for this one final sign of loyalty.

Eddie Griffin began massaging his shoulders.

"You're the man, Frank!"

As news of the game's probable starter spread throughout the bus, not everyone was quite as pleased. After a stellar season, Chris Norton felt rested and ready to go. Even more upset were the two men seated at the back of the bus.

"There is no room for sentimentality in baseball," Ferreira sniped.

"It's damned foolish if you ask me," Blair agreed. "I don't care how he's pitched, Frank's an old man. He's got nothing left."

"And Jack doesn't even consult us," Ferreira added. "What gall that man has."

Trent Blair sat pondering the whole situation for a minute.

"There's no point in even approaching Jack. He's too stubborn about these things. I can't wait until I no longer have to work with him."

Ferreira put his hand on the general manager's knee.

"That shouldn't be too much longer."

"Welcome to Fenway Park on this chilly autumn afternoon in October for the American League wild-card playoff game. This is Chuck Smith and Terry Davis, glad to have you with us!"

"A lot of people are talking about how the old curse of the Bambino is coming back to haunt the Red Sox this season. Boston has nine innings tonight to exorcise those demons."

"And if the Red Sox fail to win this afternoon, this will most definitely go down as one of the greatest collapses in baseball history."

Both managers shook hands as they exchanged lineup cards at home plate.

"No pressure," Jack Vaughn joked.

"Yeah," Casey Warren smiled nervously. "No pressure for you guys."

The hostile Boston crowd unleashed their pent up frustrations when the Pioneers took the field. They saved their loudest taunts for Marcus Dillard.

"MARR....CUSS! MARR....CUSS! MARR....CUSS!"

Dillard tried to play it off with a nervous looking smile, but every swing he took became a progressively futile attempt to suppress the crowd.

"...swing and a miss strike three, Dillard goes down swinging!"

On the mound, Frank Ringler was busy pitching a masterpiece. He was painting the corners, keeping the hitters off balance and getting by on savvy. He certainly wasn't blowing anybody away with his fastball anymore.

"Ringler's averaging less than 90 miles an hour tonight and still managing to get the outs. What a crafty veteran!"

"A lot of young pitchers could learn from a guy like this."

As Frank walked off the field after the sixth inning in a scoreless ballgame, he stroked his moustache and looked at Jack Vaughn as if to say 'don't you dare take me out.' From the corner of the dugout, the manager could see the fire in his pitcher's eyes. He tipped his cap. Win or lose, this was Frank's ballgame to the end.

The Pioneers batters were not giving him much help. Marcus Dillard came to the plate with two outs and the bases loaded in the seventh inning but failed to capitalize.

"Marcus Dillard strikes out for the third time tonight!"

"When are we gonna see Dillard come through in a big game?"

The game remained scoreless until the top of the eighth, when catcher Terry Miller stepped into the batter's box with two outs and nobody on base.

"Terry Miller is at the plate here looking to get something started."

The veteran catcher hobbled to the plate. His knees were failing and his bat had slowed, but Miller still knew how to grind out at-bats.

"The pitcher delivers....Miller hits a line drive to right field!....Davis is trying to play it....he dives!"

The ball squirted past the Boston outfielder at the foul pole and rolled all the way around the right field fence. Even with a half-crippled catcher running the bases, this one had trouble written all over it.

"It's all the way to the wall.....Miller is rounding second.....on his way to third!"

After kicking it around some more, the outfielder finally retrieved the ball.

"Miller's getting the wave home!"

The slow-footed catcher slowly rounded third. He was running out of gas.

"The throw is coming home....Miller slides....HE'S SAFE!!"

The Fenway crowd was dead silent. The impossible had a way of happening in October.

"Terry Miller is the last person I'd ever expect to hit an inside-the-park-homerun, but anything can happen at Fenway Park!"

"This is really what sports is all about! Players rising to the occasion in situations one might otherwise think impossible."

"1-0 Buffalo!"

The score held up until the bottom of the ninth when a ragged Frank Ringler finally began to tire. On consecutive singles, the Boston batters were hitting him hard.

There were two outs and the bases loaded when Red Sox slugger Don Kruckshank walked to the plate with the season on the line.

"If I'm Jack Vaughn, I'd take Ringler out. He's got nothing here."

The Fenway air was chilled as each breath coming from Ringler's mouth looked like the exhaust from an overheated motor. With his career hanging in the balance, he took the sign from catcher Terry Miller. It was all or nothing.

"Ringler is in a world of trouble here. The winning run is on second base."

Tension was running high. Television cameras captured the agony of Red Sox fans praying for salvation from another cursed season. Players from both teams crouched on the dugout steps with nervousness running up and down their faces. As usual, the camera caught a glimpse of Jack Vaughn sitting on the bench sipping his coffee. He was sticking with Ringler until the bitter end.

"Ringler delivers to Kruckshank....its belted high and deep!"

The blast had game-winning home run written all over it but the baseball gods thought differently. As the ball settled into the air over the Green Monster, an improbable, almost heavenly wind pushed it back onto the field.

"Winters is under it....AND THE PIONEERS WIN!"

"Against all odds, the Buffalo Pioneers have won 1-0 to advance to the playoffs for the sixth straight season! What an amazing comeback and an amazing story this team has been!"

"Boston's second-half collapse and Terry Miller's inside-the-park homerun really make you wonder if the Bambino really had it in for the Red Sox. What a ballgame we've seen here today!"

The players ran onto the field with an enthusiasm they hadn't shown in years. After how far they had come, just making the playoffs was something special again.

As Jack Vaughn walked towards Frank Ringler, he held out his hand. The two men hugged for over a minute as Grant Robinson noticed a small tear trickle down the manager's coarse face.

Inside the clubhouse, tears began openly flowing from the manager's eyes.

"I'll be damned if I've ever been prouder of any team," Jack said coarsely. "You boys overcame everything."

The mood in the clubhouse was an eerie mix of jubilation and sadness. With several players and coaches in the final years of their contracts and others ready for retirement, one couldn't help but feel that this might be the final hurrah.

The next day, the front page of the *Buffalo News* had a huge picture of the Pioneers triumphantly holding Frank Ringler upon their shoulders with the headline above that read: *"JUST LIKE OLD TIMES"*.

It certainly felt like the pride of the glory days was back with a flourish. The talk on the streets of Buffalo was one of flowery optimism. The Pioneers were back in the playoffs and all the old faces like Frank Ringler and Eddie Griffin were still around. The only question was whether they still had enough left in the tank.

2005 American League East Standings

Team	W-L	GB
New York	102-58	-
Buffalo	88-74	14
Boston	88-74	14
Toronto	76-86	26
Baltimore	71-91	31
Tampa Bay	69-93	33

*- Buffalo won one-game playoff

2005 Buffalo Pioneers Statistics

Player		Average	HR	RBI	SB
LF	E.J. Winters	.295	7	44	50
C	Terry Miller	.291	4	66	0
RF	Marcus Dillard	.285	44	138	8
1B	Eddie Griffin	.305	40	133	0
CF	Pete Sampson	.203	24	69	0
DH	Orlando Mateo	.291	19	73	5
3B	Dave Kelton	.270	14	68	0
SS	Tom DeVellieres	.252	2	41	8
2B	Esteban Pena	.260	4	48	13

Pitcher		W-L	E.R.A.	Saves
SP	Frank Ringler	5-7	4.94	-
SP	Chris Norton	19-9	2.67	-
SP	Johnny Turner	16-12	4.29	-
SP	Rich Lopez	13-14	4.87	-
SP	Dave Rivers	9-15	5.41	-
RP	Conan O'Shea	0-8	6.03	22

CHAPTER 17

Once the euphoria had subsided and the first two games of the playoffs had been played, there was incontrovertible evidence that the clock was ready to strike midnight. Against Texas in the first round, the Pioneers were simply overmatched.

The starting pitching was not to blame. Chris Norton left with a lead in his Game 1 start only to see it plundered by Conan O'Shea and the bullpen. It was the stagnant offence that hurt most, with Marcus Dillard going hitless in both games. During the championship years, the Pioneers made a name for themselves by capitalizing on opponents' mistakes, but they had just lost two winnable games and a lack of depth in the bullpen and bench was cited as the major culprit.

After the Game Two loss, *Buffalo News* columnist Chet Thomas cornered Jack Vaughn in the visitor's dressing room at Arlington.

"Is it possible that next game could be your last?" He asked.

"Is it possible that you could be more annoying?" Jack shot back. "Get the fuck out of my way!"

He pushed the reporter before storming out of the room.

"You're a class act Vaughn," Thomas shouted. "Right to the bitter end!"

Jack didn't feel like defending himself against the likes of Thomas anymore. It had become an act in futility. It was times like this when he took sanctuary at the Duke of York with Grant Robinson.

As he looked around the crowded pub, he was overcome with sorrow.

"I've been going to this place for six years," Jack shook his head wistfully.

"If what I read in the papers is correct," Gus the bartender said, "we're sure gonna miss you, Mr. Vaughn."

"I ain't the only one leaving," Jack added.

The bartender was aghast.

"What? They're gettin' rid of you too, Grant?"

"Looks that way," the pitching coach said softly.

"That son of a bitch, Blair," Gus muttered. "He's ruining the team."

The two men sat silently for a few minutes, watching the highlights from the previous night's loss in Arlington. The more Robinson looked at Jack, the more he sensed

150

the man was suffering from deep unhappiness. There were a few black stress marks spread over his face. Although they weren't cancerous, they could not have been healthy.

The two men took a few more drinks. Neither could describe what this night meant, but for them and almost everyone else in the bar there was a feeling that something great was coming to an end.

"I don't know what to think of this game anymore," Jack wondered. "There are some days when I'm in the dugout sitting next to you on a sunny afternoon and the world seems right...."

He took a sip of scotch.

"....but then there are others when I wonder what this game is coming to."

The pitching coach thought to himself for a minute.

"Ever think about retiring?"

The manager pondered the question for a moment.

"I'd die, Grant.....I'd fucking die. I've been playing this game since I was five."

"So the eternal flame still burns," Robinson smiled.

"Yeah," Jack pondered, as he took another sip. "When it stops, so do I."

"Then keep managing," Grant said gingerly.

"Yeah," Jack ran his hands through his hair. "I've never done anything else."

The two took another round of shots from Gus.

"Blair had me up in his office last week," Robinson said. "Who knows what he has in mind for next year."

"I have no use for that son of a bitch," Jack stammered.

"It's a shame he handled things this way."

"You're right," Jack nodded his head in agreement. "He used to be one of the finest general managers in the game. After building this organization up to such lofty heights, he's gonna run it right back into the ground."

"Who's gonna stop him?"

"Nobody," Jack shook his head. "Absolutely nobody. He's got naive, old Jenkins sitting in his back pocket."

"Not to mention Ferreira," Grant added.

"Ferreira's like a cockroach," Vaughn warned. "He'll find a way to last."

The bartender poured both men another shot of scotch.

"This one's on the house, fellas," Gus said.

Vaughn smiled faintly and grabbed the glass for a toast.

"To better days," Jack said.

"To better days," Grant responded.

The two men threw back the liquor and got up from their seats.

"So long guys," the bartender saluted. "You're always welcome here."

The fateful game came the following night. A sense of profound sadness permeated rickety, old Pioneer Stadium. In stark contrast to the crazed atmosphere at most playoff contests, this one felt like a funeral. There were more than enough subplots.

Would it be Jack Vaughn's last game managing? Would this be long-time ace Frank Ringler's final start? Was this the end of the line? All these questions weighed heavily on everyone's mind and effectively transformed Pioneer Stadium into a tomb. This was not an ordinary game and Jack Vaughn knew it as well as anyone.

"The papers are saying this is my last game," he told a depressed locker room, "but it doesn't have to happen; not tonight, not ever. We fought long and hard to even make the playoffs. We overcame insurmountable odds and showed a lot of character. I'm proud of you guys and I'll be even more proud if you come out fighting tonight."

The players felt grief in their hearts, but it only served to harden their determination. They wanted so desperately to give something back to this great man. For all the times Jack Vaughn had stuck with them during their slumps, resisted publicly berating them, and knew what to say and when to say it, they all wanted to win this one for him.

On a cold, overcast fall evening, Frank Ringler dug in and with one motion, threw both the first and last pitch.

"Ringler is in there for strike one."

"I tell you Chuck, maybe it's the weather, but the atmosphere in this place doesn't feel right. Who died?"

In the bottom of the second inning, Eddie Griffin drove in Terry Miller with a double to make it 1-0.

On the mound, Frank Ringler was being hit hard all night, but seemed to be able to get himself out of it each time.

"He's pitching on fumes," Robinson noted.

With every jam Ringler escaped, there was a fleeting dream that things might still return to the way they used to be.

"Ringler is in another bases loaded mess here...the pitch...fielded by Griffin...to second for one....back to Griffin for two...double play!"

"YEAH!!!" The crowd erupted.

"Ringler just keeps pulling rabbits out of his hat!"

A palpable sense of hope and nostalgia began to take hold. Here were Eddie Griffin and Frank Ringler, heroes from past glories, seemingly leading a brave, new charge towards another triumph. Maybe the end of the line wasn't so near after all.

When Texas slugger Jeff Hudson came to bat in the top of the sixth, any misconceptions about the reality of the situation were soon corrected. Without the ability to overpower hitters with his once-scorching fastball, Ringler had been throwing change-ups all night. Eventually the Rangers caught on.

"Once again, Ringler is in a mound of trouble here. Two outs and the powerful Jeff Hudson is at the plate. The bases are loaded for the fourth time tonight."

"Ringler sets...the pitch....its driven deep!"

The crowd hushed.

"Going! Going! Grand Slam! Texas has taken a commanding 4-1 lead here in the top of the sixth!"

The huge Texas outfielder threw his bat down and lumbered around the bases. He had crushed the ball well over 500 feet. There was never any doubt where it was headed.

"When you play with fire, you're gonna get burnt. Ringler's been in trouble far too often tonight to come away unscathed."

After Ringler induced the next batter to ground out and end the inning, the crowd cheered emptily. The veteran pitcher grabbed his arm in obvious pain as he walked to the bench.

"How do you feel?" The manager asked.

"I'm done," Frank replied.

"For today?"

"Forever," Ringler replied. "I've given you all I got. I tried to make it work for us one last time, but the arm is done."

It was one of those moments temporarily frozen in time. There were few players Jack Vaughn had more regard for than Frank Ringler. In all his years, Jack never had to cajole or motivate him and never questioned his desire. Faced with the stark realization that this forty-year-old warhorse had nothing left to give made the manager speechless. He wanted to weep, but instead chose to kiss the pitcher's forehead. It was a sign of affection he reserved for those he admired most.

"You're a fighter, Frank. You always gave me your best. You always gave this game your best."

The pitcher shook hands with long time battery-mate Terry Miller and headed to the showers for one final time.

"Could this be the last time Frank Ringler leaves the dugout? Time will tell."

The remainder of the game drifted listlessly into the cold night as Texas added more runs in the top of the eighth to take a 6-1 lead. Fans were flooding out of the stadium by the thousands by the time Pete Sampson was forced to partake in the final blow.

"Two outs here in the bottom of the ninth. The Texas Rangers are an out away from winning this series and meeting the New York Yankees in the American League Championship Series. Pete Sampson is Buffalo's last hope."

"Pete hit .203 with 24 homers and 69 runs batted in this season. What the Pioneers need here is for him to get on base. A home-run won't do it."

"The pitcher is ready....he delivers....hit weakly to Hudson at third....throw to first....the Texas Rangers have advanced to the ALCS!"

The crowd dejectedly trudged out of the stadium.

"This was a close game until the sixth inning when Texas blew it wide open. But the question weighing on everyone's mind is simple: Is this the end of an era in Buffalo?"

CHAPTER 18

"Let's make this short and sweet. You're fired."

Trent had the smug look of a man with the power to drop the axe and the capacity to wield it.

"We'll be relieving Grant Robinson as well," Blair added.

Jack Vaughn looked outside at the pouring November rain. It wasn't quite frozen yet, but it was getting there.

"It's your call. I'm wiping my hands of this mess."

"I thought I should tell you we have a successor in mind."

Jack smirked to himself

"I bet you do."

"What's that supposed to mean?" Blair asked defensively.

"You're a smart guy, Trent. I'll let you figure it out."

Vaughn glared at Jonathan Jenkins. The owner was sitting silently by the window watching the storm outside. He was almost catatonic.

"I guess you're just going to let this happen, kind of like you let everything happen," Jack said vindictively.

The old man turned around to make amends. His wrinkled face was filled with anguish as his arthritic hands reached out towards Vaughn.

"Jack, I never wanted to...."

"You pathetic old fool," Vaughn glared at the owner disgustedly. "You never had the balls to put your foot down!"

The words hit Jenkins like a sledgehammer. His mouth became temporarily paralysed as thunder and lightning raged outside.

"Don't talk to him like that!" Blair yelled sternly.

"Oh listen to you," Jack turned back to Blair. "I can't stand even the sight of you anymore."

"Buy a ticket and get in line! I'm not in this business to make friends."

"Apparently you aren't in it to win either," Jack shot back. "This team is headed nowhere."

As Vaughn walked out of the room for the final time, the room was jarred by the sound of thunder and lightning from outside. As much as Blair tried to pretend otherwise, the words stung him. Each syllable that flowed out of Jack's mouth came with a majestic authority.

"Nobody's gonna miss him," Ferreira said.

The faces of the two other men contradicted that statement.

Jonathan Jenkins walked out of the room without saying a word. The old man was completely against the firing, which made the ordeal hard enough to swallow. But Jack's verbal attack was too much to take.

For years, Jenkins took great delight in watching the manager on television. When everyone else was biting their nails, Jack would calmly sip his cup of coffee with that indiscernible expression on his face. Those that knew Jonathan Jenkins all said he died a little that night. He simply walked down to the parking garage and told his driver to take him home. The whole crushing experience left him as nothing more than a shell of a man. He would never appear in Pioneer Stadium ever again.

The next morning, there was a groundswell of mourning for the departed manager. Aside from a column by Chet Thomas, who seemed to be having an orgasm in the midst of writing it, most of the media types were sad to see Vaughn go. One of the more unbiased *Buffalo News* columnists, Paul Jones, said it right in the following day's newspaper.

A legend says goodbye

By: Paul Jones (Buffalo News)

Jack Vaughn is a man of immense proportions and rarely do men of his stature enter or leave quietly. When he swirled in here six years ago, he represented the promise of what was to come. Buffalo was a baseball city on the rise and his guiding hand appeared to be what was needed to take us to the top. It would prove to be an amazing act of chemistry. An exciting young team and this grizzled baseball legend united for three World Series Championships. It was a baseball dynasty that seemed like it would go on forever. But times change and when the chemistry was altered, things fell apart. They say he made poor on field decisions. They say that he didn't have control of his dressing room. Certainly the strip club brawls and drug busts validate the point; but ask any player who ever played for Jack Vaughn and they'll tell you otherwise. They'll tell you that he was a player's manager and that he had the respect of everyone in the dressing room. They'll tell you that he gave everyone more than their fair share of rope; some simply chose to hang themselves with it. Either way, it's

156

unfortunate that it had to end this way. Jack Vaughn was and always will be cherished in the hearts of Buffalo baseball fans. All good things must come to an end. We'll miss you, Jack.

Trent Blair called a press conference the following weekend to announce the new manager.

"The Buffalo Pioneers are absolutely pleased to announce the hiring of Norm Watkins as our manager for the 2006 season."

There was little applause in the press gallery. With Jonathan Jenkins nowhere to be seen, rumours abounded that he had handed over the reins to Trent Blair.

"I've known Norm for fifteen years," Blair gleefully pointed to the incoming manager, "and I must say he's as solid as oak. I've never met a man with a more solid demeanour. Norm Watkins is a quality baseball man and a quality individual. I'm pleased to have him on board."

As Watkins stood up only a few flashbulbs flickered from the cameras. The new manager shook hands with Blair before proceeding to the podium.

"We're gonna do baseball differently 'round here. No more free rides, no more country-club passes. The crackdown begins now."

It was tough talk, but as question period began those in the media had little interest in 'the crackdown' or Watkins at all. Most of their questions were directed towards Trent Blair and a good deal of them involved Jack Vaughn.

"For the fifth time," Blair replied annoyed, "we are sorry to see Jack Vaughn go. But we need to be moving on. Norm Watkins is our manager now. We must look forward and usher in this new era with open arms."

Nobody wanted to let the subject drop.

"Look. We're all going to miss Jack Vaughn. My heart bleeds for him. It was one of the most gut-wrenching decisions I've ever had to make, but it's over and done with. We really must be moving on and going forward."

A few days later, the Pioneers gave Frank Ringler his unconditional release. There was no farewell press conference for the potential Hall-of-Fame pitcher or even a press release from the team thanking him for his seventeen seasons of service. It was a rather unceremonious gesture for a man who had provided so many great moments over the years.

"I just found out from you guys," Ringler bitterly told a Buffalo radio host. "I guess that's the way Trent Blair operates when he doesn't need you anymore."

The widespread dissent in the city became readily apparent. Letters to the editor became frequent and fans expressed their discontent on radio call-in shows.

"Trent Blair and the Buffalo Pioneers front office should be ashamed of themselves after the way they treated Frank Ringler," one disc jockey spouted on the air. *"You won't see me at Pioneer Stadium ever again as long as Blair is in charge."*

The discord went well beyond anything in the past. While Scott Harper and Benjy Alvarez's defections to the Yankees a year earlier had caused a tremendous amount of heartache among Pioneers fans, losing two icons like Frank Ringler and Jack Vaughn was different. It marked, as BSN's Terry Davis called it, 'the end of an era'.

Trent Blair knew this. He could feel the heat and knew that a counter-move was swiftly needed. In the days following the controversy over Frank Ringler's mishandled release, the Pioneers announced that Eddie Griffin had re-signed for one final season at a modest $4 million price tag.

"I'm happy to be back and I think I still have something left to give," Griffin said congenially. "We're going to do some exciting things this season. Aside from my on-field contribution to the team, I will continue to devote my time to the Eddie Griffin Foundation. We must work hard to protect the inner core of this great city."

A reporter from the *Buffalo Sports Network* was the first to ask a question.

"You are only seven home-runs away from hitting 500. Have you set a date you'd like to get that by?"

"I really don't like to think about individual accomplishments," Eddie replied. "God willing, if I am able to hit 500 home-runs, then the good Lord is the one who deserves all of the praise."

As Eddie vacated the microphone to hug his wife and kids, there was a round of applause from the media. The entire press conference resembled a corny infomercial.

"That's why I want him back," Blair whispered to Ferreira and Watkins. "This is the type of shit our organization needs. Feel good stories."

Both men nodded their consent.

"Absolutely," they responded subserviently.

Despite whatever noble intentions Trent Blair had of turning a new page, the entire off-season was turning into one giant public relations disaster for both him and the Pioneers: the dismissal of a legendary manager, the shabby treatment of Frank Ringler, and the further bloodletting of team scouts.

The worst part was that the Pioneers could no longer afford to do anything about it. After losing $12 million the previous season, Blair was forced to further scale back the player payroll to below $40 million. The monetary demands of most players went well beyond what the small-market Pioneers could afford.

It is doubtful that any top free-agents would have even considered signing with the Pioneers anyway. There was once a time when Buffalo had been a desirable locale for free-agents, but that was no longer the case. Word travels fast in the baseball world and there were more than a few ex-players, coaches and scouts who had nothing but bad things to say about Trent Blair. It was not at all uncommon for most of the general manager's messages to go unanswered.

Baseball experts across the country were nearly unanimous in their belief that the Buffalo Pioneers were set for a big fall in the upcoming season.

<u>Pioneers head to hell in a hand basket</u>
<u>By: Tim Jubuilier (Baseball Review)</u>

The Buffalo Pioneers used to always be one step ahead of the competition. Either by stealing Pete Sampson as a Rule V pick, drafting an unheralded Chris Norton or bringing the savvy expertise of Jack Vaughn to town, these were just a few of Trent Blair's coups that paid off brilliantly. But the last few years have been a fiasco. Whether it be the losses of Scott Harper and Benjy Alvarez to free-agency, the numerous off-field scandals or the first-round flameout in the playoffs, the Pioneers have consistently shown over the past year and a half that they are headed nowhere but down. The once proud scouting corps that helped draft the foundation of the Pioneers dynasty has either been let go or resigned in protest due to Trent Blair's combative management approach. As disgruntled ex-scouts perpetrate a whisper campaign throughout baseball against the megalomaniacal general manager, it appears that the Pioneers are the ones getting caught with their pants down.

The off-season took another turn for the unexpected in late November when New York Yankees owner Vince D'Antoni fired manager Tommy Bedowes. It had been almost three weeks since New York was swept out of the World Series, but time had not quelled the impatient construction magnate's brutal temper. After assembling what was widely considered to be one of the finest arrays of talent in one dressing room, D'Antoni considered the Yankees failure to win a World Series unacceptable.

Those who knew D'Antoni best speculated that other factors were at play. His personal distaste for Bedowes played no small role in the decision. However, insiders also knew that there was someone who Vince had been eyeing for a long time and would hire the moment he became available.

It all goes back to D'Antoni's vanity. When he had needed a left fielder, he signed Scott Harper, the best one out there. When he needed a shortstop, he signed Benjy Alvarez, the finest in baseball. Now that he needed a manager, logic seemed to suggest that he would hire the biggest name out there. It didn't matter if there were several capable candidates within the organization. Vince D'Antoni wanted a manager with Hall-of-Fame credentials, someone who was a winner; someone who could deliver the World Series.

In the last week of November, when he finally landed that special someone, the Yankees owner stood in front of the microphone beaming from ear to ear.

"What can I say?" He grinned. "Jack Vaughn, welcome to New York!"

The New York media exploded in ovation. Camera bulbs flashed feverishly as Vaughn put on a Yankee jersey. It was a scene of absolute pandemonium.

Winning the respect of the tough New York media usually took years, but Jack Vaughn had them eating out of his hand on the first day. As he stood in front of the microphone for over five minutes waiting for the incessant applause to die down, the stunned baseball world looked on.

"I never thought I'd see the day when I put on Yankee pinstripes," Jack beamed, "but I suppose there is a first time for everything!"

Back in Buffalo all was quiet. The Vaughn press conference was on television in the Duke of York, but no true Pioneer fan could bear the sight of it. The blue-collar Buffalo fans had always taken pride in beating the Yankees and could always count on good, old Jack Vaughn to lead the way. Now their beloved skipper wouldn't be around to fight their battles anymore, and while many didn't blame him for what had transpired, it hurt nonetheless. It was anything but a Merry Christmas in Buffalo.

The Lassinger Steel Mill, which had long been a fixture along Interstate 90, filed for Chapter 11 bankruptcy protection during the first week of December, leading to 1500 workers losing their jobs. The recent tax increases and labour codes put into place under Governor Prentice Wulloughby had not made business any easier in New York State, but the Lassinger closing was merely part of a larger trend sweeping industrial cities across America. The blue collar worker was getting a tough shake nowadays and there was nothing the big hand of government could do in the face of it.

Baseball had once been a place of refuge for people facing hard times. As bad as things were at work or at home, one could always escape the vagaries of life at the old ballpark. Those who seemed to strike out in life could take delight at watching Frank Ringler strike out the side. Anyone born on the wrong side of the tracks could be inspired at the sight of Jack Vaughn in the dugout, proof enough that even the son of a Jersey coal miner could achieve greatness. But as old loyalties were being broken and the world was changing so fast around them, many fans came to realize that not every story necessarily has a happy ending.

CHAPTER 19

Spring training was particularly damp and overcast but the weather wasn't going to stop Trent Blair in his quest to secure a new image for the ball club. The blustering general manager was busy promoting a whole new attitude, one that would shape the way the team tackled the upcoming season. He tried to make it a reflection of the players on the field: a combination of seasoned vets and raw rookies thrown together to hopefully form a winning combination.

On the eve of the reporting date for regular players, Trent Blair unveiled the team's new slogan amid much hype. Standing in front of a huge billboard proclaiming the words, "PIONEER-ING EXCELLENCE", Blair announced that there would be signs with this very inscription all over the spring training complex, in the dressing room and eventually at Pioneer Stadium. Discipline, rather than a lack of it, was to be emphasized.

Despite the general doom and gloom surrounding the Pioneers chances among baseball experts, the youth movement did garner praise from certain members of the Buffalo media that still revered Trent Blair.

Pioneers have the right idea

By: Chet Thomas (Buffalo News)

Trent Blair has always proven himself to be more than worthy of a challenge, but this upcoming season may be his greatest glory yet. For all those doomsday pundits who said that the departures of Jack Vaughn and Frank Ringler signalled the end of the line, you'll have egg all over your faces. Why? Because Buffalo fans will finally get to see a young and exciting team on the field, because Eddie Griffin is the best tutor for the new rookies as he pursues 500 home-runs, because Norm Watkins was a perfect choice to whip this team back into shape and because Trent Blair has always emphasized player development. He proved it eight years ago when the current crop of players was coming up and it looks like he'll do it again. Outfielder Alvaro Perez has made a name for himself in AAA as one of the up and coming defensive outfielders, and pitching prospect Brian Boze has blown away hitters all through the minors. Both appear to be mature and skilled enough to make the jump this season. This could be the rebirth of something special.

Starting pitcher Brian Boze and outfielder Alvaro Perez were quickly attracting attention at camp as the players of the future. Along with Marcus Dillard, E.J. Winters and

162

Chris Norton, they were being counted upon to form the nucleus of another Buffalo Pioneers dynasty. Perhaps all the attention and expectations were unfair for the two kids. The World Series tradition was certainly an intense burden to carry and a hard act to follow. Even if they produced as expected, the Pioneer veterans still needed to step up in a big way if the team was going to return to the playoffs.

Things started smoothly in that regard. For the first time in his Pioneer tenure, Marcus Dillard arrived into camp quietly and punctually. There were no autobiographies, no yellow Ferraris, no scantily clad women and no narcissistic ranting.

"I'm happy to be here," he humbly told a reporter. "I'm coming into camp with a clear mind and want to have a great season."

E.J. Winters was a different story. After finishing third in Rookie of the Year balloting the previous season, the combustible left fielder had other plans for the new season. Over the winter he had gained 24 pounds of sheer muscle mass, most of it in his chest, to go along with a new array of gold chains. Most people were alarmed at the unnatural rate of his muscle expansion. Apparently his head had swelled at an even greater rate than his juiced upper body.

"I've got a whole new arsenal. I ain't just a base-stealer no more. I can do all kind of things. You're gonna see some power from E.J. this season."

As the players slowly arrived on the initial day of camp, they were quickly summoned out onto the field where new manager Norm Watkins was waiting keenly with a crowbar in his hand.

"Oh, what is this?" Catcher Terry Miller remarked upon seeing Watkins.

The new manager was dressed in full-body army fatigue and stood before the assembled players in militaristic fashion.

"Gentleman," he shouted at them like a general. "You are about to experience something like never before. For all you pussy-livered wimps, who are used to the easy training camps of the past, it ain't gonna be an easy ride this time 'round. This is boot camp and in one month we go to war. All of you are soldiers in my army and I am your supreme commander. Disobedience, laziness, cowardice....none of these will be tolerated. You understand me?"

Nobody responded. Watkins had only been speaking for a few minutes, but already the players had begun to tune him out.

"YOU UNDERSTAND ME?!!!"

"Sir! Yes sir!" Eddie Griffin and a few of the veterans responded sarcastically.

The manager paced back and forth in anger for a minute before continuing.

"How long do we have to listen to this shit?" O'Shea whispered to Sampson. "This guy thinks he's George fuckin' Patton."

Watkins overheard the comment.

"You got a problem, Conan?" He barked belligerently.

"I don't have a problem with you, Norm. I think you look kinda cute in that drill sergeant get-up!"

The entire team laughed.

Watkins face turned red with anger. He paced back and forth on the field.

"I think we do have a bit of a problem, Conan! You arrive here fifteen pounds heavier than last season and forty pounds heavier than you were two years ago. You're absolutely dripping with fat up and down your body and you have the audacity....no....the pomposity to question my authority?! I want all the rookies to look at this lamentable man and vow to never become like him! YOU'RE A FUCKING DISGRACE O'SHEA!!"

Before the manager could dress him down any further, the reliever began walking towards him aggressively only to be held back by Eddie Griffin and some of the other veterans. As Conan struggled to get at the manager, fat jiggled underneath his chin. The relievers' once muscular face had deteriorated into pudgy roundness.

"When did you become such a tough guy, Watkins?"

"Look who's talking," Norm laughed. "I'm going to call you the 'gas man' from now on. You don't put out fires in the ninth inning anymore, you fuel them!"

The lame attempt at humour seemed to be lost on the players.

"You're a piece of shit, Watkins." Conan yelled.

As O'Shea was taken into the dressing room to cool off, Watkins finished his inspirational message.

The manger immediately launched back into his diatribe.

"Nobody's job on this team is safe.....NOBODY!! I'M GONNA TEACH YOU ALL A LESSON YOU'LL NEVER FORGET!! I DON"T CARE IF YOU WIN 20 GAMES, I DON'T CARE IF YOU WRITE A DAMN BOOK ABOUT IT!!"

Watkins glared at Marcus Dillard, almost begging the slugger to openly defy him. He so badly wanted to make an example of Marcus, but the slugger sat there silently and refused to take the bait.

The routine for the day was rigorous: a four-mile run, followed by a session of push-ups and sit-ups. Once that was finished, everyone was supposed to complete the shuttle drill multiple times.

"This is crazy," one of the coaches told him. "You can't expect these guys to do this on the first day."

"I not only expect it, I demand it!" Watkins shouted.

It did not take long for several players to struggle through the circuit.

"Hurry the fuck up!" Norm barked at them.

By the end of the day, nearly everyone agreed it had been the hardest first day of spring training they had ever endured. As he leaned back in his locker, a sore looking Eddie Griffin turned to Marcus Dillard next to him.

"How did you like that, El Caballo?" Eddie asked.

"I still can't believe they hired this clown to be the manager," Marcus said.

"Clown is the right word," Eddie replied. "This whole camp is a circus."

A few minutes later, Watkins came bursting through the door. After surveying the room and seeing the mangled bodies of his exhausted players, a deranged smile spread across his face. He was enjoying the torture.

"Welcome to training camp boys. You're just getting a taste of what it's like to play for Norm Watkins. There ain't gonna be no passengers on my bus!"

A few groans and whispers were heard as the manager walked out of the room.

"If I knew this shit was going to happen," Eddie Griffin said, "I would have played my final season somewhere else."

"He won't last long," Terry Miller offered. "His act is already wearing thin."

Conan O'Shea began mocking the manager.

"There ain't gonna be no passengers on my bus!" O'Shea yelled.

Griffin laughed thunderously.

"Yeah," Pete added sarcastically, "you'd better watch out. Nobody's job is safe on this team."

"What's he gonna do?" Conan sneered. "Cut me?"

Upstairs in the general manager's office, Watkins was busy letting off a little steam.

"I've had enough of O'Shea, I want him outta here! Cut him, release him, do what you want. I just don't want him on my team!"

Trent sat behind his desk ponderously.

"Norm, you know I can't just do that. He's our closer. He's all we got in that bullpen next to a bunch of minor leaguers."

Watkins threw his hands in the air and paced around the room restlessly.

"What do we need him for? He had an earned run average over 6.00 last season, he's forty pounds overweight and he lips me off. I don't think I'm being unreasonable."

Ferreira rolled his eyes.

"All right, relax Norm," Trent replied. "We'll try and ride this out. If neither his attitude nor his pitching improve then we'll make a decision."

"I don't think we need Sampson around either."

"That might be a bit much," Blair demurred.

"All he does is party at night and strikeout during the day. Plus, we've got Alvaro Perez waiting in the wings. I like this kid. He runs hard and doesn't talk too much."

"Maybe because he can't speak English," Ferreira mumbled under his breath.

The general manager pondered to himself.

"We can always throw Marcus in the designated hitter spot," Blair countered.

"Yeah that would go over well," Ferreira snickered. "Marcus would never accept being a designated hitter."

"It's not his choice whether to accept it or not," Watkins barked. "I'm the manager, I set the damn rules! If he doesn't like it, I'll have to set him straight."

"We'll think about it, Norm. That's all I can say."

After the manager left the room, Blair and Ferreira were left to discuss the situation behind closed doors.

"Did we make a mistake in hiring this guy?" Ferreira wondered. "He almost makes me wish Jack Vaughn was still around."

The general manager laughed.

"He just has a different style. It'll take some getting used to."

"He seems like he's spoiling for a fight if you ask me," Ferreira warned. "This D.H. thing could spill over into the papers."

"All the better," Blair countered. "In fact, why don't you leak it yourself? It'll be easy to make Marcus look like the bad guy."

Ferreira nodded.

"I can do that."

"We'll let it play out," Blair continued furtively. "That's all I can say. There are a few ways we can go with this thing. Sampson and O'Shea both have buyouts in their contracts. The way season ticket sales are going, it wouldn't hurt to cut the budget somewhere."

A few days later, the grapefruit season got underway. Jonathan Jenkins had declined to make the trip down to Florida, leaving Trent Blair free to inhabit the owner's booth.

Things began on an excellent note. Chris Norton pitched brilliantly in the spring opener before hyped pitching prospect Brian Boze followed up with a stellar performance of his own the next day. Boze didn't mix his pitches particularly well and suffered from occasional wildness, but the young hurler seemed like he could blow away hitters at will.

After the game, Norm Watkins met with Marcus Dillard in his office.

"I want you to DH this year," he said without a conciliatory note in his voice.

"You've gotta be kidding me," Marcus shook his head. "I finally come here with a clear head and you ask me to become half a player."

"I'm not asking you," Watkins ordered him. "I'm telling you. That's the way it is."

"My defence isn't that bad."

"My mind is already made up, there's no use even trying to change it."

"Listen man, I don't want this. I don't want to DH and I really don't want another public dispute. I was hoping this season would go smoothly."

The manager stood up behind his desk.

"End of discussion, Marcus. That's an order."

The huge outfielder shook his head and sighed.

"I can't seem to avoid this shit."

The next day, the morning newspapers were filled with stories of the spat over the designated hitting role. Somehow the "private" conversation had been leaked to the media. Almost immediately, Chet Thomas jumped all over Dillard.

<u>Dillard should take one for the team</u>
<u>By: Chet Thomas (Buffalo News)</u>

Somebody tell Marcus Dillard to grow up! Aside from the fact that he is mediocre in the field and in his mental capacity, the move to designated hitter is designed to open up a spot in the outfield for young prospect Alvaro Perez. We aren't talking about somebody who has won a World Series or brought home any postseason hardware. For two seasons, all Marcus Dillard has done is pad his stats against bad pitchers and choke in the playoffs. If Marcus thinks he can hold the future of the Pioneer franchise hostage because of his fragile ego, then he has another thing coming. Norm Watkins will lay down the law and this is exactly what Marcus and his inflated head needs. After acting like a baby for far too long, what Marcus Dillard needs right now is a big spanking.

"I don't want to talk about it," Dillard told the media horde. "I need to concentrate on playing ball."

The more Marcus stonewalled the media, the more negatively they wrote about him.

"All we're asking," Blair told a reporter, "is for Marcus to be a team player. I don't think that's unreasonable."

After a few days of Dillard's continued refusal, the controversy soon reached a point where the manager realized he might lose credibility with the players and media. Before an afternoon game, Norm Watkins stormed into the locker room and confronted the burly slugger in front of everyone.

"IF YOU WANT TO PLAY ON MY FUCKING TEAM, YOU'RE GONNA BE THE FUCKING DH!! THAT'S ALL THERE FUCKING IS TO IT!!!"

Marcus stood up to defend himself.

"There's no need for any of this."

"Sit down when I'm talking to you!" Norm ordered him

Marcus continued standing.

"I SAID SIT DOWN!!"

168

"What are you trying to accomplish?" Marcus asked calmly.

Across the room, loud music suddenly started blaring out of someone's stereo.

"ARE YOU HARD OF HEARING? I SAID TAKE A SEAT!"

Watkins was salivating like a pit-bull with rabies. The two men stood face to face before Eddie Griffin decided to intervene.

"Cool it Norm," Eddie put his arm around him. "We're all on the same team here."

Before the manager had a chance to respond, his attention shifted to the yelling heard across the room.

"Turn the music down!" Terry Miller demanded.

"Hell no!" Winters yelled back. "Nobody tells E.J. what to do!"

"Turn it down!" Miller demanded again.

The catcher attempted to physically adjust the knob on the stereo.

"Man, get your hands off that!"

Punches were exchanged as players and coaches flooded in to prevent the fight from escalating. Norm Watkins and several coaches ran over from the other side of the clubhouse to step in between the two players.

"Put an end to it!" Watkins beckoned.

As the young outfielder continued mouthing off, it was obvious there was nothing anyone could do to stop him.

From the corner of the clubhouse, Eddie Griffin watched the mass heap of players and coaches piled together in a collective struggle. He shook his head wistfully.

"This place is a damn zoo."

After a few more days of public infighting, the designated hitter issue was finally resolved when Norm Watkins reluctantly agreed to keep Marcus Dillard in right field. Although it was an awkward public climb down for the rookie manager, other circumstances out of his control had conspired to force his hand.

Pete Sampson was having a horrid spring, batting .085 with no homeruns and ten strikeouts. The numbers would not have been so scrutinized had he been coming off a strong season, but Sampson had been in a free fall for almost two full years. In the bullpen, Conan O'Shea was even worse. He had already blown three saves in three opportunities and allowed a grand total of ten runs in four appearances.

With the exception of Marcus Dillard and Chris Norton, hardly any of the veterans were playing well. Greybeards Eddie Griffin and Terry Miller continued to show diminished skills and reaction time at the plate. Even E.J. Winters was having a horrid spring with the added bulk playing havoc on his once nimble hamstrings. He was hitting a few homers but had stolen only one base in five attempts

In the final days of camp, decisions had to be made. For a lineup that used to be pencilled in by December, it seemed that nothing was for sure anymore.

"I think Boze has proven himself," Blair confirmed. "He's in our rotation. What about the Perez kid?"

"I like him," Watkins said. "I want him starting in centre-field."

"He can't hit a lick," Ferreira disagreed.

"Neither can Sampson," Watkins replied. "I've had it to up to here with Pete and Conan's attitude."

"Ok Norm, I hear you." Blair agreed. "We have a few games left. If they keep playing like shit, they're gone."

The manager reluctantly agreed.

Still, it was doubtful that either of them would take advantage of their final chance. Along with E.J. Winters, they were seen at the Coconut Club until six in the morning. The following afternoon, both players looked awful.

"Sampson strikes out for the fourth time this afternoon..."

"O'Shea's sacrificial offering is sent into the heavens!...Deep!....Deep!....It's gone!"

Enough was enough. Following the debacle, Watkins summoned the two players into his office and bluntly delivered the news.

"Pack your bags and get out of here. You've been released."

"Released?" Conan thought he was kidding. "Released?"

"You do speak English, don't you?" Norm said snidely. "That's what I said. YOU'RE RELEASED!"

The news caught the two men off guard. Pete Sampson put his hands in his face and began sobbing. Conan O'Shea took a more combative approach. The rotund reliever ran into the dressing room, grabbed the water cooler and tossed it over the manager's desk.

"You motherfucker!" He screamed.

The manager ducked the incoming projectile and was spared from any further wrath when Eddie Griffin and some of the other veterans physically restrained the reliever.

After O'Shea was finally subdued, both he and Sampson were escorted from the Jacksonville complex.

The next day, the *Buffalo News* ran a huge picture on the front page of both men walking out to the parking lot with their bags packed.

The 31-year-old Sampson later signed a minor-league deal with Milwaukee, who figured he might still have some power left in him. O'Shea was a different story. Now 32, he was regarded throughout baseball as a washed up head-case and eventually forced to sign with a minor league team in the El Paso League. It was rock bottom for two players whose careers had once looked so promising.

For Pioneer fans, the departures only continued the mass exodus of heroes who had left town under acrimonious circumstances. The old gang was being torn apart and there was nothing the Buffalo faithful could do about it. Pete Sampson and Conan 'The Barbarian' O'Shea might have become more grief than they were worth in recent years, but they were still World Series heroes and many found it difficult to say goodbye one final time.

CHAPTER 20

"*Welcome to BSN Baseball. Glad to have you with us here in Buffalo for the Opening Day of the 2006 Season. I'm Chuck Smith with my co-host Terry Davis. I tell you Terry, it feels a little colder today than in years past, but opening day is still special.*"

"*It is Chuck, it really is. It's the day everyone is in first.*"

Both commentators laugh

"*The question is: who will remain there?*"

"*Well Chuck, I think the Yankees are the undeniable favourites to capture the World Series. They won 101 games last year, and we all know Vince D'Antoni will spare no expense to get a championship. I thought they had the best team in baseball last year, but now that they've hired Jack Vaughn, they have one of the best managers as well. He can act as such a calming influence on the veteran talent. Nobody is gonna touch them.*"

"*What about the Pioneers?*"

"*It's hard to say. In the past, they had a lot of veterans leading the way, but the old cast is gone and there are a lot of rookies on this team. Certainly they have some talented prospects like outfielder Alvaro Perez and pitcher Brian Boze, but they are unproven and some people in baseball wonder if these kids are ready.*"

"*How so?*"

"*The word on Perez is that he has great speed and defence, but cannot hit at the major league level. As for Boze, he's been overpowering in AAA and throughout spring, but he has a history of control problems. A lot of people are saying the Pioneers may have rushed these kids to the majors too early.*"

"*Where do you think they'll finish?*"

"*Again, it's hard to say. There are too many question marks. Will Perez and Boze perform up to expectations? Does Eddie Griffin have another good season left in his 41-year-old body? Will their no-name bullpen cost them games? Will Norm Watkins' disciplinary style go over well? Until these questions are answered, this season could turn into a surprising success or a complete and utter disaster.*"

Down in the dressing room, a heavy degree of uneasiness was felt. For some of the rookies, it was their first taste of the big leagues. All they needed was a little reassurance, but the manager did little to soothe their fears.

172

"YOU GUYS HAD BETTER GET YOUR ASSES IN GEAR!! I WANT TO SEE A WIN HERE TONIGHT!!"

Watkins stormed into his office and slammed the door. The veterans stood shaking their heads at the back of the room.

"I'm already sick of this guy," Terry Miller said.

"Jack never pulled stunts like that," Eddie Griffin chimed in.

Even the mild-mannered Chris Norton, who was set to pitch that afternoon, was disturbed by the manager's unnecessary explosion.

"I don't need this crap before I pitch. If this guy wants to yell and scream, he should go back to the army."

Norton had never been the outspoken type, so everyone understood it took a lot to get him upset.

Despite all the bad news that had dogged the team throughout the winter, Pioneer Stadium had sold out at the last minute. Opening Day was always an exciting time no matter where one's team was expected to finish.

The Pioneers were warmly greeted as they took to the field. After a three up, three down inning from Chris Norton, E.J. Winters led things off.

The cocky outfielder took his time stepping into the box. His shirt was unbuttoned several notches, exposing his collection of gold chains and recently inflated upper body.

"E.J. Winters leads off here."

"E.J.'s meal ticket last season was his slap-hitting style and his speed. He swiped 50 bases last year."

"The pitcher sets.....fires....oh a big cut there from Winters....strike one."

"He was trying to kill the ball there."

"The pitcher gets the sign....sets....the pitch......pulled to right field! Deep! Deep! It's out of here! 1-0 Buffalo!"

The crowd cheered mildly.

"Wow, a little unexpected jolt from E.J. Winters. He said he would hit with some power this year, but nobody believed him. What a way to start the season!"

As Winters entered the dugout, Norm Watkins immediately jumped in his face.

"Don't be pulling the ball. You're our damn lead-off hitter!"

"I just hit a home-run! What the hell do you want?"

"I want some accountability!" Watkins barked at him. "And I damn well better get it!"

The sullen young outfielder instinctively wanted to strike back at Watkins, but before he got a chance Marcus Dillard corralled him in his arms. The burly slugger could see the same inner rage in Winters that had once burned in his heart.

"He's pissing everyone off, kid. Don't let him make an example out of you."

Winters lips were sealed, but everyone could see that he still held a deep animosity towards the manager. His blast would turn out to be all the offence the Pioneers needed that day. Chris Norton was dynamite all afternoon.

"Top of the ninth, two outs and two strikes. Norton deals.....swing and a miss strike three! Buffalo wins 5-0 on opening day to give Norm Watkins his first win as manager."

The crowd stood and cheered.

It had been a perfect afternoon. Winters led off with a homer, Norton pitched a complete game shutout, and Eddie Griffin went deep to leave him only six home-runs shy of 500. Over in right field, team officials changed the official countdown board to 494.

Even Alvaro Perez got his first big league hit, a squeaker through the right side. Judging by Opening Day, it seemed that all the doomsday talk about falling attendance and a weak team was premature. Here was a packed house on hand to witness a resounding opening day victory.

Those illusions were corrected the next night. The second game of the season saw the lowest attendance in Buffalo Pioneer history, as only 13,000 and change showed up to watch Chicago pound Brian Boze and the Pioneers.

"The pitch....ball four! Brian Boze has walked in another run. In the top of the first inning, it is already 5-0 for Chicago."

The manager walked out towards the mound.

"And Norm Watkins has seen enough, he's signalling for the righty to come out of the bullpen."

The shell-shocked young pitcher made his way off the field as a cascade of boos rained down from the sparse crowd.

As the week progressed and the Pioneers lost game after game to dwindling crowds, the situation went from bad to worse.

"12,368 were on hand here today to see the Pioneers lose 9-1...."

"Buffalo got its road-trip off to a poor start, dropping a game in Tampa Bay 6-2...."

Everything was falling apart at once: the ticket sales, the pitching, the bullpen and the hitting. Even the manager was blowing up.

"YOU GUTLESS SONS OF BITCHES!!!"

After a defeat the following night, the same theme was heard.

"YOU GUYS ARE A FUCKING JOKE!!!"

Another night and another loss, the screaming continued.

"I'VE HAD ENOUGH OF THIS BULLSHIT!!"

The players did not take kindly to the harsh words. Everyone was trying their hardest, but the team only had marginal talent. The more Norm screamed the worse many of the younger players performed. After one particularly tough loss, Catcher Terry Miller sat in his locker attending to a bruised body with a sour look on his face.

"One of these days, I'm gonna clock that guy. He's pissing me off."

"Somebody will," Griffin nodded in agreement. "Nobody feels like listening to this shit after every game."

Rather than join in the chorus of people ripping the manager, Marcus Dillard sat in his stall without saying a word. He simply undressed and headed to the shower.

A few days later, Chris Norton ended the seven-game losing skid with a complete game shutout. The Pioneers returned to their losing ways the next day. There was little anyone could do as the carnage continued for the rest of the month and well into May.

"Ball four and Brian Boze has walked in another runner!"

More boos cascaded down onto the field. Watkins paced up and down the dugout.

"Somebody tell Bozo, the fucking clown, to throw strikes!"

The dugout was dead silent. Eddie Griffin and Terry Miller stared disapprovingly at the manager.

"Ball four! He's walked in another run! And Watkins is coming out of the dugout. He's calling for the right-hander."

"No surprise there Chuck, this is getting ridiculous."

"And Watkins is verbally undressing the young pitcher on the mound!"

Boze sunk his head in shame.

"Oh no, I don't like that one bit. This kid is struggling. You don't need to embarrass him in front of everyone. That's a very unprofessional thing to do."

Back in the dugout, Watkins wasn't finished. He continued berating the scared, young rookie in front of the entire team.

"What the hell is wrong with you? Can't you throw a goddamn strike?"

Boze timidly sat down on the bench with his face sunk in shame. The manager physically grabbed the pitcher's head.

"LOOK AT ME WHEN I'M TALKING TO YOU!!"

The rookie eventually made his way to the showers with tears in his eyes as Watkins kept pacing up and down the dugout, oblivious to everything around him. One of the coaches whispered in the manager's ear to calm him down.

"I'm not gonna go easy on him," Watkins replied loudly. "This is the big leagues. If he can't handle it, he ought to take up lawn bowling!"

"Be reasonable," the coach continued.

"I'll do whatever I want!" Norm screamed back. "This is my team."

The coach sat down.

Watching the massacre from the comfort of Jonathan Jenkins' vacant owner's box, Trent Blair and Al Ferreira wore dreary looks on their faces. Not only was their team receiving a battering on the field, but Blair was feeling the heat in the newspapers. While Chet Thomas remained supportive of the general manager, he was clearly in the minority among the Buffalo media. One columnist pulled no punches in his assessment:

Pioneering Ineptitude
By: Paul Jones (Buffalo News)

The time has come to clean house. The pitching staff is a mess, the batting order is not producing, and errors are being made at an alarming rate. The Buffalo Pioneers have become a team that snatches defeat from the jaws of victory. In many ways, they don't even resemble that. Several players, E.J. Winters among them, seem intent on doing their own thing while Norm Watkins' so-called discipline goes by the wayside. There is no Jack Vaughn around to blame anymore. This is Trent Blair's team, this is Trent Blair's hand picked manager, and this is even Trent Blair's slogan. The only thing this team "pioneers" day in and day out is last-place baseball. Far from providing *"excellence", ineptitude should be the new mantra, because that's about all these sad group of players are accomplishing.*

     The article hit a chord around the city. Midway through May, the Pioneers were reaching a crisis point. This time, Jack Vaughn's guiding hand and steely demeanour were nowhere to be seen. Aside from the stellar play of Marcus Dillard and Chris Norton, everything seemed to be imploding from within. The usually steady Eddie Griffin was starting to show his age, E.J. Winters was in a prolonged slump, while rookies Brian Boze and Alvaro Perez turned out to be complete busts.

     After his hit on opening day, Perez had gone hitless in 20 at-bats and was batting .184. Even worse, he had already committed an astonishing 12 errors in centre-field, a bad sign for a defensive outfielder. Perez truly made infamy for himself against Boston when he committed four errors and had five strikeouts in one game. The *Baseball Review* later nominated him for their Hall-of-Shame team.

     On the mound, Brian Boze wasn't much better. His main problem was a lack of control and the inability to fool major league hitters with a 97-mile-an-hour fastball that had no movement. In seven starts, he had gone 0-4 record with a 7.98 earned run average.

     "We're demoting them both to AAA for further seasoning," Trent Blair told the assembled media. "Their play has been nothing short of disappointing."

     As Eddie Griffin approached his 500th career home-run, the hype machine began churning. Despite all the bad vibes surrounding the team, Griffin's chase of the historic mark was garnering plenty of positive media coverage as fans temporarily flocked back to Pioneer Stadium.

     For a few days in early June, the right-field billboard stood at 499 until the day of destiny finally arrived.

     "Eddie Griffin steps to the plate here in a scoreless ballgame and nobody on base."

     The crowd stood up in anxious anticipation.

     "There hasn't been a lot to cheer for in 2006, but you can just feel the electricity in Pioneer Stadium right now."

     "The pitch.....belted to left...it could be.....it's gone!"

     "YEAH!!!" The crowd roared.

"That is number 500 for Eddie Griffin and they're giving him a standing ovation here at Pioneer Stadium!"

Griffin rounded the bases slowly and took his batting helmet off to salute the crowd.

"Congratulations, Eddie Griffin. Nobody deserves this more than you!"

An official from the Pioneers presented Eddie with a plaque at home plate and the applause from the crowd seemed like it would never cease. Griffin certainly wasn't going to be the one to end it. The larger than life first baseman always knew how to savour a moment.

As other Pioneers came out to congratulate him, Marcus Dillard hugged the elder first baseman.

"Congratulations, man. This is unreal."

"This will be you in ten years," Eddie smiled and whispered in Dillard's ear. "You've got the talent to do it, Marcus."

Dillard smiled as the two men walked back to the dugout.

Once the euphoria surrounding Griffin's accomplishment subsided, reality came back with a vengeance. The Pioneers were in last place and nobody was more responsible for that than E.J. Winters. The lack of offensive production from Winters at the top of the order was one of the biggest disappointments of the season. With all the muscle he added during the winter, he kept repeating to anyone who would listen that he was no longer just a slap-hitting base stealer.

"Winters is really struggling this year, hitting .205 with only one steal."

"Call it the sophomore jinx, but he is having a terrible season. I don't know how much longer they can leave him in the lead off spot. He isn't getting on base and he isn't stealing bases."

"He's trying to be a power hitter and failing miserably at it."

"His only home-run came on opening day."

The pitcher quickly went up two strikes on Winters.

"The pitch....Winters takes a big cut and goes down swinging!"

The crowd booed vehemently as E.J. limped back to the dugout. With his hamstrings still bothering him, he took his batting helmet and threw it at the bench in anger.

"Maybe you should show that emotion at the plate!" Watkins yelled.

178

"Yo fuck you, man!"

"WHAT!!" Watkins screamed. "DON'T YOU TALK BACK TO ME!!"

The manager jumped up in the left-fielder's face.

"Please!" Winters yelled back rebelliously. "I'll say whatever I want to you!"

"Oh yeah?" Watkins replied in a confrontational tone. "You're suspended Winters! Indefinitely!"

The young outfielder was incensed. His face was stricken with chemical imbalance as his biceps pulsated feverishly. There was little human left in Winters' body and no telling what he might do next. In a display of speed he had seldom shown since last season, E.J. unleashed his fury.

"You mother fucker!" Winters screamed. "You can't do this to me!"

He belted Watkins with an upper cut that bloodied the manager's nose. With every punch, his enraged fervour grew. By the time Eddie Griffin came in to split it up, Watkins face was full of blood. Nobody could control Winters. With tears running down his face, he let out a crying moan as he kept wailing away at the manager.

For everyone in the dugout, it was the most bizarre moment they had ever witnessed in their lives. By the time Winters was escorted away by security, tears were running down his face and his voice could be heard above everything.

"He can't do this to me! They can't do this to me!"

E.J. tried to resist the security guards in vain.

"Get your fuckin' hands off me!" He screamed at them.

The game on the field now became secondary as everyone wanted an explanation for what had just happened.

"What's that kid on?" Terry Miller asked Eddie Griffin.

"Who knows," the veteran first baseman shook his head. "You just never know anymore."

It did not take long for highlights of the attack to be played and replayed on national sports telecasts. Every television crew had a perfect shot of the senseless beating Winters laid on his manager and there was no hiding it from the thousands of people who had seen it in person. Norm Watkins face was so bashed in that he needed to be taken to the hospital for precautionary reasons.

After the game, with both men long gone from the stadium, Trent Blair was left to field the media's questions. As he stood with his back against the clubhouse wall, his face gave away the shame he was feeling. After all the drug-busts and controversies of years past, he had gone to great pains to make sure this season ran smoothly. But as Trent Blair stood in front of the inquisitive media horde, it seemed that nothing he did went as planned anymore.

"What measures are you planning to take against E.J Winters?" A reporter asked.

"That will be discussed internally," Blair responded despondently.

As he continued to stonewall the media's attempts to get beneath the surface, the reporters only got bolder.

"Is it possible you erred in hiring Norm Watkins?"

"Frankly I resent that comment. If you guys are going to turn this into pot-shot corner, then I'm leaving."

He stormed out of the room and sent the reporters scurrying for a delicious quote from one of the players. The gregarious Eddie Griffin was more than happy to accommodate them.

"I'm glad I wasn't involved," Griffin joked. "E.J. looks like he has a good right jab. I wouldn't want to be caught on the receiving end of one of those!"

The reporters laughed at Griffin's uncanny wit, making him the only person to come out of a bad situation smelling like roses.

Each time it seemed like the Pioneers hit a new low, things just kept getting worse. Back in his mansion, Jonathan Jenkins watched the madness on television. All he could do was meekly shake his head in agony.

"What the hell has happened to this team?"

He had believed for so long in the infallibility of Trent Blair, but that faith was dying with everything else. As he lay in bed, the chilling realization dawned on the old man that there was nothing he could do about it. Everything he had built, everything he lived for was crumbling before his weary eyes.

The following day, the Pioneers suspended E.J. Winters indefinitely and designated him for assignment. Unlike the spring training squabble with Terry Miller, there would be no making up this time.

"I want him gone," Watkins ordered. "Gone! You hear me?"

The manager removed the bandage from his face. His face was a mess.

"I'm talking to several teams about a deal," Blair responded, "but you have to understand, we can probably get more for him if we wait for things to cool down. Who knows, maybe we can even help him. God knows we need his bat."

The manager rubbed the stitches on his face.

"Fuck him," Norm said. "He doesn't have the maturity to play at this level. I'm sick and tired of babysitting him. As far as I'm concerned, he can go to hell."

Blair and Ferreira rolled their eyes.

"Why don't we just sleep on it? When we wake up everything will be fine."

CHAPTER 21

"And in sports news, tragedy has struck the Buffalo Pioneers. Once promising young outfielder E.J. Winters has died of an apparent drug overdose. Winters was discovered unconscious in his apartment late last evening and pronounced dead at 6:25 this morning. Initial reports from the coroner's office are inconclusive."

The news left the city in complete shock. Interest in the Pioneers had been low with their slide into last place, but last night's bizarre events combined with this tragic and unexpected death suddenly vaulted them back into the forefront. As the days went by and the mysterious death was examined more closely, suicide became apparent as the root cause.

Everything had happened so fast that the players and fans could be excused for feeling blown away. The police found several vials of unidentifiable substances along with numerous bags of cocaine littered throughout the apartment. The front page of the *Buffalo News* showed the grim reality. Winters was lying face first on his apartment floor with a pool of blood flowing from his temple.

The incident was an attack on everything good and decent, leaving many with a nauseating feeling in their stomach. E.J. Winters was a pathetic example of wasted youth and untapped potential, a boy who never grew up. In the morning newspaper, *Buffalo News* columnist Chet Thomas did his best to sum it up:

<u>Winters time came much too soon</u>
<u>By: Chet Thomas (Buffalo News)</u>

The life and tragic suicide of E.J. Winters is not something that can be pinned on any particular person. You can't blame Trent Blair, Al Ferreira, Norm Watkins nor anyone in the Pioneers organization. Something happened to the misguided E.J. Winters between the time he arrived in Buffalo and the time he departed for a higher world. His innocent Bambi eyes and skinny, boyish demeanour were stolen and replaced by a drugged, bloodshot glare and steroid induced upper body that we came to know. It is hard to say what happened to this troubled young man during his year and a half stint in the big city except that he was thrust into the spotlight too early and paid for it with his life. E.J. Winters wasn't perfect when he arrived in the majors. Far from it, he showed a degree of spunkiness that clearly needed some disciplining. Instead of helping this process however, the *majors only reversed it. Baseball chewed E.J. Winters up and spat him out. That is nothing less than a tragedy of epic proportions.*

The following day, a pall set in over the dressing room. Emmanuel James Winters was not a particularly easy person to like. He was cocky, foul mouthed and immature, but he was also a teammate, as much as he sometimes played for himself. Even Terry Miller, who had his share of run-ins with Winters over the years, wore a grim expression on his face the next day.

"E.J.'s a sad case," Miller told the reporters. "He was like a little boy in a grown man's body."

The following night's game went ahead as scheduled with a pre-game ceremony honouring E.J. Winters' tumultuous life. It was hard for the players and fans to come to grips with his death. It had all happened so fast. Most of them looked like they wanted to be at Pioneer Stadium for a game as much as the 15 000 fans who bothered to show up. The Pioneers were soundly trounced 10-3.

After the game, Eddie Griffin strolled over to the Duke of York. It was a lonely walk to the tavern. In happier times, he would regularly go for drinks with Jack Vaughn or Frank Ringler after a ballgame, but it wasn't like that anymore. A lot had changed since he had been there last, but at least Gus was still around.

"Eddie!" The bartender exclaimed. "So good to see you!"

He grabbed Eddie a wine cooler from the refrigerator.

"I'm all right. How are you doing, Gus?"

"Look around," the bartender pointed around the half-empty tavern. "With the crowds from the ballgame down, we ain't doing so hot in here."

"That's a shame," Griffin replied disinterestedly.

Gus had followed the Pioneers since their inception and came to know many of the players personally. He had the eagerness of a man who had little else going in his life.

"I'm sure you don't want to hear about my problems," Gus continued anxiously. "After all, you guys have enough problems as is."

Eddie yawned and looked up at an old picture of Jack Vaughn.

"I guess we do," Eddie shrugged, "but I don't care too much about it. I'm done after this year."

"I hear you might take a job in the organization," the bartender said hopefully.

Eddie laughed thunderously.

"Not this organization!" Griffin leaned over the bar. "You think I wanna be around when the roof caves in? H-e-l-l-l-l no"

The bartender had a big lump in his throat. Something he held near and dear to his heart was withering away.

"What do you think of the new rookies? Any promise?"

"You'd have to ask them," Eddie scoffed. "I haven't met any of 'em and I don't care to. Frankly Gus, I'd prefer not to talk about baseball. This year was a mistake and I can't wait to get the hell out of town."

The bartender could barely conceal his disappointment. He had always held Eddie Griffin up on a pedestal as a pillar of the Buffalo community and imagined the veteran first baseman staying late after games to help the young rookies before returning home to his wife and family. The more Eddie opened his mouth, the more that image was shattered.

"Well, I guess that's your prerogative," Gus replied disappointedly. "It seems everyone is leaving Buffalo nowadays."

"Yeah, a real pity," Griffin said without really caring. "Could I have the bill? I'm supposed to meet some Russian bimbo at the Crazy Eight. You should see the guns on her. WOW!"

"Have fun," the bartender replied. "Here's your bill."

He tossed the piece of paper at him disgustedly

"See you around, Gus."

"Yeah sure," the bartender muttered as he walked away.

The team headed out on a road-trip, but nothing changed.

"The Pioneers opened up their seven game road trip, but it made little difference as they dropped a 6-2 decision in Seattle tonight. The longer this season goes on, the worse it seems to get."

"I don't want to get too biblical here, but a day of reckoning is approaching. Changes will have to be made before the trade deadline at the end of the month."

With every loss, Watkins began feeling the heat more and more. Critics questioned his disciplinary tactics, his handling of the pitching staff, his effect on young players and his questionable on-field decisions. As the losses continued to mount, the pressure from the media rose with it.

"How do you hope to turn this terrible slide around?" One reporter asked.

"For one thing," Watkins replied, "We need our veterans to step up. They're just not getting the job done. Marcus Dillard needs to be more of a leader."

"Dillard's having a great season," the reporter persisted. "He's second in the American League in homeruns."

"You think I don't know that?" Watkins snapped back. "That's why bums like you are working the sports beat. The bottom line is that we need more leadership from Marcus. He's been nothing short of a cancer in our dressing room."

The comments were front and centre in the following morning's *Buffalo News*. When Eddie Griffin came into the dressing room the following day, he gleefully threw the paper upon Dillard's lap.

"How do you like that, El Caballo?" Eddie seemed to be taunting him.

"Get that shit out of my face," Dillard threw it back at him.

"Don't bother denying it," Eddie said. "You are officially the scapegoat."

"I'm trying hard to forget about it," Dillard frowned at him.

"Ah lighten up. I could see this coming from a mile away."

"What can I do?" Marcus shrugged. "I'm not exactly on the best terms with the media in this town. I guess I'll just try and ride it out."

As the road trip ended and the team returned home, that was looking next to impossible. Dillard was booed unmercifully at Pioneer Stadium, even after he slugged a homerun.

"This stadium is 1/2 empty, but by the way the fans are booing Dillard, you'd think there was a full crowd here."

"The pitch......Dillard takes it for strike three!"

"BOOOOOOO!!!"

The Buffalo fans jeered with every grain of energy in their bodies. It was almost as if they had channelled all of their disappointment from the season into crucifying him.

"Look at this place," Blair said from up in the private box. "It's empty!"

"The attendance has been a disaster," Ferreira added.

"Disaster doesn't even begin to cover it. Accounting tells me we're on pace to lose $15 million. The team is losing, Jenkins is dying; this whole fucking operation is out of control."

Blair grabbed his hair in frustration.

"What are you gonna do?" Ferreira asked.

"I can think of one way to save $11 million," Blair responded. "He's standing there in right field."

Ferreira looked over at the towering Dillard.

"After the way he's played this season, you'd be crazy to trade him."

"It's not as if we're going to win anyway," Blair added. "Everything will be fine if we handle it right."

"How do you plan on doing that?" Ferreira asked

"Watch and learn."

Following the game, Blair strolled into the clubhouse and made himself unusually available to the beat reporters thirsty for something to give their demanding editors.

"What do you think of Norm Watkins' comments regarding Marcus Dillard?" One scribe asked.

Blair looked around the room and when he was unable to spot Dillard among the throng of players and media, he provided a verbose answer.

"I agree wholeheartedly. We've been trying for two and a half years to get Marcus to take up more of a leadership role, but like the saying goes, you can only lead a horse to water. He can't always be so focussed on his individual achievements. Until he realizes that, he'll never be anything but a one dimensional slugger."

The reporters had the look of miners who had just struck gold.

"Can I quote you on that?" The writer asked eagerly.

"You sure can," Blair smiled back at him.

When the comments were brought to his attention, Marcus was ready to explode. He felt like defending himself, but managed to keep his emotions bottled up.

"I don't have nuthin' to say," he told the reporters, before putting his shirt on and heading onto the bus.

Marcus was merely trying to be a professional, but instead came off like a brooding malcontent. On most days, Blair's verbal salvo would be sure to make headlines the following day, but this time his criticisms were overshadowed by news that would shake the very foundations the franchise was built upon.

The news anchor's grim face conveyed the seriousness of the situation.

"We have just received a report that Buffalo Pioneers owner and supermarket millionaire Jonathan Jenkins has suffered a massive heart attack! We are told that he has been rushed to a Cheektowaga hospital where he is listed in critical condition. We will update you as this story breaks."

The story tore a hole in the hearts of almost every Buffalo citizen. 'Get Well' cards flooded in from throughout western New York. In baseball circles, there was an even greater outpouring of sympathy expressed for the Pioneers owner. Unlike some owners who were constantly pushing their own agenda at the league meetings, Jenkins had garnered a reputation as an easy man to deal with. Commissioner Smalls even phoned Rose Jenkins personally.

"We can only hope and pray," Eddie Griffin told a group of reporters the next day, "that the good Lord Jesus Christ has Mr. Jenkins in his divine plan."

It could be said that the old man's health problems mirrored those of his beloved ball club. On the field, the Pioneers didn't seem to have much of a pulse themselves. With the exception of Marcus Dillard and Chris Norton, and the steady if unspectacular play of veterans Eddie Griffin and Terry Miller, nobody on the team was doing much of anything. Seven and eight game losing streaks were becoming commonplace.

Through it all, Norm Watkins wedged himself tighter and tighter in his managerial chair.

"These guys don't have the heart to win," he would tell reporters after games. "In war, you have to be strong. I don't think half of these guys know what that word means."

"What about Marcus Dillard?" The reporter asked in an attempt to uncover another land mine. "Does he know what it means?"

"Marcus is lost in space doing his own thing. I've been challenging him all season to turn himself into a complete player, but I don't even bother talking with him anymore. He's just.....out there. You know what I mean?"

"No," the reporter smiled, "but that'll do."

The manager's comments were splashed all over the next day's sports section. Watkins had managed to manufacture a controversy where none previously existed and spawn long-winded discussions on sports talk radio. Despite the fantastic season Marcus Dillard was having at the plate, most of the public's opinion ran against him.

"*It's too bad Norm Watkins had to be saddled with these head cases in his first season,*" one radio host stated on the air. "*First he had to deal with the troubled EJ Winters and now Marcus Dillard. It's no coincidence that the Pioneers went downhill the minute this albatross arrived in town.*"

Only 10 000 people were bothering to show up at Pioneer Stadium and many of them had paper-bags covering their faces. It seemed the only reason many even came was to show their disdain for Marcus Dillard.

He was not even safe during the national anthem

".....and the Rocket's red glare!....The bombs bursting in air!"

"DILLARD....YOU BUM!!" A drunk screamed from the upper deck.

The heckling continued throughout the game.

"BOOOOOO!!" They yelled after every Dillard strikeout.

Even after his eighth inning homer put the Pioneers on the scoreboard, the incessant jeering would not subside.

"BOOOOOO!!"

With all the contempt the fans were showing him, it was safe to say that Dillard had become the most hated player in Buffalo sports history; even more vilified than a certain field goal kicker who had blown the Super Bowl fifteen years earlier. Throwing his excellent statistics aside, the fans and media had placed all of the club's failures on his shoulders.

The Yankees came to town the following weekend and the local media temporarily devoted their attention to the Jack Vaughn homecoming. Ticket sales were significantly more brisk for the three-game series as the town prepared to welcome home an old hero. Before the game, Dillard was the first to see Jack behind the batting cage.

"Seeing you is like a breath of fresh air," Marcus told him.

There were no stress marks on Vaughn's face and nary a coffee cup in sight. The manager had a newfound vitality to him.

"Ah," Jack blushed. "You're exaggerating."

"No I'm serious," Marcus repeated with a straight face. "You look great. How are you doing?"

"Never been better," Jack answered, his eyes sparkling. "I've got a good situation here. I haven't felt this refreshed in a long while."

"I wish I could say the same thing, but I don't know how much longer I can take it. I'm gonna blow up soon."

"That bad, huh?"

"Everything I do is criticized. If I hit a homerun, they boo. Even when Norm or Trent rips me in the papers, I keep my mouth shut and the press says I'm a recluse or a malcontent."

Vaughn nodded understandingly.

"I know what you're going through Marcus, I really do. I had to work with those jackasses for six years."

"Then there's Eddie," Marcus rolled his eyes. "Nothing he ever does is scrutinized. He's like Mister Wonderful in the town."

Vaughn smiled mischievously.

"He really is a phony bastard, isn't he?" Jack chuckled.

It was the kind of cackling laugh only Vaughn was capable of making.

"You know," Marcus laughed, "you're the first person that I've heard say that. I thought I was the only one who noticed."

The two men laughed heartily.

"If you listened to Eddie all day, you'd think God was only on his side," Vaughn said wryly. "He's one of a kind, that guy. Whenever we needed a big hit in the playoffs, that son of a bitch was the one to get it for us."

Marcus bent his head.

"How are you two getting along?" Jack asked

"We're gettin' along," Dillard answered. "Eddie knows how to play the media game, so he keeps his distance sometimes. After all, anyone that's ever befriended me is either dead or playing in the El Paso league."

The two men laughed.

"Can you blame him?" Jack smiled. "Eddie can have any front-office job in baseball after he retires. He sure doesn't want to fuck that up by hanging out with a low-life like you!"

Marcus smiled.

"I guess he's got his image to uphold."

As rain drops began falling, both men scurried into their respective dugouts.

"Keep your head up today," Vaughn warned him. "I might have some of my pitchers bust you high and inside."

"They'd better hit me!" Dillard replied bombastically. "Otherwise Marcus might have to deposit a few balls into Lake Erie."

Jack laughed heartily.

"I'm glad to see you haven't lost your sense of humility."

When he was introduced before the game, Jack Vaughn received a lengthy standing ovation from the Buffalo faithful.

"They're really giving Jack a warm welcome back to Buffalo!"

For many fans, it was a tearful moment; an old hero coming back to town wearing enemy colors. Nothing could contain the groundswell of affection many Pioneers fans still held for the man. Blue-collar towns love their blue-collar heroes and nobody personified the working man quite like Jack Vaughn.

When the game itself finally began, the Yankees did not take long to assert their dominance over their cross-state rivals.

"Nobody out.....LaRocque and Alvarez have both drawn walks.... and Scott Harper is at the plate."

Boos rained down on the field.

"They still haven't forgiven Scott Harper in this town."

"The pitch is drilled to right field!...It's gone!.....3-0 New York!"

The blast traveled over the bleachers, putting a large dent in the "Pioneering Excellence" sign hanging over right field.

After three innings, heavy rain began falling on the field, forcing the umpires to postpone the game until a later date.

With the afternoon suddenly available, Jack Vaughn walked over to the nearby hospital where Jonathan Jenkins was recovering from his debilitating stroke. The two men had not spoken since the acrimonious firing of the previous fall, so the manager could be forgiven for feeling a little awkward.

As he entered the hospital ward nervously, Jack was immediately put at ease when he saw Rose Jenkins waiting outside Jonathan's room. She was always so pleasing to the eye; a woman of warmth and substance.

"Oh Jack," she squeezed him hard. "It's so good to see you."

"Good to see you too, Rose. You look ravishing as always."

"Oh," she blushed and did a little twirl. "Why thank you Jack!"

"How is he?"

"He's hanging on," the smile eased off of her face, "but find out for yourself. He's been waiting for you."

Jack slowly and uncomfortably walked into the room, where the pale-faced Jenkins lay in bed with his eyes closed. The old man's frail eyes opened and the color rushed back into his face at the sight of the manager. Vaughn hadn't the slightest idea what to say.

"Jack," Jenkins painstakingly reached out to touch his arm. "I'm glad you came."

"How are you, Johnny?"

"I'm better now that I'm seeing you," he smiled. "I didn't want to go without talking to you one final time."

"Look Johnny," Jack responded with a pained expression. "That stuff I said to you last fall, I didn't mean it. It was heat of the moment...."

Jenkins looked out the window gloomily.

"You meant it," he replied. "But I can't say that I blame you. For years I had nothing but blind faith in Trent Blair, but I watch on television and read the newspapers. It's all coming home to roost now. I was so damn stupid."

The old man placed his feeble hands on his face.

"Your heart was always in the right place, Johnny."

"Everything came so easily," Jenkins drudged on. "We were winning games, the money was rolling in. I thought it would never end. I don't know what happened or how it did, but we pissed it all away. I'll go to my grave bearing that heavy burden in my heart."

Jenkins pressed his hand on his face to conceal the grief that would otherwise be pouring out of him fluidly. Watching the old man struggling to articulate his final thoughts filled Jack with a profound sense of sadness. He was still tortured by what could have been in Buffalo and why it had all come to such a screeching halt.

"I guess we all must die at some point," lamented Jenkins. "I should have realized that when I bought this team. None of us can keep going on into eternity."

Jack closed his eyes and covered his ears in denial. He desperately wanted the old man to stop, the truth hurt too much. He thought when he moved to New York that he had escaped it all: the internal bickering, the angst over the Pioneers long-term future in Buffalo. Jack now knew that was impossible. He refused to believe that everything must eventually come to an end.

"Don't be saying things like that," Jack tried to reassure him. "You still have many vibrant years ahead of you. You've got a great wife. Things are looking great."

"Things are not good at all," Jenkins corrected him with surprising force for a man in his predicament. "I'm gonna go any day now and who knows who'll take over the team?"

He paused for a moment. The rain outside was coming down harder than ever.

"Look Jack, I'm not looking to wear you down with my problems. You gave us six wonderful seasons. I always respected you and I'm just glad we could patch things up."

The manager stared out the window blankly.

"They never should have been un-patched."

Jenkins painstakingly reached for Jack's hands and patted them gently.

"You're a good man, Jack."

The manager was never adept at saying goodbye. His crustiness made him awkward in expressing himself during times when conflicting emotions rendered him unable to think. After summoning up all of the love he felt for this wonderful old man, Jack kissed Jenkins on the forehead.

"You get better," Jack insisted. "And next time we're in town, I'll come up again."

"I certainly hope so."

"All right, Johnny. Get well."

It was still raining heavily by the time Jack walked back outside the hospital entrance. He stood there frozen, the pathetic image of Jenkins still tormenting his mind.

Jonathan Jenkins epitomized the old-world values of courtesy and class that were dying out in this new age.

For as long as Jack could remember, baseball had been his lifeblood. He was slowly realizing however, that there were more important things in life. The possibility of limited youth had finally entered into his consciousness.

That night, news came that Jonathan Jenkins had fallen into a deep coma. The doctors weren't quite willing to pronounce him dead, but the prognosis was not promising. The news cast a dark shadow over the team.

"This series came in with a whimper and ended with an even bigger one. Yesterday the Pioneers dropped both ends of the day-night doubleheader before losing 8-1 this afternoon. I think the question on everyone's mind is the status of long time owner Jonathan Jenkins."

"Definitely. And as we sit here before all-star weekend, his situation looks grimmer and grimmer with each passing day."

Chris Norton and Marcus Dillard were the only Pioneers chosen for the annual All-Star Game. It was hard to argue with either selection. Norton had won 10 games and posted a 2.25 earned run average on a last-place team, while Dillard had slugged 26 home-runs by the beginning of July and was leading the American League in runs-batted-in.

Any notion that Dillard's strong season was appreciated by the Pioneers front office quickly went out the window prior to the first game back from the break. All Trent Blair could see was an $11 million salary and money hemorrhaging from the team's financial bottom line.

After each game, Watkins and Blair kept persisting in their efforts to antagonize their star right fielder into waiving his no-trade clause and accepting a move elsewhere. Both of them knew it was only a matter of time until Marcus cracked.

"We think we can still turn things around," Blair told reporters. "But some things need to change. It's hard to win ballgames when someone like Marcus Dillard refuses to buy into the program. I think it's both unreasonable and indecent of him."

Then against Cleveland, Marcus dropped an easily catch-able fly ball in the sixth inning after losing it in the lights. Boos rained onto the field from bitter fans.

"Two runs come around to score on the Dillard error and its 5-0 Cleveland!"

Norm Watkins immediately called a time-out and sent one of his backup infielders to replace Dillard in right field. The move seemed deliberately intended to provoke as much humiliation as possible.

"And what is Norm Watkins doing! He's pulling him in the middle of the inning!" *"Oh, that's not right. You don't do that to a player. I don't like that one bit."*

The manager glared at Dillard as he walked back into the dugout, almost inciting him to say something. The huge slugger refused to retort or throw his glove in the dugout. He simply proceeded back to the bench and sat down. His internal nuclear reactor was ready to detonate, but Marcus still managed to keep it all inside.

After the game, Watkins refused to let the incident go.

"We have too many one-dimensional players on this team and Marcus is one of them. All he cares about are his homeruns and I really can't tolerate that. There is no room for selfishness on this team."

Dillard was in the shower when the manager gave his critique, but the reporters quickly brought it to his attention.

Sitting in front of his locker, with nothing but a towel around his massive torso, Dillard's rage began spinning out of control. He put a dent in the wall with his fist and stormed around the dressing room in anger. Just by looking at him, every reporter in the vicinity knew he was ripe for the picking. All they had to do was turn on the tape recorders.

"FUCK TRENT BLAIR! FUCK NORM WATKINS! FUCK THE PIONEERS! GET ME THE FUCK OUT OF HERE!"

"Do you want to leave Buffalo?" A reporter asked.

"THESE FANS DON'T APPRECIATE SHIT! I BUST MY ASS.....THEY DON'T APPRECIATE NUTHIN!"

The damage was done. With many contenders looking for an outfielder with Dillard's power, Trent Blair was only too happy to oblige his request. It was only a matter of time until the deal was consummated.

A few days later, Marcus Dillard joined the growing list of ex-Pioneers.

"The Buffalo Pioneers have dealt 31-year old outfielder Marcus Dillard to Colorado for pitching prospect Dan Lee and cash considerations. We now go live to Buffalo where Trent Blair is addressing the media."

The general manager had a huge grin on his face as he wiped his brow.

194

"Out of sight and out of mind," Blair said. "That sums up how I feel about it. We rid ourselves of a troublemaker and in return acquire a young pitcher who can help us sometime down the line. It's a trade that is beneficial to all the parties involved. We get to send Marcus Dillard two thousand miles away....."

Blair smiled.

"....and now that he's playing in the thin air of Denver, who knows?" Blair added sarcastically. "Maybe he'll be able to hit his eighty home-runs now."

The general manager had spun the story into the perfect parameters he saw fit. As he tried to tell everyone, the team was doing the honorable thing and improving themselves for the long-term. Indeed many people bought the story. Chet Thomas, whose record in getting the story right has been checkered to say the least, wrote a searing indictment of Marcus Dillard the following day:

Marcus Dillard's legacy: Egoism, Choking and 2½ years of Disappointment
By: Chet Thomas (Buffalo News)

On paper, the Pioneers may be a weaker team today, but in reality they've finally cleared the decks of all the baggage Marcus Dillard brought with him during his disappointing stint in Buffalo. It wasn't about the 26 homeruns he hit before the break, the 44 he hit last year or the 41 he hit the year before that. It was about his horrid performance in the playoffs, his lack of regard for anyone but himself, and the questionable influence he had on the likes of Conan O'Shea, Pete Sampson and E.J. Winters. With Marcus it was always about what Marcus wanted, about what Marcus needed, and about how Marcus felt. That is no longer necessary. When all is said and done, the trade of Marcus Dillard is simple math of addition by subtraction.

Not everyone felt so negatively about Marcus Dillard. On that evening's telecast, BSN's Terry Davis had a more objective spin on it.

"Despite what Trent Blair is trying to make it out to appear, this was a salary dump. Marcus Dillard was not the problem on this team. This is a group of players who had little chance of contending coming into this season. Anyone who thought this team had World Series talent was deluding themselves. The rotation bottoms out after Chris Norton, the bullpen is non-existent and Eddie Griffin is ready for retirement. If anything, Marcus Dillard was one of the few bright lights in this dull season. You have to wonder what the Pioneers will do now, especially since the kid they picked up, Dan Lee, is considered only a marginal prospect."

The commentator was correct in predicting dark times ahead. In the weeks following the trade, the Pioneers fell into an even greater tailspin. By the July 31st trading deadline they were a full 35 games behind the New York Yankees for first-place. The season was essentially over.

That evening, Trent Blair officially threw in the towel by sending catcher Terry Miller to Philadelphia for a player-to-be-named-later. It was just another day and another hero from the days of yore being shipped out of town. Miller wasn't the heart and soul by any stretch of the imagination, but he had still been a valuable cog on a once powerful dynasty.

"You're stripping this team to the bone," Ferreira cautioned. "There's nobody in the organization to replace him at catcher."

"I'm not really interested in that right now. We can save on his salary and finally think about building for the future."

"What if the future never comes?"

"It will and sometime soon I'm going to play an even bigger role in ensuring that. We just need to wait until an old horse gets taken to the glue factory."

CHAPTER 22

"In the club's second tragedy in less than two months, Pioneers owner Jonathan Jenkins was pronounced dead at 2:13 am, eastern standard time. After suffering a massive heart attack in early June, Mr. Jenkins had fallen into a coma just under a week ago and was on life-support."

"It wasn't an easy decision," Dr. Gerry Harris told the media, "but it was made with the full consultation of the medical authorities and the Jenkins family. We can only hope that they have the strength to make it through this grievous period."

Devastation began to set in for friends and family members. This was something that went far beyond baseball. Jonathan Jenkins was loved and admired in the community not just for his role in bringing the World Series to Buffalo, but for his philanthropy and civic mindedness. It was for all the supermarket employees he had paid equitably and treated fairly over the years.

His departure was another loss in a year when many things valuable seemed to be slipping away. In his morning column, Chet Thomas called him *"the Pioneer of Pioneers."*

When pressed for comment, Trent Blair too expressed his "shock and dismay at the loss of so great a man."

The death resonated throughout the community. At the baseball game later that day, the sparse crowd on hand observed a moment of silence in his honor. Then in a most grand gesture, Jenkins was afforded presidential treatment when his funeral included a solemn march through the streets of Buffalo en route to the cathedral. An American flag was draped over his coffin as the city said goodbye to its favorite son.

The funeral service, which was televised by the Buffalo Sports Network and several local news outlets, was capped off with a stirring eulogy from Rose Jenkins. As she walked up to the podium, Rose exuded the same strength and composure that her friends had come to know and respect. She was hurt by the loss more than anyone but refused to reveal it.

"We all congregate here today to mourn the loss of Jonathan Jenkins," she began. "For over forty years, I have come to know this man first hand. But I want to start off by saying that this should not be a day of sadness. My Johnny would not want it that way. We should come here to remember his life and celebrate his passing into a higher world. What a man he was...."

She smiled and took a few breaths.

"A World War Two naval officer at twenty-two years of age, he helped defend the country against the threat of fascist imperialism. A graduate of Canisius College, he epitomized the post war generation that sought to make a new start for themselves. As a man who made his life in the supermarket, nobody could outsmart him...."

She took another breath.

"....In those early years, he lived and breathed groceries. Jonathan was a man who treated his employees and customers with respect and dignity. He owned many stores, but never acted like he owned the people working in them. When it came to business, Johnny was a man who made his way by applying smarts and morality to every decision he made. Business however, was not his only forte..."

She looked at the crowd once more.

"....I can attest to a man who was the quintessential husband. Gentle, caring and compassionate, I've had the pleasure of living with him for the better part of my life. I certainly don't know what I would have done without him. He was faithful and devoted in every aspect, but I was not his only love. Baseball was his mistress....."

A few whispers were heard around the cathedral.

"And over the years I learned to live with her. Jonathan was utterly consumed by the game and in many ways it transformed him. He was like a little boy when it came to baseball. The way he held out such hope for it, unaware that like everything else in this world, it too was plagued by human weakness. Such was the way with Jonathan. He loved baseball more than anyone I know...."

She panned the cathedral for familiar faces.

"....I can recall one cold winter afternoon when we were eating at a downtown restaurant and there must have been at least three feet of snow outside. You know how it is at that time of year. Its right in the middle of hockey and football season, but not for Johnny. I'll never forget him looking outside and saying, 'only nine weeks until spring training!'"

The entire cathedral erupted in laughter

"But that's how it was with him. He could sit there in an absolute blizzard and all the poor bugger was thinking about was summer and baseball! His hunger for the game was insatiable and I don't think I ever saw him more content than when the Pioneers won the World Series. The look of pride on his face, I don't think I've seen it since......well.....our wedding day of course!"

She elicited more laughs from the packed cathedral

"Jonathan had many friends in this game and many friends in life. He was a great owner, a wonderful man and an ideal husband. God has played an essential role in his life and I just know that my Johnny is in good hands. So long, my love."

As she stepped down from the podium, the entire congregation gave her a rousing ovation. The television cameras panned the cathedral, which was filled with a who's who of power brokers: former New York Governor Tom Murdoch, Buffalo mayor Art Dingleman and Baseball Commissioner Richard Smalls were all in attendance.

As the procession made its way outside the cathedral, Rose finally caved into her emotions and began to sob slightly. She was slowly walking down the stairs in front of the cathedral and into the range of television cameras when Trent Blair put his arm around her in a grand gesture and helped her into a waiting car.

The media ate it up. The next morning, the *Buffalo News* ran a picture on the front-page of Trent Blair and Rose Jenkins walking down the stairs together. The photo led to endless speculation in the weeks to come.

"Rose Jenkins set to control Pioneers?" one headline read.

Making an even bigger jump to conclusions, one supermarket tabloid reported that *"Rose Jenkins and Trent Blair are suddenly an item."*

Forget the thirty-year age differential between the 43-year old and the elderly widow or that relations between the two had never been particularly warm. In the wake of the Pioneers' collapse, the city was looking to clasp onto anything and everything that served as a reminder of the past.

With all the innuendo that was surfacing, Rose Jenkins decided to pay a visit to the general manager's office on a sunny August afternoon. As she walked in, Blair and Ferreira were reviewing minor league reports behind the general manager's desk.

"Rose, what a surprise!" Trent stood up. "How have you been holding up?"

As the general manager put his arms around her, the widow tried to wiggle out before taking a seat. There were few people Rose disdained more than these two. She often wondered about their relationship, especially the way Al Ferreira seemed sycophantic to everything Blair suggested. Ferreira's sly face and thin mustache led her to wonder what lay beneath the surface.

"I'm just fine," she replied coldly. "I didn't come here to chat. I'm here to set things straight."

"And set them we will!" Blair continued in his car salesman's voice. "I've been meaning to discuss a few possibilities with you."

"Look Trent," she said. "This isn't what you think."

"It is what I think," he eagerly interrupted her again, "and it can be more! I have a grand vision for this team in the post-Jonathan Jenkins era."

"Oh yeah?" She wondered skeptically. "And what would that be?"

As he readied to discuss his proposal with her, Blair became so excited that he could barely get the words out of his mouth.

"As the man who engineered the success of this organization, I have organized a consortium of local investors that would not only keep the team in Buffalo, but who would carry on the winning tradition of Pioneer baseball......with me at the helm!"

There was an eerie silence in the room.

"Look Trent, before you go off on a tangent, we need to get a few things straight. I don't like you......"

The smile vacated his face.

".....I never liked you. In fact, I despise you with every bone in my body. I have a slightly different version of events than the one you're trying to invent. I don't credit you for the success of this organization, in fact I blame you for making a mess of it. You may have been able to sucker my husband for all those years, but I see right through you. And you know what, Trent?"

"What?" he asked nervously.

"I don't like what I see one bit. You are an arrogant, self-centered manipulator and I'll be damned if I allow Jonathan's treasure to be plundered into your hands! Do I make myself clear?"

"Crystal," he answered back.

"That'll be it, boys."

The conversation was over. Rose had simply walked into the office, done her business and left on her own terms.

As she left the room, Trent desperately called her back.

"Rose, wait! Who are you planning to sell the team to?"

Her voice pounded with a sharp brutality.

"Anyone but you!"

She slammed the door behind her and walked away.

"You okay, Trent?" Ferreira asked.

The general manager sat shaken in his chair.

"Trent, you all right?"

There was no response.

"Trent?"

The general manager looked at Ferreira with desperation in his eyes.

"Can I trust you, Al?"

"Of course," Ferreira reassured him.

Trent stood up and walked out of the room catatonically.

"Trent, what the hell are you doing? Where are you going?"

"I need a beer," he finally answered.

"You never drink! Where are you...."

The door closed.

The setting sun was peering its way though the window shades as Ferreira glanced at a faded picture of Trent holding up the World Series trophy with an ecstatic Jonathan Jenkins beside him. The old man had his arm placed affectionately on Trent's shoulders. They looked like father and son standing together with smiling faces. It was a reminder of better times.

As Ferreira examined the general manager's desk, he noticed the table was made of some of the finest oak. The more he stared at it the more he desired to touch its fine edges and feel the contours of its long body. He clutched the leather on the general manager's vacant chair and wondered how it would feel to sit there.

"Mr. Blair?" the receptionist paged him.

"It's me, Wendy. Trent went out."

"Oh," she replied. "Tell him that someone from the Internal Revenue Service just phoned. It sounds pretty serious."

"Can do," he answered back.

The remainder of the season went by almost like a blur. As the losses continued to pile up, everything had become meaningless. There is nothing more depressing than a baseball team fifty games out of first-place in September. With an autumn frost permeating the air, the fans stayed away from crumbling Pioneer Stadium in droves.

The players even lost interest. Not even Watkins' daily explosions were lighting a fuse underneath them.

"YOU GUYS ABSOLUTELY STINK!! I'M SICK OF YOUR HALF-ASSED EFFORT!!"

The team had become numb to his brand of discipline. Most of the players never took Watkins seriously from the start, but now they weren't even flinching when he raised his voice. Instead of his words going in one ear and out the other, now he wasn't even making it inside.

In the midst of a five-game losing streak, the manager predictably blew his fuse once again.

"YOU GUTLESS PIECES OF SHIT!! IF YOU DON'T WANT TO PLAY HARD, THEN I'LL FIND PLAYERS WHO WILL!!"

The players sat in their stalls and stared at the ground despondently when a garbage can was suddenly flung across the room, spewing refuse all over the room. It was just an ordinary day at the ballpark, but all of the kicking and screaming had finally added up for Eddie Griffin.

"Why don't you take it easy, Norm."

"Why don't you sit back down in your stall, Griffin!"

"I'm gonna stand here all day," Griffin pumped his chest in the manager's face. "And there isn't a damn thing you can do about it!"

Watkins paced around the room thinking of how to respond.

"You're right Eddie. There's nothing I can do about it. After the way you've been hitting all season, I'd rather not see you at the plate ever again!"

In a room filled with young players who held Eddie in higher esteem there was much silence and little approval for the manager's words.

"Your lame jokes aren't funny, Norm."

A few snickers were heard around the clubhouse.

"I'll fine you, Griffin!"

"I don't care what you do.," Eddie scoffed at him. "You sit there and blame us. You say I'm having a bad year. What the hell did you expect? I'm 42 years old! Maybe if you hadn't chased Marcus out of town, we wouldn't be in such a mess."

"One more word out of you! And I'll...."

"You'll what!" Eddie screamed back. "What are you going to do, Norm? You know, maybe you and I do have something in common."

"What would that be?"

"We'll both be retiring soon," Eddie smiled at him vainly. "The only difference is that I'm headed to the Hall of Fame and you're headed to the unemployment line. Maybe the army will hire you to mop the floors!"

The dressing room cracked up in laughter.

"SHUT UP!! ALL OF YOU!!"

The players continued laughing.

"I SAID SHUT UP!!" Watkins repeated.

The manager was forced to retreat to his office in humiliation. Whatever credibility he held previously was now stripped right off him. Norm Watkins was like a guard dog without bite, an attack cat without claws. He was neutered.

"That was beautiful," Chris Norton said to Griffin. "I've been waiting for someone to do that all season."

"Look man, you need to get out of this place," Griffin responded with a more serious look on his face.

"What do you mean?" Norton asked.

"A good pitcher like you with several good seasons left. You don't want to be stuck playing on a loser."

Norton remained silent, but began to ponder his own situation. Once the idea of leaving Buffalo was put into his mind there was no turning back. All he could do was continue to pitch well and let his agent handle things at the end of the season.

"On one of the worst Pioneer teams in recent memory, Chris Norton has been brilliant, winning 16 games and posting a stellar 2.48 earned run average. He continued it tonight, throwing a complete game shutout and ending Buffalo's five game losing streak."

September usually mattered at Pioneer Stadium, but not this season. There was no playoff spot on the line and no excitement to speak of. With a half-empty crumbling stadium, a dispirited team on the field, and 112 losses, playoff fever was a thing of the past. Pioneer Stadium had come to resemble a mausoleum.

The only thing that broke up the monotony was a ceremony surrounding Eddie Griffin's final game. Only 13 000 bothered to show up. Still, what every desperate soul wanted to see on that cold, overcast September afternoon was a reminder of how it used to be.

Trailing 5-0 heading in the bottom of the ninth, with one out and nobody on base, Eddie Griffin got his chance to go out with a bang.

"Eddie Griffin comes to the plate now in what may be the final at-bat of his illustrious career."

The crowd stood to cheer.

"You can only tip your cap to a man like Eddie Griffin and what a fantastic career he has had. He played fourteen years for the New York Yankees before signing a free-agent contract with Buffalo. He has hit well over 500 homeruns and been a tremendous role model throughout his career. It's been a pleasure watching you play, Eddie."

"Well that was lovely, Terry, but he still has one more at-bat here. He steps in.....the pitcher sets....takes the pitch for ball one!"

The fog from Lake Erie made its way into the stadium. Even the large bank tower across the street, which always seemed to hover over the stadium, was barely visible.

"Eddie just slipped a little there, the surface is a little wet."

"The pitcher sets.....delivers.....THIS ONE IS BELTED!"

"Get out!...Get out baseball!"

The announcers threw any delusion of partiality out the window.

"This one is long gone!"

"Yes! Yes!"

"What a way to finish off! For Griffin that is his 17th home-run of the season in what may be his last at-bat!"

"And these fans want a curtain call!"

Eddie popped out of the dugout and tipped his cap to the small crowd.

The image of a hobbled Eddie Griffin hitting a homerun in his final at-bat was a powerful one. The ovation the fans gave him was for the six years of service in Buffalo; all the clutch hits in the playoffs and the times he made the city feel good about itself by saying the right thing at the right time (....half the time he actually meant it). It was the fans' final glimpse at the man who had brought them so much excitement over the years.

2006 American League East Standings

Team	W-L	GB
New York	109-53	-
Boston	91-71	18
Baltimore	86-76	23
Toronto	72-90	37
Tampa Bay	65-97	44
Buffalo	50-112	59

2006 Buffalo Pioneers Statistics

Player		Average	HR	RBI	SB
LF	E.J. Winters	.205	1	13	1
C	Terry Miller	.267	2	45	0*
1B	Eddie Griffin	.263	17	79	0
RF	Marcus Dillard	.285	26	81	8*
DH	Orlando Mateo	.260	15	64	4
3B	Dave Kelton	.249	11	54	0
SS	Tom DeVellieres	.221	0	34	2
2B	Esteban Pena	.234	2	40	8
CF	Alvaro Perez	.214	0	11	5

* Statistics prior to trade

Pitcher		W-L	E.R.A.	Saves
SP	Chris Norton	17-12	2.31	-
SP	Johnny Turner	12-14	4.97	-
SP	Rich Lopez	9-15	5.34	-
SP	Dave Rivers	3-8	6.57	-
SP	Brian Boze	0-4	7.84	-
RP	Dan Lee	2-5	5.96	8

CHAPTER 23

"*And the New York Yankees are the 2006 World Series Champions! I have Vince D'Antoni with me here. Tell me Vince how does this feel?*"

The owner's face was beaming.

"It feels wonderful," D'Antoni answered. "I have to thank Jack Vaughn for the professional job he did all season. He ran this team like a well-oiled machine and he deserves praise for that."

Back in Buffalo, Trent Blair and Al Ferreira watched the proceedings at the general manager's home. The television was suddenly turned off.

"What did you do that for?" Ferreira wondered.

The pervasive smell of alcohol stunk up the room. As Trent Blair tightened his bathrobe, his breath absolutely reeked of it.

"I don't feel like listening to it!"

"Relax, it's just a post game interview."

The general manager stumbled sideways before regaining his balance

"Whatever...(belch)," Blair replied drunkenly. "I hate both those men."

"Well, its gonna take a little more than hatred to compete with them next year. What are we gonna do about it?"

The general manager's eyes were spinning.

"Trent?" Ferreira repeated

"I dunno....(belch).....why don't we call an organization meeting and discuss it.....huh? How does that sound?"

"You fired all of the scouts," Ferreira reminded him.

Blair sat in a chair stroking his beard. It had grown across his once clean-cut face like a weed infested garden.

"As long as we still have Chris Norton there's no problem. Frank Ringler stayed, Norton will stay...."

Trent continued rambling on as he looked out the window.

".....and the prospects will develop. We'll be back on top in no time."

A demented smile expanded across his face.

"I never thought I'd say this," Ferreira interjected with a dose of reality, "but you're making all these evaluations without scouting reports. We need more than just minor league statistics to rate a player."

"That's bullshit," the inebriated general manager stammered. "Just get the laptop out. That's always been enough."

"No its not," Ferreira warned him. "Boze and Perez aren't even hacking it at AAA and this Dan Lee kid you got from Colorado got pummeled when we called him up."

"Don't be such a pessimist....(belch)...positive thinking always prevails."

Ferreira never dared cross the general manager before, but was no longer in the mood to waste time with a drunkard.

"Live in reality, Trent! This team is in serious trouble both financially and on the field. We don't even have an owner."

Trent snapped with an intoxicated vehemence.

"Are you trying to stab me in the back?"

"What are you talking about?" Ferreira denied. "Where did you get that idea from? I would never think of it."

The general manager's face, which had looked so bold and resolute during his zenith, now appeared so despairingly human. Over the past few weeks, his once smooth face became grizzled with the hairy residue of lapsed hygiene and disheveled hair. He had been showing up at the office later and later everyday. His mind, once so razor sharp, was becoming increasingly sporadic.

"I'd never turn on you," Ferreira reassured him before leaving the house.

During the off-season, several issues hung over the team, beginning with the sale of the team. Rose Jenkins made no secret of her intention to sell, but aside from Blair's group there were no credible local buyers coming to the forefront.

When he formed his consortium, Trent Blair shrewdly included just about every conceivable local buyer to limit her alternatives. As the stalemate with Rose Jenkins dragged on, Blair knew he was her only local option and it was assumed that Mrs. Jenkins would eventually be forced to sell to him. One day all of that changed.

"Reports out of Buffalo today indicate that Portland billionaire Roger Reich, head of the telecommunications giant Reich Systems has purchased the Buffalo Pioneers for $120 million. Details at 11."

Roger Reich was one of the most powerful men in America. Starting in the mid-1990's, he had built his small internet start-up into a vast telecommunications empire whose strongest market lay in the Pacific Northwest. He was the master of the hostile takeover, snatching companies through bitter and acrimonious battles that ended in a courtroom more often than not. Reich was known in the business world as a scrapper, not afraid to get his hands dirty in order to build up his empire and often doing so just for the fun of it.

The transfer of control from the Jenkins estate to Reich Systems was entirely symbolic of a larger trend in the game. Huge corporations were running the teams nowadays, so often able to promote their clubs through the media outlets they owned. For small-time entrepreneurs like Jonathan Jenkins, they were quickly becoming extinct in this brave new world.

Rose Jenkins got what she wanted, the sale of the baseball team to someone other than Trent Blair, and Roger Reich got what he wanted, the team itself. However, it took only a few questions to reveal that Buffalo fans were in for what they least wanted.

"Answer the question Mr. Reich," a reporter demanded. "Are you planning to move the team to Portland?"

"As I have stated time and time again, I am not coming here with any predisposed ideas on what I will or will not do. The situation will play itself out and a decision will be made in due course moving forward."

The diminutive businessman looked like he was enjoying himself.

"Why can't you answer the question?" The reporter persisted

"This press conference is over."

Reich stepped down from the podium and took a quick exit.

As rumors abounded throughout baseball that the Pioneers could be on the move, the lords of baseball cast long frowns.

The next day, Commissioner Richard Smalls telephoned Yankees owner Vince D'Antoni at night to feel out his opinion on the subject. The Commissioner had a habit making important phone-calls after midnight to catch people in their less guarded moments.

"A good evenin' to you, Mr. D'Antoni," the Commissioner said in his southern drawl.

"This better be important," D'Antoni said groggily.

208

"I wanted to talk with you about some very disturbing news, and for once it's not about you."

"That's a first," D'Antoni laughed.

"No Vince, I believe we have an even bigger problem. This Roger Reich fellow thinks he can buy a team and move it just like that. I have other ideas and I am prepared to fight tooth and nail to keep that team in Buffalo."

"I don't see how this involves me," D'Antoni replied indifferently.

"I wanted to get a sense of how you feel about this."

"I hope the guy moves the team," D'Antoni said bluntly. "Get the Pioneers out of New York State."

"I was hoping you'd be a little more selfless when it came to these matters."

"I don't have time for selflessness."

"Even if you lose a geographical rival?"

"I don't see it," Vince refuted. "And if you expect me to act out of charity or whatever the fuck you wanna call this, you can forget it."

"I see," the Commissioner surmised. "You know, Mr. D'Antoni. I grow weary of your ways."

"And I grow weary of your raspy voice calling me up to make threats at two o'clock in the morning!"

The Commissioner sighed.

"You Yankees have always been a selfish bunch."

"What the fuck is that supposed to mean? Aren't you still hanging black men from trees down there in Louisiana?"

The Commissioner sighed impatiently.

"You have yourself a pleasant evenin', Mr. D'Antoni."

A few days later, Roger Reich arrived in Buffalo to acquaint himself with the city. Everyone in the organization was walking on eggshells to please him. His tour of the city began through the downtown core and wrapped up with a visit to Pioneer Stadium. The small businessman wore a gold turtleneck under his white blazer.

"What a dump this place is," he commented as he looked around the decrepit stadium. "We actually play our games in this place?"

"We'd be moving into a new stadium right about now," Blair replied, "but the Governor nixed the stadium proposal when he was elected two years ago."

"What's wrong with him?"

"Apparently he doesn't believe in sports," Blair responded.

"A real egghead, huh?"

The two men laughed.

"You could say that," Blair smiled nervously.

Reich's volatile demeanor suddenly changed as he struggled with his new gold plated cell phone. After a few minutes of frustration, he impatiently threw the device into the garbage to the general manager's shock.

"Did you just throw that phone out?" Blair asked in astonishment.

"I'll buy another one tomorrow. I can't be bothered to get it fixed."

The two men walked into the general manager's office and sat down. Once inside the privacy of Trent Blair's office, Roger Reich wasted no time in expressing his opinion on the current state of the team.

"This franchise is an absolute mess. The team stinks, the financial statement says it lost $16 million last season and we play in this ancient pile of rubble. When I see something like this, you can only look to who has been in charge. That appears to be you."

"Yes," Trent defended. "It certainly appears that we have mismanaged this team, but you really must understand, Roger...."

"Call me Mr. Reich."

"What?"

"Call me Mr. Reich," he reiterated forcefully.

"Yes," Blair continued apprehensively. "What you really must understand, Mr. Reich, is that this game goes in cycles. Just three years ago we were celebrating our third World Championship in as many years...."

"I don't care about what you did three years ago," Reich interrupted him. "If my company is losing billions of dollars, do you think my shareholders give a damn what I did three years ago?"

"Not likely."

"They don't. And neither do I. Just tell me about the future, your farm system, your scouting staff, anything. "

210

"Well," Trent answered anxiously. "We are currently in a transition phase with our scouting department."

"Don't bullshit me."

"I wouldn't call it bullshit."

"I can smell bullshit from a mile away," Reich remarked icily. "What about the farm system? The major league team obviously isn't any good otherwise you wouldn't have lost 112 games. Are there any prospects coming up?"

"Brian Boze, Alvaro Perez, Dan Lee to name a few."

"Did you say Alvaro Perez?" Reich said in disbelief. "Isn't he the guy who had four errors and five strikeouts in one game?"

"That kid has a lot of potential," Blair defended.

"So does my ten year old son! That doesn't mean I'm ready to anoint him as the savior of a $120 million baseball team."

The general manager looked annoyed.

"For a man with little to no baseball background," Blair said. "You certainly act like you know better."

"Based on the answers you're giving me, I'm beginning to think I do! Are you a complete incompetent or what?"

"If you would allow me to finish, Mr. Reich, I have built winning teams in the past and I am on course to building another one."

Reich pounded his fists into the desk.

"For the last fucking time," Reich yelled. "I don't care about the past!"

The general manager was taken aback.

"I don't know how things worked around here when the old man was giving you the run of the house," Reich continued ranting, "but you have a few months to put some life back into this moribund operation or else you're toast. You can start by firing whatever circus clown you had managing this team."

"I can do that," Blair nodded in agreement

"I shouldn't have to tell you this," Reich remarked icily. "It seems like the only one who knows what he's doing around here is Al Ferreira."

The general manager's ears perked up with curiosity.

"And when were you speaking with Al?" Blair asked.

"We've been in constant contact over the past week, but enough about that...."

Reich looked at his watch impatiently.

"....I need to get back to Portland for a seven o'clock."

As the owner stormed out of the office, Trent wondered to himself whether the end was near. His mind raced in a fit of paranoia as he remembered all of the enemies he had accumulated over the years. He pulled out a bottle of whiskey stored in his desk.

The next day Trent Blair announced that Norm Watkins had been dismissed as manager.

"This was a difficult decision and one that was made after great deliberation on my part," Blair explained to the handful of reporters. "The Buffalo Pioneers will not be retaining the services of Norm Watkins for the 2007 season."

There was little outcry over this move. Nobody in the media or on the team was going to miss Norm Watkins. Even the normally supportive Chet Thomas described Watkins one-year tenure as manager an *"abominable failure."*

After cutting the rope with Watkins, Blair focused his energies on signing ace pitcher Chris Norton to a long-term deal. Norton was the centerpiece of the organization's rebuilding efforts just as Frank Ringler had been ten years earlier. Trent Blair was confident he could get a deal done.

The following afternoon, the general manager put a call in to the pitcher's agent.

"We are prepared to offer Chris a five-year deal that would total in upwards of $50 million," the general manager began. "We want Chris Norton in Pioneer colors for the rest of his career."

"I'm sorry to disappoint you," the agent replied, "but you'd have to offer my client a hell of a lot more than that to entice him into staying in such an odious situation. He doesn't want to play on a last place team."

"We're working to change that. I'm trying my best to rebuild this team."

"You're living in the past, Blair. With this market and your reputation, that'll never happen again."

The general manager began clutching at straws.

"All right," he said desperately. "I'm asking you as a favor. Chris has been a life-long Pioneer and I'd like him to remain one."

The agent laughed thunderously.

"A favor?" The agent asked. "A favor!"

The agent continued chuckling to himself.

"That's a good one," the agent hollered. "It's doubtful that I'd do such a favor for a friend of mine, but I certainly don't count you in that category."

"I'm serious here," Blair replied.

The agent would not stop laughing.

"Oh, I'm sure you are," he continued chortling uncontrollably. "That's what makes this so damn funny!"

"I'll take that as a no," Blair said despondently.

The agent only began laughing harder before Blair hung up the phone.

Later that day, Blair was disconsolate about the news.

"There's no loyalty nowadays," Blair lamented. "Frank Ringler stayed in Buffalo, Chris should be doing the same."

Al Ferreira had a stern look on his face. After years of apprenticeship, he no longer wanted anything to do with Trent Blair.

"Why would he?" the assistant G.M. said bluntly. "This team is going nowhere."

"What's that supposed to mean?"

"You're losing it, man."

Blair immediately raised an eyebrow.

"And what's this I hear about you talking to Reich behind my back? Are you trying to pull a power-play on me behind my back?"

"I don't know what you're talking about."

Trent snapped.

"You son of a bitch!" He pointed at him accusingly. "I know what you're pulling."

"Don't be so foolish," Ferreira said.

The assistant slyly opened the door.

"After all I did for you!" Blair rambled on. "You have the nerve to pull a stunt like this. Get out of my sight!"

"I was just leaving."

"GET OUT!!"

The assistant general manager grabbed his coat and quickly walked out of the room. The general manager sat down behind his desk and had another glass of whiskey.

"He thinks he can outfox me," Blair muttered to himself. "Not over my dead body."

It would turn out to be a long night for the general manager. That evening, he drank his sorrows away at one of the local watering holes until well after 2:00 am.

The next morning he arrived five minutes late for his own press conference to announce the Pioneers new manager.

"The Buffalo Pioneers are pleased to introduce Gene Dennis as our manager for the 2007 Season...."

It was a low-key announcement. Nobody could figure out why Blair hired Dennis, but the scrutiny was hardly overbearing. The team was still paying off the remainder of Norm Watkins' contract and Roger Reich had given Blair little money to spend on a new manager. Blair had asked three of his minor-league managers whether they wanted the job and each refused. Eventually Blair turned to Dennis, who was managing at the single-A level.

"....it was an exhaustive search and I truly believe we got the best man available moving forward."

A few days later Chris Norton went public with his demand for a trade on a BSN interview show with baseball analyst Chuck Smith.

"I have mixed feelings about this," Norton said, "but it's the right thing to do. The truth is that I never wanted to leave Buffalo. The team left me. Terry Miller, Grant Robinson, Jack Vaughn, and Frank Ringler, those guys are all gone. They were like father figures to me and taught me everything I know."

"Trent Blair has vowed to rebuild this team," Chuck Smith reminded him.

"I don't see a light at the end of the tunnel," Norton countered. "There are absolutely no prospects to speak of and we're drawing flies. It's a ridiculous situation."

"What about Eddie Griffin?" Chuck Smith wondered. "Has his hasty retirement cemented your decision?"

"I'd be lying if I said it didn't. Look, I don't want to be the bad guy here. A lot of great things were done in this city. I just don't want to be the only one left on a sinking ship."

With Norton just a year away from free agency and making noises about leaving town, Trent Blair's hands were tied. He either had to trade the star pitcher or risk losing him for nothing the following year. Every general manager in baseball knew Blair's predicament and remembered how ruthless he had been in the days when he was on top. They remembered all of the scouts he had fired and the baseball people he had disrespected. Now that Blair was falling down, they certainly weren't going to help him get back up.

Luis Toca was one such person. After being fired by Trent Blair two years earlier, the highly regarded scouting director landed on his feet as general manager of the St. Louis Cardinals. Time had apparently not healed any of his wounds either. Toca was offering only marginal prospects in return for Chris Norton.

"Come on!" Trent couldn't believe his ears. "Chris Norton is worth a hell of a lot more than the guys you're talking about. I need at least one player who can step in right away."

"That's my final offer," Toca replied.

"Work with me here," Trent pleaded. "The owner is on my case. I need an impact player."

The Dominican laughed.

"Work with you?" Luis said. "I did work with you and it was pure misery. You treated everybody in this game like dirt. I'd be surprised if you get a better offer than mine."

"I see how it is," Trent charged. "This is collusion!"

"I prefer to call it fucking you over," Toca quipped, "but I'm not fussy. Maybe we'll all throw a party when you get fired!"

"I'll find somebody who is prepared to pay what he's worth."

"Check around," Toca said confidently. "Just keep my number on your speed dial. You're gonna need it."

A week later, the Pioneers dealt Chris Norton to St. Louis for two talented shortstop and third base prospects and a mediocre minor-league pitcher. It was not nearly enough, especially since none of them would be ready for the majors in the upcoming season. But with dissent against him so widespread, Trent Blair had no alternative but to pull the trigger. No team came close to St. Louis' paltry offer.

At a press conference, the general manager tried to put on a brave face.

"I'm excited about the prospects we acquired in this deal," Blair lied through his teeth, "we've really put together a solid foundation for the future."

Blair could wax eloquently all day about how the deal set the Pioneers' future, but for shell-shocked fans it was merely another link to the World Series team being broken. The events of the past few years had given Pioneers fans so many reasons not to care anymore and this was merely another one of them.

A stale atmosphere hung over the town that winter. Season ticket sales plunged to an all-time low of 3500, the club was under constant threat to be moved by new owner Roger Reich, and somehow the worst team in baseball became even worse.

CHAPTER 24

For the first time since Trent Blair arrived in Buffalo nearly a decade earlier, the Pioneers entered spring training with absolutely no preconceived notions of contention. As bad as last year's team had performed, at least the season had begun with traces of hope. After the disaster from that season sunk in and the team was stripped of its veteran talent heading into 2007, the buzzwords heard around camp were no longer 'playoffs' or 'contention'.

"If we could win 60 or 70 games, I'd be a happy man," Blair told a reporter in Florida. "We're working to develop our young talent. I feel like I did eight years ago, when we were building a champion for the first time. I'm excited about the possibilities. We have a new manager and a new attitude."

Out was the tyrannical Norm Watkins, the old guard left over from the World Series years, and the combustible mix of players that had begotten one of the most wretched seasons in baseball history. In came rookie manager Gene Dennis and an entire crop of blue-eyed rookies looking to stick it in the big show.

The local press ate it up for a while. With the sun shining and the grass green in Florida, this spring training seemed like the calm after the storm. The old warship had fought some mighty impressive battles over the years but in the aftermath of its wreckage, it only made sense to start building a new one.

For the ardent baseball fan, there was little on this team to be enthusiastic about. The games on the field had become less important than the ones off it, of which there were no shortage. New owner Roger Reich and New York Governor Prentice H. Wulloughby continued to play cat and mouse over the possibility of a new stadium.

Rumors abounded for months that the Governor was softening his anti-stadium stance. As the story went, he had recently shown up at Pioneer Stadium for a conference with city officials and was disgusted at what he saw: insufficient seating, crumbling infrastructure, not to mention rat and cockroach infestation. If the experience had changed his outlook, he certainly was not showing it.

"The state refuses to become a black hole for baseball subsidies," Wulloughby told Reich at a meeting. "We aren't prepared to unconditionally surrender hundreds of millions of dollars for a new stadium. That's insanity."

"What's insane," Reich disputed, "is that this hasn't been taken care of yet...."

He pointed at the Governor accusingly.

"....and that's a failure on your part."

The Governor's advisors were flanking him on both sides, while Buffalo mayor Art Dingleman sat at the end of the table. Not much had changed with Dingleman since the last round of stadium negotiations. His hair was still greased, the synthetic smile was still permanently implanted on his face and he was as publicly popular as ever.

"Like I've always maintained," Dingleman assured everyone. "I'm an ardent supporter of this project. Getting support from the City of Buffalo is the last thing you two need to worry about."

The mayor's two-faced act was well known, but Reich was growing impatient.

"Mr. Dingleman, I've heard all I care from you about promises. What are you willing to deliver?"

Dingleman's smile suddenly frowned the moment he was put on the spot. The time for evasion was over.

"What can you deliver?" Reich repeated sternly.

The mayor squirmed around in his chair and looked over his notes.

"The city is willing to match whatever contribution the state makes," he answered.

Suddenly his smile reappeared. A game of political hot potato was being played and he had successfully thrown it back onto the Governor's lap without getting burned.

Reich turned his attention to the former university professor.

"What's it going to be, Governor?"

"Like I told you earlier," Wulloughby said. "The state will not turn itself into a black hole financing your team. The economy is going bad, people are unemployed....."

"Cut the shit," Reich interrupted. "You can play that card in public if you wish, but I don't have time to listen to it. What are you saying?"

"The bottom line?" Wulloughby asked.

"That's all I ever care about," Reich replied.

"We'll support a new stadium on two conditions. Number one, the final price tag must be equal to or less than the average cost of the previous five baseball stadium constructions in North America."

"I can live with that," Reich's said, as his eyes glowed a little.

"The second and most important condition," the Governor continued, "is that the state will be involved in every step of designing and constructing the stadium. Every decision must have state approval."

Reich shook his head. The agreement had been so close before this extraneous clause was thrown in.

"That's ridiculous," Reich scoffed. "Absolutely ridiculous. If you insist on that, you're asking for cost overruns."

"It's a recipe for safeguarding the state's interest."

The Governor closed the book with stadium figures in it

"It's a recipe for disaster! This is exactly the kind of needless bureaucratic garbage New York has become know for under you. Back in Oregon, your proposal would be laughed at."

"This isn't Oregon, sir."

Reich looked around the room and noticed at least twenty people sitting around the table. He needed a captive audience for the live theater he was about to perform.

"I sometimes wonder about you socialist egghead types," Reich observed. "You hire these bureaucrats to work everything out on paper but there isn't an ounce of practicality in any of it. And when it finally is put under the litmus test of reality, the whole plan folds like a cheap suit. This is the real world, professor. Feel free to join it anytime."

"There is such thing as a world outside big business," Wulloughby replied.

"And what would you know about business?" Reich shot back. "You've never had to earn a penny in your life."

As the conversation slowly descended into an exchange of personal insults, Art Dingleman could barely control the smarmy smile of self-satisfaction that was spreading across his face. He was a safe distance away from vitriol being tossed back and forth.

"Mr. Reich, you truly are an impressive specimen," Wulloughby responded. "I'm sure your brand of oratory works well in the bloody seas of the corporate world, but it doesn't wash with me. I've spent my entire life fighting people like you because of the greed that you represent. You're a shark, Mr. Reich, a man akin to coming in and getting whatever it is he desires. Not this time. My morals aren't up for sale."

The Governor glared down the table at Dingleman, who suddenly stopped grinning.

"You forgot one small detail, Governor," Reich smiled.

"What's that?"

"Roger Reich always gets what he wants. It's been a pleasure meeting both of you, but I really must be going."

"You're walking out?" The Governor said in a fit of shock. "The meeting hasn't been adjourned yet."

"Consider it adjourned."

Mass chaos spread throughout the room as Reich swiftly walked out of the room. The owner almost seemed pleased by the outcome.

"What the hell just happened?" Wulloughby asked one of his aides.

The meeting had taken place in private, but judging by the leaks to the media it might as well have been televised. Reports in the *Buffalo News* and on BSN sportscasts were rampant regarding the team's delicate situation. According to many reports, the Pioneers were as good as gone.

Over time a group of diehard fans formed a political action committee called "SAVE OUR PIONEERS." Its goal was simple: keep the baseball team in Buffalo. Whether that took lobbying, fund-raising or protesting, the S.O.P was determined to make a difference. As the days and weeks passed with no announcement from Mr. Reich or the club, it was beginning to look as if the group was fighting a phony war against an invisible enemy.

Then, on the eve of opening day, Roger Reich dropped the bombshell. It was a message delivered without sympathy or tears; notable only by its arbitrary resemblance to a corporate takeover.

"Following the conclusion of the 2007 season, the Buffalo Pioneers will be relocating to the City of Portland with the intention of playing there in 2008. In the aftermath of a dearth of public support both in attendance and from the state government, it was the only viable option remaining."

Reich took a sip of water as the stunned media looked on, many of them visibly dejected. Al Ferreira stood to Roger Reich's immediate left, towering over the small owner. Trent Blair was nowhere to be seen.

"It's not easy to uproot a team, especially one with as much history as the Buffalo Pioneers. But I'm a forward thinking person in a forward thinking world. Without a new stadium, baseball has no place in Buffalo. I made every attempt to work with Governor Wulloughby, but we have reached a critical impasse at this juncture."

As Reich finished up his speech, one look at Chet Thomas' face gave away what was coming next. Whenever Thomas had an axe to grind his facial features contorted, his upper lip expanded and his eyes zeroed in on his intended prey. On this occasion he was the first in line for questioning.

"I have to ask you a question, Mr. Reich. Did baseball have no place in Buffalo when the Pioneers were consistently selling out games? Did it have no place when the Buffalo Pioneers were the best team in baseball?"

With every question, the partisan media officials rallied behind Thomas. With every mounting challenge, they roared their approval.

"Did it have no place when this was considered the best baseball town in America by several publications? Tell me Mr. Reich, how can you come to judge a team you just bought a few months ago?"

The owner took a deep breath. He was facing over one hundred cameramen, beat reporters, columnists and commentators all passionately opposed to what he was telling them. Roger Reich was used to hostile corporate takeovers, he was used to having egg thrown at him in boardrooms and generally being despised, but it had been a while since he had faced something like this. He loved every minute of it.

"You tell me," Reich shot back. "A team averages 10 000 fans to their games in a relic of a stadium and the Governor pompously serves up platitudes about needing to pay for hospitals. Does it sound like this town deserves a major league team?"

"How can you sit here and tell us these lies! You know as well as anyone that if you spent some money and put a winning team on the field, Buffalo fans would come out. You expect people to watch a minor league outfit?"

The owner was becoming visibly upset.

"You of all people should not be lecturing me. I've read your stuff. You're nothing but a sensationalist reporter."

"And you're nothing but a notorious carpetbagger," Thomas shoved it back in his face. "You've been doing it to companies on the West Coast for years. I believe I speak for everyone in this room and in this city when I say take a hike!"

"I would like nothing better than to do just that," the owner replied with a look of delight on his face. "This press conference is over."

Chaos spread throughout the press conference as Reich left without answering any more questions. Interest in the Pioneers may have been low at the time, but nobody in Buffalo wanted the team to completely skip town. These were their Pioneers. The three World Series Championships were a part of their collective consciousness, something they could never easily let go. This was one fight the fans would not relent.

CHAPTER 25

"Welcome to Opening Day 2007 Season here on the Buffalo Sports Network! It's a cool, overcast day here in Buffalo and there is some doubt as to whether they'll be able to get this game in. In any case, there's plenty to talk about."

"It's been another hard winter for Pioneer fans, but after yesterday's announcement by new owner Roger Reich it's been an even harder night."

"Why would he make such an announcement the day before the season starts?"

"If his intentions really are treacherous, then what better day to make the announcement? Opening Day usually guarantees a sellout crowd, no matter how bad your team is. The Pioneers were expecting a big walk-up crowd for this afternoon's game. Roger Reich was obviously trying to rip the hearts out of every Pioneer fan."

"I don't think these fans will give up that easily. It'll be interesting to see how this plays out."

"Definitely. I guarantee that there is more underway. The league should have something to say about it. This thing is far from over."

The fans jammed into Pioneer Stadium in a noble attempt to show Roger Reich they were not ready to roll over and die. As impressive as the crowd may have been, the game itself was a comedy of errors. The Pioneers made six errors and lost in extra innings on a dropped fly ball by Alvaro Perez. Even with the tremendous outpouring of support from a capacity crowd, the energy in Pioneer Stadium seemed negated by the overcast skies and bank tower across the street casting an ominous shadow over the festivities.

For years, opposing teams dreaded trips to Pioneer Stadium. When the Pioneers were winning and the stadium was full, the grand old ballpark could be one of the most hostile environments in baseball. With a lackluster team on the field that was no longer the case. The Pioneers were soundly swept by Kansas City to open up the season.

The following day, Roger Reich received a phone-call from the Governor.

"I've reconsidered," Wulloughby said. "I'd be willing to re-open discussions on the stadium deal."

Reich snickered.

"You're about a day late and several millions of dollars short, Governor. The moving vans are backed in. This thing is gonna happen whether you like it or not."

"Don't be unreasonable," Wulloughby pleaded. "I'm willing to talk. There's no reason to be jumping to conclusions."

"On the contrary," Reich answered. "I never intended to keep this team in Buffalo in the first place. You merely provided me with a convenient excuse."

The Governor paused for a moment. He was beginning to realize that he had been bamboozled.

"If that's the case, then stop publicly blaming me for refusing to finance a stadium."

"I sure can," Reich laughed again. "You already refused my noble attempt in a room full of people. Dingleman even saw it."

"Excuse me," Wulloughby differed, "but Art Dingleman doesn't exactly inspire confidence."

"Perhaps not," Reich shrugged. "But everyone knows you're gonna be wiped out in the state elections next year. So tell me, Governor, who are they more likely to believe?"

The former university professor was trapped in a corner. Prentice H. Wulloughby might have been a brilliant and articulate man, but he was a mere novice in the art of the cutthroat. In only 33 months of office, the Governor had proven that all of the sociological problems he spent years theorizing about in the ivory towers of academia proved to be far harder to solve in reality. Before the end of his first term, Prentice H. Wulloughby was already considered to be a political has-been.

A few seconds passed with nothing said.

"You still there, Governor?"

More seconds pass.

"You won't get away with this," Wulloughby finally answered.

"Governor," Reich laughed once more. "You really should go back to teaching. You ain't cut out for this kind of thing."

A final resolution seemed to be on the horizon.

"In baseball news, the league has announced that it is planning to vote on the relocation proposal put forth by Roger Reich at the ownership meetings in early June."

For public consumption everything still remained in limbo. No baseball team had relocated in decades and many owners, whose heritage in the game went back generations, wanted it to remain that way. The deck may have been heavily stacked against him, but Roger Reich was never one to give up without getting what he wanted.

The next day, Reich personally phoned the head of his corporate legal department to focus their energies on the upcoming legal battle with Major League Baseball.

"I want the entire legal division of Reich Systems to go full throttle on this case. And I mean everyone."

The lawyer on the other side of the line was flabbergasted.

"But....but...."

"But nothing!" Reich stammered. "I want everything else put on the backburner. Everything! I've never wanted to win a fight as badly as I want to win this one."

"This is impossible," the lawyer stuttered. "We have a lawsuit pending and we're under investigation by the Justice Department. Do you really expect us to throw all this stuff up in the air for.....for a baseball team?"

Reich breathed heavily into the phone.

"When I say something, I want it done! And your failure to realize that has just cost you your job. You have until 10 o'clock tomorrow to pack your things and get the fuck out!"

Click.

On the field, the Pioneers somehow managed to fall fourteen games out of first place by the end of April. With a rag-tag collection of no-name players led by an equally unknown manager, the results were thoroughly predictable. What bothered Roger Reich most was the way they were losing. Errors and strikeouts were becoming all too common.

"That team on the field is a disgrace," Reich pointed out the window of his private box. "You should be ashamed to put your name to it."

Trent Blair sat and listened, taking the abuse much like a certain Dominican scout named Luis Toca had endured from him years earlier. There was nothing he could do or say as long as the fast talking Internet tycoon continued his verbal assault.

Al Ferreira sat across the room silently. The two had not spoken in a month.

"Failure doesn't sit well with me," Reich mouthed on. "It's a cancer that eats away at every healthy bone in the body. You seem to be cultivating this disease."

"Baseball goes in cycles," Blair defended himself. "We've had a sustained run of success and are merely in a rebuilding phase."

"Don't feed me that shit!" Reich shouted back. "Its one thing to finish in last with young players, but I don't see any progress. These prospects you were telling me about haven't done a damn thing all season. If you can sit there and tell me that you planned this then...."

He paused.

"....then I'm going to re-evaluate who's running my team. I'm going to be making some changes and you're going to have to start being accountable for your actions."

Reich patted Al Ferreira on the back.

"I have nothing further to say to you."

As Trent Blair looked at Roger Reich, a man weaned on instant gratification, he knew the patience and benefit of the doubt he had received from Jonathan Jenkins was gone. Dynasties were not built anymore they were bought. A process that used to take five years could now be reduced to one month during the off-season when all of the big names were for the taking. Trent knew right then and there that it was over for him.

He dutifully walked out of the room, leaving the other two men alone for several hours.

By the time Al Ferreira walked down to the office at 1:30 in the morning to grab car keys, there was a glimmer of light coming from the door of the general manager's office. The closer he moved towards the office, the more his interest piqued. What he heard were the disturbing sounds of a grown man sobbing, accompanied by the loud bang of a half-empty whiskey bottle being placed on the table. As he glanced inside the office, every muscle in his body froze in a state of temporary paralysis.

It was Trent Blair, whose shirt was undone and was evidently drunk out of his mind, moaning and wailing away his sorrows as he looked through an old photo album. There were pictures of him with Frank Ringler, Eddie Griffin and Jack Vaughn as the four of them joked around before a spring-training game five years earlier. It was a reminder of happier times. Above was a newspaper snapshot of him in his early thirties when he was first introduced as general manager. His face back then had been so vibrant, so full of youthful energy. He had the world at his feet.

"Everything I built is gone," he cried amid a drunken stupor, "my life, my friends, everything!"

Blair cradled the photo album as if it was the dearest thing to him.

"All I have are memories."

It was a sight Al Ferreira would never forget: the collapse of a man who once stood so imperiously in board meetings, the man who would shout down anyone that dared challenge him. Trent Blair had once been a bold visionary, but he was now the architect of a baseball dynasty that lay in ruins. Watching Blair in his pathetic state became too much for Ferreira to handle.

The next morning, newspapers were rife with leaked reports that Blair was set to be fired within days. When pressed for comment, Roger Reich adamantly denied it.

"I don't know where you people get your information from, but we have never discussed the possibility of firing Trent Blair. Let me make the point clear, so that there will be no confusion. I give Trent Blair my complete vote of confidence. He's done a fantastic job."

In any event, Trent Blair had bigger problems. For months, agents of the Internal Revenue Service had been circling him like vultures. One day, they finally came in for the kill.

"Turning to baseball now, it is more bad news for the Buffalo Pioneers. State authorities are reporting that Pioneers general manager Trent Blair has been arrested for alleged tax evasion and embezzlement. He is currently being held in a North Tonawanda jail."

The next day, the *Buffalo News* had a picture of Blair being led out of the Pioneer Stadium front office in handcuffs. Bad news definitely comes in bunches for some people and his arrest sent shockwaves throughout baseball. Never before in modern baseball had a general manager been indicted for having a hand in the cash register of his own team. The charges were damning. With former team accountant Paula Lombardi as the corroborating witness, the district attorney had all the evidence he needed.

What made the alleged crimes even more repulsive for the baseball world was the timing of them. A majority of the hundreds of thousands of dollars had been taken in the year leading up to Jonathan Jenkins' death. For a man who was so widely respected around the league to be taken advantage of in his final hour was something that sickened most people.

Within a few days, Blair was released on $10 000 bail, but the damage had already been done. It mattered little if he was innocent or guilty, although the evidence conclusively pointed to the latter. What mattered was the image around him. Up until that point, Trent Blair always had a loyal following of Buffalo fans and media willing to cut him a little slack.

"Sure the team is bad," some would say, "but Trent Blair brought the World Series to Buffalo and he can do it again."

In the aftermath of his arrest and evidence that he had taken advantage of an owner considered to be so innocent and pure, there could be no such forgiveness. Out of the 8500 people who bothered to show up at the next home game, they were unanimous in their dissent.

"BLAIR MUST GO!! BLAIR MUST GO!!" The crowd chanted.

In the past, Trent Blair would have fought hard to shut up his naysayers. He would have barged into his office, ordered people around, mouthed off to a reporter, and called a press conference to give his version of events. But with a sense that his world was collapsing around him, he sat there absently and absorbed the punishment that was being dished out to him. When television cameras panned up to his private box hoping for a reaction, all they got was an emotionless, blank stare.

Much like Hitler hiding in his bunker or Napoleon during his last secluded days on St. Helena, Trent Blair spent his final days hunkered in his office. There would be no more grand conquests. Every day seemed like one more tick on his countdown of destruction. Eventually the timer reached zero.

"As of today," Roger Reich announced, "Trent Blair will no longer be a part of the Buffalo Pioneers organization. This was a decision that I have grappled with for months, but I would be a liar if I said that recent events hadn't added an air of expediency to his dismissal. The time was right and a change needed to be made."

Reich sipped a glass of water.

"I can only say how lucky we are to have a man of honesty and fortitude such as Al Ferreira to step in his shoes. This is a day the Pioneer organization must move forward."

With the criminal charges and summary dismissal from the Pioneers, even the most ardent Trent Blair supporters could no longer defend him.

Blair's time in the game has passed

By: Chet Thomas (Buffalo News)

There were always a lot of things about Trent Blair that made you want to like him. He always dressed well and spoke with a certain charisma that made its listener believe that he was always one step ahead of the competition. For many years that was the case. When he and Al Ferreira assembled a three-time World Series champion, they did it without the monetary advantages so many other teams in bigger cities use. They did it by building a strong farm system, being creative and bringing quality people on board. But Blair soon got away from his strengths and turned into a megalomaniac. He thought buying the mercurial Marcus Dillard could guarantee him a fourth World Series, when all it did was tear the team apart. Then he fired most of his scouting staff out of the mistaken belief that he could evaluate players by himself using an unproven statistical method known as sabermetrics. But worst of all, when it all came crashing down, it was revealed that Blair had bitten the tender hand that was feeding him. This is not just about him stealing from Jonathan Jenkins. For anyone who has been paying attention, it was obvious some time ago that Trent Blair was leading this team nowhere.

Having Al Ferreira usurp his power must have been an especially bitter pill for Blair to swallow. His underling and companion had latched onto his star just when it was on the rise and jumped off just as quickly when it faded.

Trent Blair's slow demise from greatness ended with a resounding thud three weeks later when he pleaded guilty in a Cheektowaga courtroom to charges of embezzlement and tax evasion. It was part of a complicated plea bargain, but he was still looking at anywhere from 3-6 years in prison. For a man who had been named the Executive of the Year just a few years prior, the fall was steep.

Trent Blair died a thousand public deaths that week, eternally damned in the hearts and minds of true Pioneer fans everywhere. It appeared that even after violating everything sacred, he had profited nothing. Once his temporal success had run its course he was now condemned to wither away in the earthly Hades of prison.

All the media attention on Blair was finally diverted by the onset of the long awaited ownership meetings. They got underway on a Friday afternoon in early June as several owners filed into the downtown New York hotel. It was shaping up to be a long weekend where anything could happen, especially with several owners publicly expressing their displeasure with Roger Reich.

In the face of all the dissent, Reich did have Vince D'Antoni on his side. Both men were self-made billionaires with maverick mentalities. The Yankees owner respected Reich immensely and recognized that he had the same insatiable appetite for winning. Sooner or later that hunger would have to be satisfied, and since Reich had both the money and resources to assure success, D'Antoni had no problems with him taking the Pioneers out of New York State and eventually somewhere other than the American League East Division.

Getting other votes would prove to be more difficult. The rest of the owners, many of whom had owned their teams for generations, did not take kindly to some telecommunications upstart buying an established club and trying to move it immediately. Roger Reich hadn't paid his dues and many league officials were looking to show him just that.

As Commissioner Richard Smalls walked into the hotel lobby, he immediately held court with a gang of reporters.

"I believe Mr. Reich is going to be in for a rude awakening," the Commissioner said in his southern drawl. "He's gonna find that winning our votes ain't as easy as one of his corporate takeovers."

CHAPTER 26

The ownership meetings were widely regarded as the final hope for keeping the team in Buffalo. Reich needed the support of 24 of the 32 owners for any move to be ratified. With the Commissioner and several owners firmly opposed to any move on principle, popular sentiment seemed to be against Roger Reich.

As the ownership meetings stretched on from Friday evening through Sunday afternoon, a sense of anticipation was building. Everyone was keenly aware that Sunday's vote was about more than the simple transfer of a franchise from one city to another. It was about precedent and whether a new well-heeled owner could blow into the league and immediately move an entrenched team.

On Saturday night, the eve of the big vote, Roger Reich received a telephone call in his hotel room.

"Mr. Reich," the Commissioner answered in his southern drawl. "I want you to call off the vote."

"I will do no such thing," Reich stammered. "I'm moving that team come hell or high water."

The Commissioner sighed.

"You have a promising tenure in this league, Mr. Reich. Don't let it be ruined. I have 20 votes in my back pocket and all of them will vote against you. If you lose this vote, your name will be tarnished."

"The vote doesn't matter," Reich was equally adamant. "That team will be playing in Portland next year whether you like it or not."

"The Buffalo Pioneers have a storied past," the Commissioner countered condescendingly. "They've won championships and been around since you were just a little boy. If you think you can just walk in and erase all of that, then you'll never learn how this league works."

"You don't know how I work!" Reich shouted back at him. "This vote is only the beginning. I have 20 legal experts preparing a lawsuit as we speak."

The Commissioner clammed up.

"Am I being threatened?"

"That all depends on your perspective," Reich replied.

"What are you saying?"

His nose knew what was coming next.

"I'm saying that just as I can make your life a living hell if my proposal is defeated, I can make your life extremely profitable otherwise."

There was a long silence.

"How profitable?" the Commissioner asked curiously.

"Very profitable," Reich answered assuredly.

There was another uncomfortable silence.

"You know that this is against my every principle," the Commissioner responded sarcastically, "but I suppose I have a duty to act in the best interests of the league."

The two men laughed impishly.

"I'm glad I could count on the integrity of the Commissioner to see my point of view," Reich said happily. "Have a great evening."

"I believe I will," Smalls replied.

A full media blitz descended upon the hotel the following day. Every move was scrutinized, every bathroom break was reported and there were reporters crawling all over the hotel. It was hard to predict what was going on behind the boardroom walls. When the meeting finally adjourned at 6:35 p.m. on Sunday night, Commissioner Richard Smalls emerged to deliver the verdict.

"After long and fruitful discussions on the request for relocation put forth by Mr. Reich, we have reached a decision. By a close vote of 25 to 7, the team owners of both the American and National Leagues have voted to accept...."

Jaws dropped across the room and hearts sank all over Buffalo.

"...the Pioneers proposal to relocate in Portland beginning next season. I deliver this decision with a heavy heart. Nobody wants to see a city lose its baseball team and I can only say to the fans of Buffalo that I tried my best. As the game of baseball grows and grows and becomes more and more financially rewarding for all involved, we are left with the unfortunate economic side effects. This world isn't perfect and I believe we've all seen why tonight."

The past twelve months had already been rough for Buffalo fans. They had witnessed two tragic deaths, two major firings, the departures of a long-time catcher, star right fielder, ace starting pitcher, and Hall-of-Fame first baseman. Pioneer fans had grown accustomed to heartbreak, but nothing compared to losing the baseball team entirely. For the fans of the team in question, it is comparable to losing a loved one.

Like any death however, a cause must be found. The following day, Buffalo mayor Art Dingleman tried to play the role of coroner. In a prepared statement to the media, he lashed out at Governor Prentice Wulloughby for usurping a potential stadium deal.

"The Governor has consistently blackballed the city of Buffalo and the Pioneers in their honorable attempt to build a new stadium for a new era of baseball in Buffalo."

For the first week, much of the tide of public opinion turned against the beleaguered Governor. He was greeted with jeers and catcalls every time he stepped foot in Western New York and his already dismal popularity level sank well below 20%. Several political columnists openly called for his immediate resignation. After almost three years of ineptitude on the Governor's part, fumbling the stadium deal was the straw that broke the camel's back.

It wasn't as if everyone was a baseball fan, certainly a good portion of the population was not; but for the vendors that made their money on the pre-game rush, the hundreds of employees who worked for the Pioneers and men like Gus at the Duke of York, their livelihoods were threatened. Baseball had provided so many things to Buffalo over the years: an influx of money into the economy, a sense of civic pride and the distinguishable definition of being a big league city. The game added a certain luster to the town, a special spot on the map. That would no longer be the case.

Even those unattached to the game, felt the sting of the loss. Baseball was played for half of the year, so it was not as if everyone watched every game. Just knowing that it was there, that one could buy a Pioneers hat for their little boy on his birthday or take them out to the old ballgame was enough in itself. Suddenly all of that was gone. There would be no game to watch on those hot and hazy summer afternoons, no longer any reason to read the sports section in the morning to check the standings. It was still business as usual in the city, but suddenly the empty 9-5 ritual, which became so monotonous during the winter, was extended year round.

No longer would there be businessmen sneaking out of work or students skipping school to catch a day game at Pioneer Stadium. Baseball would still be played in the parks and city diamonds of urban Buffalo, but suddenly there were no heroes to emulate. There would be no more little kids pretending to be Scott Harper or Frank Ringler. Instead they would be forced into the ignominy of watching highlights of the Portland Pioneers on the late night sportscasts.

The remainder of the season dragged on tediously. Buffalo had adjusted to having a losing baseball team, but at least it had been theirs before. Now they were being asked to support a team with no chance of winning so that it could turn things around in Portland. Paid attendance dropped steadily, reaching lows of 5000 by September. For anyone actually present, they knew the real attendance was much less.

The city was given three months to digest the loss of the team. Many bade their final farewell on that Sunday night in early June. The game had long since alienated them. Baseball no longer spoke to them with the romantic innocence of their childhood. Heroes and villains still existed, but only so far as the almighty dollar would allow. The truth is, for many people, baseball had already left Buffalo. Others had a harder time removing it from their consciousness.

The S.O.P. hadn't yet given up hope for last minute resuscitation through a class action suit aimed at keeping the team in Buffalo. When matched against the legal behemoth that Roger Reich had assembled their weak attempts to 'Save Our Pioneers' were squashed like a bug.

"If the rest of your motion is as laughable as this," the district judge ruled, "then I'm going to dismiss it immediately. The judgment is for Reich."

Public protests were organized for downtown, but it all had such an air of futility to it. Police came in to squash some of the uprisings that got out of control. The whole affair made front-page headlines in the *Buffalo News* when a disturbing picture was printed of a little boy wearing a dirty, old Pioneer jersey and crying amid the mayhem. Eventually the S.O.P was forced to fold its tents.

As autumn arrived the air grew crisp, the leaves fell over Buffalo, and the team drifted listlessly onward through the cruel month of September. With each passing day, the giant bank tower across the street loomed larger than ever over desolate Pioneer Stadium. The day of reckoning was fast arriving.

On days when the Pioneers were not playing, the television in the empty Duke of York pub was tuned into the New York broadcast as Jack Vaughn and his fantastic New York Yankees made another run at the World Series. Each Yankees victory on the backs of a Scott Harper homerun or a Benjy Alvarez catch made the bar patrons wonder what might have been.

Amidst it all, Vince D'Antoni took great delight in Buffalo's misery.

"There are a lot of bleeding hearts in this town," he told the *Buffalo News* after the Yankees swept through town, "but Buffalo doesn't deserve major league baseball. The corporate community didn't step up. If they really wanted that team, a local group would have bought it."

D'Antoni cracked a large smile.

"But you never know," he mused. "Baseball could always come back here. I know we're looking for a place to move our minor league team."

The final game of the season was played on a breezy Sunday afternoon, but few people paid attention. It hurt too much to watch.

"*.....there are two outs here in the ninth inning and the Pioneers are down to the final at bat of their season. Alvaro Perez is up to bat.*"

A cold wind was blowing in from Lake Erie.

"*After being heavily hyped as a prospect, Alvaro has been a major disappointment in his first two seasons. We can only hope he'll get himself untracked next season in Portland.*"

"*Perez steps in....the pitcher delivers....grounded feebly to third base....flip to first and this season is in the books.*"

The cold, crumbling stadium was filled with embittered boos from the few thousand rowdy fans that bothered to show up. Many of them had brown paper bags over their heads and began ripping out seats. A minor melee ensued when security tried to restrain them.

"*It's a shame it had to end this way. I have so many great memories of sitting here in this booth covering the Pioneers for the Buffalo Sports Network. It's been such a pleasure working alongside you Terry....*"

The commentator choked up.

"*Thanks Chuck, you don't know how much that means to me. I've had a wonderful time working in Buffalo. For all of those who say that this town doesn't deserve baseball, I ask you to remember what it was like when these fans had a reason to care. Sure, you can harp on about the disgraceful attendance this season, but that has come after years of heartbreak. I remember the day Jack Vaughn came to town, the day this team made the playoffs for the first time and the day the*

Pioneers captured that first World Series title. The stadium was full and the city was buzzing with excitement. Don't let anyone ever tell you that this wasn't a baseball town. For I have seen with my own two eyes that it undoubtedly is. For the final time, this is Terry Davis for Chuck Smith and the rest of the BSN crew saying so long from Buffalo."

2007 American League East Standings

Team	W-L	GB
New York	111-51	-
Boston	98-64	13
Baltimore	83-79	28
Toronto	78-84	33
Tampa Bay	70-92	41
Buffalo	45-117	66

CHAPTER 27

The two men took a knee and placed flower petals in front of the grave before bowing their heads in reverence. It had been almost four years since Jonathan Jenkins passed away, but fond memories of him still lingered.

"All right," Jack said solemnly. "Let's get outta here."

As Vaughn stood up, an old friend kissed the grave. Grant Robinson seemed to become a little more bent over each year and there were noticeably more gray streaks in his hair.

The two men slowly walked out of the cemetery and headed downtown. Twenty minutes went by before Jack and Grant reached the intersection of Oak and Swan Street. The street behind Pioneer Stadium had once been so packed, vibrant and full of life, but was now rundown and barren. There were some teenagers making a transaction in one of the alleyways, although neither man cared to find out the seedy specifics. So much had changed in so little time.

The stadium that had once housed one of the greatest teams in baseball history was falling apart before their very eyes. The bricks that once proudly carried Pioneer colors looked shaky and decrepit. Even a large billboard that used to proclaim 'Home of the Buffalo Pioneers' was shattered into pieces by some of the hoodlums now inhabiting the area. The three World Series banners still hung over center field, but the years of wind and rain had taken their toll. It was a horrific sight.

The two men turned around and proceeded across Swan Street to the bar where they had enjoyed so many good times, but instead of seeing Gus's welcoming face, they were abruptly greeted by a boarded up entrance. Both men remembered the pub had always been full of life. There were so many great post-game memories locked in the history of that little tavern.

"They closed the Duke of York?" Jack asked disappointedly.

"Guess so," Robinson responded softly.

The more they looked around the area, the more they noticed how much things had changed. The souvenir shops and outdoor vendors, which were usually busy at this time of year selling Pioneer merchandise, were nowhere to be seen. The grass, which had once been so thoroughly maintained by the city, had grown long and was sprouting weeds.

They began walking down Seneca Street. The streetscape was littered with pawn shops. Old storefronts that once dominated the streetscape were either boarded up or demolished. Finally, the two men came across a coffee shop.

"I'll have a coffee," Robinson said.

"And for you, sir?" the young attendant turned to Vaughn.

"I'm okay," Jack said.

They sat down at a table by the window. The shop was filled with street vagrants and unemployed laborers. Most of their eyes were fixed on Jack Vaughn. It was hard not to notice him. His hair had kept a good deal of its color and his face had a dynamic vitality to it. He seemed rejuvenated, in a way defying nature.

"So how's retirement been treating you?" Jack asked.

"I've been keeping busy," Robinson smiled. "It's a calming experience. You ought to try it sometime."

"Well," Jack nodded in agreement. "After I finish this season, I just might."

Robinson laughed.

"Mm...mm...mm. The great Jack Vaughn as a retiree. I'll believe that when I see it."

"I'm dead serious, Grant. After this season, I might just walk away."

Robinson stared at him to make sure he wasn't pulling a prank.

"Damn, you are serious," Grant replied. "You still regret what happened here?"

It was a question that Jack found difficult to answer. He had to summon up so many hidden and complex emotions to explain the grief he felt for the fate of baseball in Buffalo. His career in the game had been long and fruitful, but his six years here in Buffalo stood out above it all. The champagne celebrations of nearly a decade earlier still danced in his mind.

"I have such conflicting memories. There were those first years when everything went right, when all the hits dropped in and the bounces went our way. It was a beautiful thing we had going...."

His smile dimmed.

"....But it didn't last, nothing in this world seems to last. We were coming off such a high, and it all just seemed to implode at once. Power, sex, money, drugs, it all took its toll. Everything seemed to wither away."

238

He could see a glimpse of Pioneer Stadium over a bevy of crumbling apartment complexes and long since vacated industrial warehouses that dotted the depressed street. It was a pitiful view. His face swelled with sorrow and he paused before staring out the window again.

"I guess it's all a part of the game today," Jack shrugged. "When the players are on the field and every team has a chance, nothing tops this game. But it ain't like that no more. A good baseball town like Buffalo goes without a team and you have kids like Marcus Dillard and A.J Winters thrown millions of dollars before they know how to handle it."

Grant took a sip out of his mug and continued listening.

"It's funny though," Jack continued. "With all its warts and deficiencies, there is something about this grand old game that keeps drawing me back. No matter how much they try, they can't screw up the game of baseball."

The two men laughed.

"Then what is it?" Robinson asked. "If you love the game, why would you want to leave it?

Jack ran his hands through his hair.

"I'm almost 70," he shrugged. "There's no way I can keep this up. The road trips, the flings with girls a third my age...."

Robinson looked on approvingly.

"When I look back on my life," Jack continued, "I've accomplished everything I ever set out for. I won some rings, got in the Hall and made enough money to live in comfortable retirement. But beneath it all, something is missing."

Jack seemed to be searching for words to describe an unfulfilled angst that he could neither grasp nor comprehend.

"Is it guilt?" Robinson wondered.

The old pitching coach read him like a book.

"Maybe a little," Jack said as he sadly stared out the window. "All of those afternoons at the ballpark. I've given up a lot for baseball and I'm beginning to wonder if it was worth it. You couldn't possibly understand how much it hurts when your ex-wife and kids won't even talk to you. Everything I won, everything I accomplished; I feel like I traded them in for it all. I can't live with that."

"Who is to say you can't make up with them," Grant asked.

"The time for reconciliation has passed. All those years when Beth was begging for just a small sign of affection from me, when my children were craving some attention from their father, I ignored them all. It was just baseball, baseball, baseball, non-stop. I used to look at Beth and wonder how she got so strung out.....well.....there's my answer."

"Don't beat yourself up," Grant said stoically. "Life is too long a journey to not make a wrong turn occasionally."

"I suppose," Vaughn considered.

Over the next few minutes, several vagrants came and went from the shop. While Robinson continued drinking his coffee and filling out the crossword, Vaughn flipped through the morning newspaper.

The headlines were dominated by the financial scandal involving Reich Systems. With his once powerful telecommunications corporation in shambles and under investigation by the Justice Department, Roger Reich had been indicted a day earlier for defrauding investors out of billions. The front page of the *Buffalo News* had him being led out of his Portland office in handcuffs.

Jack could not be bothered to read any further. The minutiae of business and white collar crime bored him like nothing else. He flipped to the sports section where his Yankees sat atop the American League East Division. Even after all these years, there were few subtle delights in life that compared to seeing one's team first in the baseball standings.

"You seeing anyone these days?" Grant inquired after a lengthy delay.

"Yeah," Jack answered. "I met a woman at one of those Manhattan law firms. She just turned 36."

"A little young for you, but at least it sounds better than those some of those other girls I've seen you with."

"Thanks for the seal of approval," Jack smiled, "but I'd actually like to keep seeing this one and if things get serious, I don't want to fuck it up like before. I have enough regrets already."

Grant returned his coffee mug as the two men walked towards the door. They weren't headed anywhere in particular on this day, but the sun was out and the endless concrete jungle seemed inviting.

"So what's next for you?" Grant asked.

"I guess we'll see after the season. Maybe I'll do some part-time stuff in the minors, maybe I'll help out in spring training...."

Jack paused for a moment, almost struggling to say it.

"....but I'd really like to settle down with this woman. I'm getting old, Grant, and I ain't gonna be around forever. Nothing lasts forever."

ISBN 141202210-X